"A TOUCHING c...
thing...

...REATIVE...
with a generous amount
of humor."
—VO...

"CLEVERLY CRAFTED.... This novel
presents just the right mix of
'scary and humorous.'"
—ILA Literacy Daily

"*Coraline* meets *Monsters, Inc.*"
—Publishers Weekly

NIGHTMARES!

THE LOST LULLABY

Books by Jason Segel and Kirsten Miller

Nightmares!

Nightmares! The Sleepwalker Tonic

Nightmares! The Lost Lullaby

*Everything You Need to Know
About NIGHTMARES! and How to Defeat Them*

JASON SEGEL
KIRSTEN MILLER

NIGHTMARES!
THE LOST LULLABY

~ ILLUSTRATED BY KARL KWASNY ~

 A YEARLING BOOK

Copyright © 2016 by The Jason Segel Company

All rights reserved. Published in the United States by Yearling, an imprint of Random House Children's Books, a division of Penguin Random House LLC, New York. Originally published in hardcover in the United States by Delacorte Press, an imprint of Random House Children's Books, New York, in 2016.

Yearling and the jumping horse design are registered trademarks of Penguin Random House LLC.

Visit us on the Web! randomhousekids.com
Educators and librarians, for a variety of teaching tools, visit us at RHTeachersLibrarians.com

The Library of Congress has cataloged the hardcover edition of this work as follows:
Segel, Jason, author.
Nightmares! The Lost Lullaby / Jason Segel, Kirsten Miller; illustrated by Karl Kwasny.
pages cm
Summary: "Twelve-year-old Charlie and his friends are in new danger as a visitor from the Netherworld is in Cypress Creek and is intent upon connecting the two worlds. It is up to them to stop that from happening or risk losing all that they've ever known"— Provided by publisher.
ISBN 978-0-385-74429-4 (hc) — ISBN 978-0-375-99159-2 (lib. bdg.) —
ISBN 978-0-385-38405-6 (ebook)
[1. Dreams—Fiction. 2. Nightmares—Fiction. 3. Friendship—Fiction.] I. Miller, Kirsten, author.
II. Kwasny, Karl, illustrator. III. Title.
PZ7.S4533 Ni 2016
[Fic]—dc23
2016010539

ISBN 978-0-385-74430-0 (pbk.)

Illustrations by Karl Kwasny with illustration assistant Stephanie Pepper

Book design by Stephanie Moss

Printed in the United States of America
10 9 8 7 6 5 4 3 2 1
First Yearling Edition 2017

As a boy, Ron Daly survived the bombing of Glasgow.
His stories of wartime Britain helped inspire this book.
His life inspired everyone who knew him.

PROLOGUE

She bent down and peered through the keyhole. On the other side of the door lay a dimly lit hall. She couldn't reach it, but she knew exactly where it was: on the second floor of a purple mansion in a town called Cypress Creek. Three doors along the hall led to bedrooms, and there were four people asleep inside. She'd been watching them through the keyhole all evening, the two boys and their parents. And she'd been deciding what to do with them when she got to the other side.

She tried the doorknob for the thousandth time. It

twisted, but the door wouldn't budge. It wasn't just locked. It was barricaded. She knew she was the one they were trying to keep out; there was no doubt about that. The people who lived in the purple mansion had left her a letter.

The anger raged like a bonfire inside her. She squeezed her eyes shut and clenched her fists, digging her fingernails into her palms. She had to find a way to control it. One wrong move and the family would burn down the tower, destroying its secret and leaving her stranded. She had only one option: she'd have to wait. Sooner or later, her twin sister would find her.

At last she left her post at the keyhole and climbed the stairs back up to the tower. The mansion's owners had boarded the tower's windows, but moonlight managed to sneak inside. The portal she'd come through was still open. The Netherworld, the land of nightmares, lay beyond it. For decades, she'd been passing back and forth between the two realms. Now the family downstairs was trying to stop her. She'd never imagined that people like them could ever muster the power, but they had managed to foil her last big plan.

The only piece of furniture in the tower was a giant oak desk. They had left it behind when they'd cleaned out the room. It must have been too bulky to get down the stairs.

She climbed on top of it and lay down in the moonlight. Then she picked up the letter she'd found waiting for her when she'd arrived. It was far too dark in the tower for an ordinary human to read. But it had been a long time since she'd been ordinary.

Dear ICK,

We are the guardians of this portal, and we know you share our power to pass through it. We cannot stop you from visiting the Waking World, but we can keep you from going any farther than this room. If you try to leave, we will burn down the tower and everything in it. The portal will be destroyed, and you will never see your sister again.

Hopefully, the Netherworld authorities will find you and punish you for the horrible crimes you've committed. Until they do, stay out of our dreams.

Charlotte, Charlie, and Jack Laird

Charlotte, Charlie, and Jack Laird. She repeated the names in her head. They belonged to the two boys and the girl who'd grown up. How interesting that only three people had signed it—when four people lived in the house.

ICK was almost positive she knew what it meant, and she saw an opportunity. Three of the people downstairs knew she'd be coming. But the fourth person wasn't expecting her.

CHAPTER ONE

THE BEASTS

Just down the hall from a strange door covered with locks, Charlie Laird was writhing in his sleep. When he'd closed his eyes earlier that evening, he'd been looking forward to visiting the Dream Realm. But that wasn't where he'd ended up.

Charlie didn't know where he was. He couldn't see anything. It was darker than any place he'd ever been.

"Don't panic," Charlie ordered himself. "Remember—you're a pro at this stuff."

He reached out an arm and swept his fingers through the darkness. He felt nothing but the wind pressing against his palm. He took a step forward, and his bare foot made a wet, slurping sound as he wrenched it out of the swampy ground. He was outside, that much was certain. A few more steps followed, and then Charlie stopped and sniffed the air. The warm breeze that embraced him carried the stench of manure. He hoped it wasn't coming from the muck that squished between his toes. He managed to control his fear, but he couldn't help being totally grossed out.

Eager to keep moving, Charlie lifted a leg. Then he froze with his foot still dangling in midair. He thought he'd heard something. Nothing much—just a soft grunt, as if someone close by had been clearing his throat.

Utterly blind, Charlie spun around in the darkness, listening carefully for the source of the sound. "Hello?" he called. "Is there anyone out there?"

He stopped moving and held his breath, waiting for— and dreading—a reply. Thunder rumbled in the distance and the wind picked up speed. Not only was he outside, there was also a storm heading his way.

Seconds passed, and no one answered. But something *moved*. Charlie heard a slurp of mud and a light splash: a footstep. He stood perfectly still and heard a second footstep, followed a few moments later by a third and then a fourth. The creature in the darkness was moving slowly, but it seemed to know exactly where it was going. It was making a beeline for Charlie.

"This is only a nightmare," Charlie whispered to himself. It had been a while since he'd needed such reassurances. He knew how nightmares worked, and he knew how to beat them. But there was something very different about this dream.

The creature was so close now that Charlie could smell it. It stank like a toilet crammed with nasty old sweaters. Charlie's legs twitched as the thing moved closer. He desperately wanted to bolt. But the worst thing you can do is flee from a Nightmare. It makes no difference how fast you run; it'll always hunt you down in the end. So no matter how scared he was, Charlie had no choice but to stand his ground.

"What are you and what do you want?" he demanded, hoping he sounded a lot braver than he felt.

Charlie could hear the beast's teeth grinding rhythmically. When Charlie wondered what it was chewing, a million horrible images began to flicker in his brain. Then he heard something that brought everything else to a stop.

It was a song coming from somewhere in the distance. A sweet female voice was humming a lullaby—a lullaby Charlie knew well. His own mother had sung it to him years earlier, when he was little and she was still alive.

"Mom?" Charlie shouted, his hopes rising. "Mom, is that you? Are you out there?"

The woman kept humming peacefully, as if she hadn't heard him.

"It's dark! I can't see you!" Charlie tried again. "Can you find me? Can you help me?"

His question was answered with a torrent of rain. The storm drowned out the song and crushed Charlie's hopes— just as he felt an enormous beast brush against him. He yelped and tottered backward, falling with a splat in the mud.

Charlie held his arms out to brace for an attack, and his mouth stretched wide to scream. Now that he was down, there was no telling what the creature might do. Then a bolt of lightning lit the sky, and Charlie saw that the beast that had been stalking him was far from alone. There were dozens of identical creatures hovering above him, chewing in unison as he struggled in the muck. Each beast was four feet high and almost as wide, with a jet-black pelt and amber eyes that shone in the light.

They were sheep, Charlie realized. *Black sheep,* just like the ones from the song.

Charlie sat bolt upright in his bed. His chest was heaving and his heart racing. Both the covers and his nightclothes

were drenched with sweat. He'd never experienced a nightmare like the one he'd just had.

And as his heart slowed and he caught his breath, Charlie realized why it had felt so unusual. The nightmare wasn't *his*. He was absolutely positive that he'd just been inside someone *else's* worst dream. And whoever the dreamer was, he or she was *very* afraid.

CHAPTER TWO

THE NEW GIRL

Charlie felt his eyelids growing heavy. He'd woken up at four a.m., and he hadn't been able to get back to sleep. He'd never thought much about sheep before, but now he seemed to be obsessed with them. Eight hours had passed. It was almost noon. Charlie was in the middle of the most important surveillance mission of his twelve-year-old life. And he *still* couldn't get those smelly beasts out of his head.

He peeked through the gap he'd made between some books on a nearby shelf. The girl he was watching was still there. She'd been hogging one of the library's computers for the last forty-five minutes, but no one had dared bother her. When she'd sat down at the terminal, Charlie's heart had started racing. He couldn't even imagine what a real-life supervillain like India Kessog would search for. Where to find explosives at bargain prices? How to breed man-eating rats? Poisons that mix well with cafeteria ketchup? But as it turned out, the girl wasn't interested in research. It had taken her twenty minutes to figure out what to do with the mouse, and after that all she'd done was watch cartoons. Not even the awesomely weird kind either. She was giggling away at shows that only the lamest toddlers would watch.

Then the bell rang and the girl stood up and smoothed the old-fashioned outfit she was wearing. It looked like a uniform of some sort, Charlie thought. Beneath a navy-blue pinafore, she wore a crisp white shirt with a red tie poking out from the collar.

When she pushed her chair beneath the table, no one else budged. Even for a library, the room was oddly quiet. There were two dozen kids nearby, but none were talking. Their eyes were all glued to the girl. They weren't gawking because they found her appearance unusual. They were staring in horror. They'd all seen India Kessog before. And not at Cypress Creek Elementary.

Either the girl didn't notice or she didn't care. After the bell rang, she gathered her things and blithely skipped toward the door. The other kids wisely stayed put, while Charlie cautiously followed behind her.

As she walked down the school's main hall, India never stopped moving her head. She was obviously taking everything in. She paused to laugh at a vending machine that sold bottles of water for a dollar apiece. A few steps later she plucked a purple combination lock right out of another kid's trembling hand and studied it as if it were some kind of rare gem. The girl was gathering information, Charlie concluded. If only he knew what she planned to do with it.

The crowds parted as India made her way through the school. Wide-eyed kids stood with their backs pressed against the walls. Others ducked into nearby classrooms, and Charlie saw a seventh grader stuff himself into an open locker. He didn't blame his schoolmates for acting totally petrified. Their worst nightmare had appeared in real life and was walking through the halls of their school.

Charlie squatted behind a janitor's cart as India stopped to gaze in wonder at a digital clock on the wall. It had just turned noon. It was hard to believe that only four hours had passed since Charlie's eighth-grade year had begun. The first day of school already seemed destined to become the longest day of his life.

Which was a shame, Charlie thought miserably, because aside from the lack of sleep, it had all gotten off to such a wonderful start. His stepmom, Charlotte, had fixed regular pancakes for breakfast. Golden brown and delicious, they hadn't contained a single fleck of kale. Then Charlie's little brother, Jack, discovered he'd outgrown his beloved Captain America costume—and had gone to school dressed like a normal human being for once. And on the drive to Cypress Creek Elementary, Charlie's dad, Andrew Laird, had kept them in stitches with a story about his own first day of eighth grade, when the seam of his new pants had burst in front of the cutest girl at school as he bent over for a sip at a water fountain.

When Charlie had taken a seat in homeroom, his mood couldn't have been better. And then everything went horribly wrong. He heard a sweet voice with an English accent coming from a girl seated at the front of the room. She was new to Cypress Creek Elementary, she told the class, and her name was India Kessog. But it didn't matter what the creature called herself. Charlie would always know her as INK.

India Nell Kessog (INK) and her sister, Isabel Cordelia Kessog (ICK), looked like ordinary twelve-year-old twins. But thanks to a black-and-white photo of the girls dated 1939, Charlie knew they hadn't aged a day in almost eighty years. At some point in time, the girls had simply stopped growing older. Charlie had no idea how they'd managed the feat—but he suspected it had something to do with the desolate lighthouse where ICK and INK had dwelled for almost a century. Located on a dreary, windswept beach in Maine, the twins' home possessed a powerful secret. Just like Charlie's purple mansion, the lighthouse held a portal to the land of Nightmares.

Charlie had always believed that he, his little brother, Jack, and his stepmother, Charlotte, were the only humans who were able to pass between the Waking World and the Netherworld. Then he'd discovered that ICK and INK had been traveling back and forth between the two worlds for decades. Perhaps the twins had been regular kids when they'd first begun making the trip, but the time they'd spent in the Netherworld must have changed them. After they'd stopped aging, ICK and INK started plotting against mankind. Just this last summer, the girls had hatched an astonishingly evil plan. Joining forces with the Netherworld's goblins, they'd invented Tranquility Tonic, a potion with the power to stop humans from dreaming— and turn people into zombielike Walkers.

No one could figure out why ICK and INK had chosen the neighboring town of Orville Falls as the first place on earth to sell their tonic. But once the vile potion had the people of Orville Falls drooling and shuffling like the walking dead, the twins had turned their attention to nearby Cypress Creek. They started appearing in the nightmares of Charlie's schoolmates and neighbors, and as soon as the town's residents were all too scared to sleep, ICK and INK opened a store on Main Street in Cypress Creek and advertised their tonic as the cure for bad dreams.

The tonic worked as promised. But it prevented more than nightmares—it stopped good dreams too. And when people stop dreaming, bad things start happening. With no dreamers to rebuild it every night, the Netherworld began to collapse down a giant hole—and a cloud of pure Nothingness threatened to swallow the Dream Realm.

If Tranquility Tonight hadn't been put out of business, three entire worlds could have perished. Charlie and his friends had managed to prevent *that* disaster, but ICK and INK remained at large. A fire that INK started had destroyed the twins' lighthouse, leaving the sisters stranded on different sides of the portal. ICK was still in the Netherworld, but Charlie and his friends had lost track of INK. After the fire, she'd vanished into the Waking World.

Charlie had always known they'd need to find INK one day. Now he and his friends didn't have to look any farther. One of the villains who'd nearly destroyed three worlds had come straight to them.

At Cypress Creek Elementary, INK was on the move again. Charlie slipped out from behind the janitor's cart. The warning bell rang, and the hallway began to clear. It was Charlie's lunch period, so he was in no hurry. He wasn't about to lose sight of India Kessog. He'd track her for hours until he found out what she was up to. Wherever INK went, he'd stay right behind her.

Then a door swung open and closed, and INK disappeared. Charlie came to a halt. He'd follow INK anywhere . . . *except the girls' room.* Charlie glared at the door with its skirt-wearing icon and considered kicking it in frustration. Should he follow INK inside? There was no telling what kind of trouble she might be brewing. But what if there were innocent girls in there, doing . . . *girl stuff?* Charlie had faced some terrifying things over the past year, but he worried there were some sights from which even he might never recover. He checked to his left and then to his right. There didn't seem to be anyone watching on either side of the hall. Charlie reached out his hand to push the door open and a horrible squeal blasted through the crack. It wasn't the kind of noise human vocal cords usually make. It sounded more like a terrified beast.

Charlie yanked his hand back from the door, and a split second later, a boy burst out of the girls' room. Charlie instantly recognized Ollie Tobias. As always, Ollie's yellow hair was perfectly parted, and he wore a natty bow tie and suspenders. But his face was the color of Elmer's glue, and his clothes and his fingers were splattered with what looked to be bright red blood.

"Ollie!" Charlie gasped.

"Charlie!" Ollie grabbed Charlie's shirt and clung to it, the fabric wadded up in his fists. "I saw her! The one from my nightmares. She's here, Charlie. She's here!"

Ollie Tobias had been one of the first kids in Cypress Creek to be stalked by ICK and INK in his dreams. He'd taken the tonic to get rid of his nightmares, but the stuff hadn't worked on him at all. He was immune to Tranquility Tonic. And as it turned out, Ollie's immunity was just the clue Charlie had needed. By figuring out what was protecting Ollie, Charlie and his friends had discovered the antidote to Tranquility Tonic and saved every last one of ICK and INK's victims.

Charlie pried Ollie's fingers away from his shirt and tried to get a better look at the boy's wounds. "I know! I saw her too. What did she do to you in there?" He'd figured INK was dangerous, but he'd never expected her to *attack* anyone.

"What?" Ollie asked, still panting. He followed Charlie's eyes to the splotches of red on his skin and clothes and managed a mischievous grin. "Oh, that's just nail polish."

"Nail polish?" Charlie asked.

"Yeah." Ollie gestured toward the girls' room. "I was making a few improvements for the ladies."

For a moment, Charlie would have given almost anything to see what Ollie Tobias had been painting in the girls' restroom. Ollie was not only the school's most notorious delinquent, he also possessed impressive decorating skills. But there was no time to appreciate Ollie's artistic achievements. Charlie grabbed the boy's arm and dragged him into an empty science classroom across the hall. It was time to call for backup.

"Give me your phone," he told Ollie.

"Phones are not allowed at Cypress Creek Elementary," Ollie said with a perfectly straight face. For someone who'd been about to pee his pants with terror a few seconds earlier, he'd recovered his sense of humor with impressive speed.

Charlie held out his hand in response.

Ollie grinned. "Would you prefer to use my smartphone or a burner?" the boy asked.

"What's a *burner*?" Charlie asked.

"Tsk, tsk." Ollie rolled his eyes. "And you call yourself an eighth grader," he said, slapping a smartphone into Charlie's open palm.

Charlie punched ten digits into the keypad.

"Calling Paige Bretter?" Ollie teased. "What am I asking? Of course you are. She's the only other kid here with a phone. They let her carry it because her mom's always sick. And look at that—you've got her number memorized. Nobody knows anyone's number anymore. Unless they . . . *love* them."

Charlie was used to people teasing him about Paige, but that didn't make it any less annoying. "Paige has been one of my best friends since kindergarten," he snipped.

"That's really sweet. Your grandkids are gonna love that story," Ollie said with a cackle.

"Shut up, Ollie, unless you want to go hang out with your new friend in the bathroom. I bet she'll think all your jokes are hilarious," Charlie said, turning his back to the boy. He didn't want Ollie to see his face burning red.

Paige picked up immediately, and her voice was a frantic whisper. "Charlie! Where have you been? We're in the lunchroom, and we've been looking all over for you. Have you seen the new girl?"

"She's in the first-floor girls' bathroom," Charlie said. "Get Alfie and Rocco and meet me in the hall outside. We need to have a chat with her."

CHAPTER THREE

DISAPPEARING INK

When Charlie saw his friends round the corner, he breathed a deep sigh of relief. Backup had arrived, and it was capable of kicking some serious butt. Rocco Marquez, the school's star athlete, was the second-tallest kid in the eighth grade—at least a foot taller than dainty blond Paige Bretter, who had a giant personality that more than made up for her lack of stature. As usual, Alfie Bluenthal was rocking one of his geektastic science T-shirts. It featured a cartoon diamond with a scowl on its face above the line UNDER PRESSURE. He may have been the least athletic of the bunch, but whenever there was a problem to be solved, Alfie and his impressive brain could do some serious heavy lifting.

Alfie, Paige, and Rocco had been Charlie's best friends since kindergarten. They were smart, brave, and resourceful—just the sort of people you'd want by your side in a crisis. Which, as it turned out, was extremely convenient. Over the last six months, crises had gotten quite common in Cypress Creek.

"We're here. What's the plan?" Paige cracked her knuckles.

"INK's still in the bathroom," Charlie said, pointing at the girls' room door. "Let's go."

Alfie's eyes bulged and his jaw dropped. "In *there*?" he asked nervously.

"It's a bathroom, Bluenthal," Paige said with a huff. "It's just like yours—except a whole lot cleaner."

"It's prettier too," Ollie added, showing off the nail polish splotches on his clothes. "I've been working on it all morning."

Rocco gave Ollie a hearty slap on the back. He didn't seem to be nervous at all. "A chance to see Ollie's latest art *and* have a conversation with a supervillain? Sounds like the girls' bathroom really has it all. What the heck are we waiting for?" When he stepped forward and pushed through the door, Paige followed him inside. Alfie groaned and reluctantly trailed behind her.

"Stay here and stand guard," Charlie ordered Ollie. "Don't let anyone in."

"Sure thing, but what do you want me to do about the other door?" Ollie asked.

"Other door?" Charlie said.

"Yeah. You mean, you've never been in there? There's another door on the opposite side of the bathroom."

"What?" Charlie groaned. While he was watching one door, INK could have escaped through the other. "No, Ollie, I *haven't* been in there."

Just then, Rocco popped his head out of the bathroom and confirmed Charlie's fears. "Unless INK's invisible, there's nobody in here. Nice work, by the way, Ollie. Reminds me of the time my mom took me snorkeling in Mexico. . . ."

"These aren't *Mexican* species," Alfie called out behind Rocco, his voice echoing off the bathroom's tiles. "They're all native to Australia's Great Barrier Reef." He stuck his head out below Rocco's. "You paint a mean turkey fish, Ollie!"

"What are you talking . . . ," Charlie started to ask as he pushed past his friends and entered the bathroom. "Whoa," he said, temporarily forgetting his reasons for visiting the girls' room.

The blue tiles on the bathroom's walls had been trans-

formed into an underwater world teeming with sea creatures. Brightly colored fish swam in circles around them,
while the unmistakable silhouette of a giant hammerhead
shark passed across the ceiling. A pair of flipper-clad feet
appeared to be sticking out of the beast's mouth. Anemo-
nes waved at Charlie from atop the paper towel dispenser,
and a giant octopus embraced one of the toilets with its
many arms.

A trash can in a corner was filled to the rim with nail
polish bottles, and the air reeked of varnish.

"Yes, remarkable, isn't it?" Alfie said. "And to think
Ollie must have done it all with his mom's nail polish collection. By the way, this is so much nicer than the boys'
room, Paige. You even have toilet paper, and doors on the
stalls!"

"Yeah, yeah, yeah," Paige said. "The girls here are all
so civilized and clean. Too bad one of us is a homicidal
maniac who may not be human. What are we planning to
do about her, anyway?"

"I don't know," Charlie admitted. He closed the lid on
one of the toilets and took advantage of the seat. He'd
been trying to figure it out all morning, and he still hadn't
come up with an answer.

"Why is she here?" Rocco asked. "After INK burned
down that lighthouse, she could have gone anywhere and

we never would have found her. Why would she come to Cypress Creek, where every kid in town will recognize her from their nightmares?"

Charlie looked up at his friends, surprised. Did they really not know? Maybe they didn't. None of them had any siblings. "She came here because there's a portal to the Netherworld inside the purple mansion," he told them. "And her sister is trapped on the other side." Charlie didn't have a sister, but he had a brother. And as annoying as Jack could be, Charlie would never leave him stranded.

One of the bathroom doors slammed open against the wall. Charlie's friends flinched, and he jumped up from his seat. A woman had just barged into the lavatory. She was small—barely taller than Charlie. Her thick black hair was cut in a sleek bob, with bangs that brushed against her eyebrows. She wore a slim black dress and black heels, and her mouth was painted crimson. Ms. Abbot was Charlie's new homeroom teacher—and the latest addition to the Cypress Creek Elementary staff. She taught Charlie's science class and was also filling in for a history teacher who'd broken his collarbone in an unfortunate longboarding accident on the way to school.

Ms. Abbot had moved to town from New York in the middle of August—and she'd been the subject of her neighbors' gossip ever since. Rumor had it that the new teacher lived in a run-down old house deep in the woods outside Cypress Creek. She kept to herself, which just made everyone curious. People whispered about her black clothing, her unusually pale skin, and her penchant for bright red lipstick. Some people speculated that Ms. Abbot was hiding a terrible secret, though no one seemed to know what it was. But her reputation for being a bit odd had been cemented that morning, when she kicked off the school year by showing the class her collection of preserved animal brains. Charlie had dealt with Nightmares of all shapes and sizes, but Ms. Abbot gave him the creeps. She may have been small, and she may have been pretty—but there was something about her that wasn't quite right.

Ms. Abbot was supporting a little girl whose feet did not appear to be working properly and whose eyes seemed unable to focus.

"It's going to be okay," the teacher promised the child. "The principal is calling your mother and father to come get you. We're just going to put a little water on your face."

Paige ran to the sink and turned the faucet on for the pair. "Is that Ellie Hopkins? What's wrong with her?" she asked.

"Ellie's not feeling very well," Ms. Abbot responded. "But she'll be . . ." Her voice trailed off as she finally noticed Ollie's artwork and the boys who'd gathered round. "Did you just paint the walls in here?"

Charlie sighed. The last thing any of them needed was to be collared for vandalism on the first day of school.

"No, ma'am, we didn't." Alfie's voice quavered. A suspension would blemish his otherwise perfect academic record. "I swear we had nothing to do with this!"

"Well, when I find the person responsible, I'm going to ask them to decorate my house too. The kid's got crazy talent," Ms. Abbot said, returning her attention to the girl in her care. "Will one of you hold Ellie while I wet some paper towels?"

Alfie and Paige each took an arm. "Is there anything Charlie and I can do?" Rocco asked. He lived to be helpful.

"Yes, thank you. You can start by getting out of the girls' bathroom. Then would you mind going to the lunchroom and collecting Ellie's things? She fainted near the condiment stand."

"She fainted?" Charlie asked. A chill trickled down his spine.

Ellie opened her mouth. The four words that exited were barely whispered, but Charlie still managed to catch them. "I saw the girl," she said.

Charlie nudged Rocco with his elbow. "Let's go," he said.

CHAPTER FOUR

THE PROMISE

"She looks so . . ." Rocco paused to search for the right word.

"Diabolical? Homicidal? Bloodthirsty?" Charlie was happy to fill in the blank.

"Harmless," Rocco said with a sigh. Charlie heard the pity in his friend's voice, and it sounded like trouble. Though Rocco was taller than almost everyone else at school, beneath that strapping exterior was a soft spot the size of a kindergartner. Rocco Marquez was way too nice.

But Charlie had to admit it—his friend was right about INK. She was sitting on her own at a table in the center of the cafeteria. Not only was her table empty, but so were the four tables that surrounded it. All the other kids were keeping their distance. At the tables on the edge of the cafeteria, a hundred students had crammed into half as many seats, and the air around them swirled with whispers. Charlie knew what it was like to feel so alone. It wasn't a very nice feeling.

INK was examining the items on the lunch tray in front of her like a scientist dissecting a particularly revolting specimen. She picked up a nugget and gave it a sniff. Her face wrinkled with disgust, and she dropped it back down to her plate.

"Looks like INK's sense of smell is working just fine," Charlie noted. "All you need is one whiff of those nuggets to know they're not made of chicken."

"But she seems to really be into the tater tots," Rocco said. INK had already popped one into her mouth. Her face registered surprise, followed by delight. She immediately reached for another. "Maybe she's not so bad after all."

"Everyone likes the tater tots," Charlie replied. "They're the only things on the menu that actually taste like food. But we didn't come here to watch INK eat lunch. Let's go talk to her."

"Uh-oh," Rocco said. "I guess somebody else had the same idea."

A kid was pushing through the crowd, trying to reach the empty center of the cafeteria. "Excuse me! Sorry! Excuse me!" Charlie winced at the sound. He couldn't see the kid's face, but he knew the voice all too well.

His nine-year-old brother, Jack, emerged from the mob and set his Captain America lunch box down in front of INK. The whispers stopped and the lunchroom was eerily silent. Standing by the door, Charlie and Rocco could hear every last word. "Mind if I take this seat?" Jack asked the girl.

INK looked up, and the sides of her mouth twitched as if she were struggling to smile but didn't know how. "Hello, Jack," she replied in her elegant accent. "I was hoping I'd see you here."

Jack beamed as if he really meant it. "Hi, Indy," he said.

Charlie had almost forgotten that the two knew one another. Over the spring, Jack had taken dozens of secret trips to the Netherworld while Charlie and Charlotte were asleep. During one of those visits, Jack had met INK. He later told Charlie that he'd kept the girl company because she'd seemed lonely. But Charlie suspected their friendship was just part of the twins' devious plot. There was only one reason a villain like INK would hang out with a nine-year-old. She must have been gathering information on the Laird family, their purple mansion, and the town of Cypress Creek.

Jack opened his lunch box and pulled out a sandwich. "You're from England, right? Have you ever tried a PB&J? It stands for peanut butter and jelly. Or peanut butter and *jam,* if you're fancy. It's kind of an American delicacy— sort of like tater tots. My stepmom makes the best PB&J in the whole world. She finds these weird berries in the woods and turns them into jam." He held out half of his sandwich and INK accepted it.

What was Jack doing? Charlie fumed. This time his brother couldn't claim he didn't know any better. Was he trying to get himself killed? Who knew what INK would do if someone upset her. What if she hated PB&Js? Charlie took a step forward, planning to push his way through the crowd.

Rocco put a hand on his shoulder. "Don't, Charlie," he said softly. "I think Jack's got this one covered for now."

The old jealousy flared up for an instant before Charlie got control of himself and it died back down. His brother had a way with people—and ogres, gorgons, and changelings—that Charlie would never share. Jack could charm the pants off just about anyone or *anything.* He'd been sitting with INK for less than a minute and he literally had her eating right out of his hand.

"So do you go to school here now?" Charlie heard Jack ask.

INK nodded. She clearly wanted to speak, but her mouth was sealed shut with peanut butter, and it took several attempts before she could swallow it. "A bomb destroyed my old school in London. I always wanted to find a new one."

Charlie felt ill. Was that what INK had in mind for Cypress Creek Elementary?

"A bomb?" Jack asked casually, without a hint of concern in his voice. He really was good at this, Charlie thought bitterly.

"Oh yes," INK said. "It blew the whole place to smithereens."

"Gee," said Jack. "That's terrible."

"Not really. It happened at night," INK said, taking another bite of her sandwich. "There was no one inside."

"Whew," Jack said, wiping imaginary sweat from his brow. "Well, welcome to Cyprus Creek Elementary! I'm glad you're here, but I'm kind of surprised. I thought you'd want to go to school in Orville Falls."

INK stopped chewing. Something about her eyes had changed. "Why would you think that?" she asked.

Jack didn't let the question throw him for a second. "Oh, just because there's a big house there that they call Kessog Castle. Since your last name is Kessog, I figured you must be related to the guy who built it. Was he a cousin or something?"

"He was my uncle," INK said. "But I will *never* go back to that horrible place again. The people there are the worst I've ever met."

The tone of her voice made it perfectly clear that her uncle and Orville Falls were not subjects she cared to discuss. "Interesting," Charlie mumbled, wishing he had a pen to take notes. His brother and INK chewed their PB&Js in silence while Jack seemed to think about what to ask next. Suddenly the whispers from the kids at the edges of the cafeteria began to grow louder.

"Oh no," Rocco groaned. "Things are about to get way *too* interesting."

A hulking figure had stepped out of the crowd at the edges of the cafeteria and into the center of the room. A smaller creature scurried behind it, darting among the chairs. The hulk was a girl named Jancy Dare—star line-backer for the Cypress Creek Elementary football team, which Rocco captained. Jancy was taller than Rocco by three full inches, wider than him by at least six—and meaner than a sack of snakes. The nightmare of eighth-grade football players throughout the state, she was leg-endary for tackling quarterbacks—even those who weren't on the field. The imp trailing behind her was a kid named Lester. No one could figure out whether he was Jancy's boyfriend or her servant. His only functions seemed to be lugging Jancy's backpack around, taking her abuse—and handing it right back out to everyone else.

Jancy stomped up to the table where Jack and INK were sitting. "I know you," she said.

"I know you too," Jack said. "We've gone to school together for five years. How are you today, Jancy? When does football season start?"

Lester tittered.

"I wasn't talking to you, Captain America," Jancy snarled. "I was talking to her." She pointed a finger directly at INK. Its tip was less than an inch from the red tie tucked primly into the top of INK's navy-blue pinafore.

"Cute outfit," Lester said. "What are you? A Halloween-edition American Girl doll?"

INK said nothing. She was staring at Jancy with a look that Charlie would have called *scientific*—as if there were something about the linebacker's bright red face that intrigued her.

"I had a million nightmares this summer about a kid who looked just like you," Jancy said. "She wouldn't leave me alone or let me get a good night's sleep. She'd keep popping out from behind things or locking me in dark rooms. Well, now you're in *my* world, sister. I don't know how you got here, but I'm gonna pay you back. And I'm really gonna enjoy it too."

INK's eyes hadn't left Jancy's face. "I'm sorry. I've never seen you before, and I have no idea what you're talking about. I'm afraid you must have me confused with someone else," she said politely.

Jancy shook her head. "Nope, I'd recognize that weird outfit anywhere. And you've got the accent too. So stand up and take your punishment like a woman."

"You seem quite agitated," INK observed, rising from her seat. "And you're perspiring heavily. May I ask you a question? Have you recently been on the front lines of a war?"

"What the . . ." Jancy looked around to see if anyone else had understood. "Are you threatening me?"

"Not at all," INK said. She didn't look afraid.

But Charlie was worried. And he wasn't scared that INK might get hurt. He was terrified of what was about to happen to Jancy. "I've seen enough," he told Rocco. "Let's go."

They rushed toward the group in the center of the cafeteria. As they drew closer, he noticed that Jancy was indeed sweating buckets. There were beads of perspiration across her forehead, and the back of her shirt was soaked.

"What do *you* want?" Jancy demanded when she spotted Rocco heading her way.

"I want you to stop what you're doing," Rocco ordered the linebacker. "May I remind you that you're still on probation for giving that quarterback a concussion last season?" Charlie recalled the incident. Jancy had been on the field—but the quarterback she'd tackled had been sitting in the stands when she'd attacked. He hadn't even been involved in the game. "You so much as flick this girl with one finger and you're off the team for the rest of the year."

Jancy's nostrils flared with rage. She was so tall that Charlie could see up her nose and halfway to her brain. "Don't you know who this is, Marquez?" she demanded. "It's that creepy girl we all saw in our dreams. And haven't you and your little friend Laird been going around telling everyone they shouldn't run from their Nightmares? Well, I'm standing right here until this one hits the road. She's not even a real kid. She's some kind of ghost or demon or something! Just watch!"

Jancy darted to the right and delivered a pinch to INK's upper arm with two of her meaty fingers. Charlie saw the linebacker's face change the moment she made contact. Whatever Jancy had been expecting, it wasn't what she'd found. And the yelp of pain that issued from INK's mouth made it perfectly clear that her arm was made of flesh and blood. For a moment, it seemed as if time had frozen. No one in the cafeteria moved a muscle. Charlie wasn't even sure he was breathing. Something horrible was about to happen.

"That's it!" Rocco charged toward Jancy, shoving Lester out of the way and sending him sailing across the cafeteria floor on his rump. "I warned you." He stood nose to nose with the girl known across the state as the Quarterback Killer. There was no telling what might have happened if Ms. Abbot hadn't entered the cafeteria at that very moment, searching for Ellie Hopkins's backpack, which Charlie had completely forgotten.

"You two!" she shouted across the room. "I don't know what's going on over there, but you both just won a trip to the principal's office!" The two football players were still on the verge of blows, each waiting for an excuse to tackle the other. "Now!" Ms. Abbot bellowed at the top of her lungs. It might have been Charlie's imagination, but the lights overhead seemed to flicker.

As Rocco and Jancy marched across the cafeteria, the sound of a pencil on paper drew Charlie's attention back to INK. She appeared to be taking notes.

"Remarkable." INK closed the little book in which she'd been writing. "How long has the girl been like that?" she asked Charlie.

"Forever," Charlie said. "Come with me." He took INK by the arm, which was just as solid as any he'd ever felt, and guided her toward the door. Jack rushed after them, leaving his lunch behind on the table.

"Are you okay, India?" Ms. Abbot asked INK as they passed.

"I don't suppose I'm the one you should be worried about," INK replied.

Then Ms. Abbot glanced over at Charlie and Jack. "Is your school always so crazy?" she asked.

"Oh, this is *nothing*," Jack replied. "You should have been here when we had a monster for a principal."

Out in the deserted hall, Charlie stopped and let go of INK's arm. He, his brother, and the strange girl stood in a circle. For the first time, Charlie had a chance to study INK up close. Her auburn hair was perfectly parted and pinned back by a tortoiseshell barrette. Her skin was the bluish white of skim milk, and the apples of her cheeks were a delicate pink. With her big brown eyes and long black lashes, she really did resemble a doll. But not the sort of doll you'd find on a toy store's shelves. Looking at INK was like opening a forgotten trunk in a dusty attic and discovering a perfectly preserved doll from another time tucked inside.

"I know who you are. Why are you here?" Charlie asked her. "What do you want?"

"Geez, Charlie. Way to break the ice," Jack muttered sarcastically under his breath.

"I want to go to school," INK told him. "The world

seems to have changed a great deal while I've been away. There must be a lot for me to learn."

Charlie shook his head and laughed. "Nice one. I don't believe that for a *second,*" he sneered. He pointed back toward the cafeteria. "The kids in there won't believe you either. You've got something planned. What is it? Are you going to blow up our school, or burn it down, like you did to that lighthouse in Maine?"

Jack gasped at his brother's rudeness. "Charlie!"

INK stared at him with her giant brown eyes and nodded as if she finally understood. "My sister warned me it would be like this. But that's all right. I'll show you all *exactly* what I have planned."

Then, without warning, INK bolted. She was faster than she looked, and within seconds, she'd rounded a corner. Charlie and Jack did their best to keep up, but INK had already disappeared.

CHAPTER FIVE

THE DEADLY DOZENS

Charlie and Jack raced through the streets of Cypress Creek, darting around baby carriages and leaping over dogs. Charlie reached Hazel's Herbarium a split second before Jack did. He stood spread-eagled in the front door, blocking it so his brother couldn't get into their stepmother's store. But Jack just dropped to his knees and crawled between Charlie's legs.

"Boys! What in the—" Charlotte Laird stepped out from behind the cash register and Jack sprinted across the shop to reach her. A customer watched the scene with bulging eyes and growing alarm, clutching a jumbo-sized container of fungus remover to his chest.

"INK is here!" Jack managed to shout before he fell to the floor at Charlotte's feet, panting like he'd just carried the news over the mountains and all around town. As soon as the secret was out, Charlie's knees buckled. He collapsed and sucked in as much air as his burning lungs could hold.

Charlotte left the boys on the floor and hurried over to her customer. "I'm so sorry, Mr. Hainey," she said, taking him by the arm and guiding him toward the front door. "I'm afraid we have a little emergency here. Would you mind excusing us? Your fungus remover is on the house today. But please don't forget the two rules we discussed— use it only on your feet, and a little goes a long way. Let's avoid making the same mistake three times, shall we?"

"Of course," the man assured her, stepping over Charlie on his way out of the shop. "Thank you for understanding, Mrs. Laird."

As soon as he was out the door, Charlotte locked it and flipped the sign in the window to CLOSED.

When she spun around, the coils of her curly red hair were writhing like snakes. "What in the blazes is going on?" she demanded. "I'm trying to run a business here!"

Charlie began the painful work of peeling his body off the floor. "INK was at school today."

"No!" Charlotte grabbed a table to steady herself. She looked like she'd just jammed a fork in a toaster. "At Cypress Creek Elementary?"

"Yeah, and Charlie chased her away!" Jack added.

"I did not!" Charlie growled as he stood up and brushed himself off.

Jack jumped to his feet. "Did too!" he shouted at his brother. "Charlie was rude to her and she disappeared."

"Well, what was I supposed to do?" Charlie shouted back. "Offer her a peanut butter and jelly sandwich?"

"Boys!" Charlotte shouted, and the arguing stopped. "Both of you! Take a seat at the counter this instant."

Charlie and Jack swapped snarls as they pulled stools up to the counter. Then a strange sight caught Charlie's eye. More than two dozen potted plants sat on the floor in a corner of the room. His stepmom's herbarium was wild and green, but she never left plants on the floor, where they might get knocked over. The pots always stayed in the windows or on the shelves. Someone had purchased these and was coming to pick them up, Charlie figured. They were packaged in clear plastic bags, and a receipt was pinned to the largest one. None of this would have been all that remarkable if it hadn't been for the plants themselves. Charlie worked for his stepmom every weekend, and he knew the plants in the bags weren't species Charlotte usually sold. He recognized devil's breath, jimsonweed, foxglove, and wolfsbane among them. There were a couple of tropical specimens he couldn't identify. But he was willing to bet that they shared one thing in common with every other plant on the floor: they were all poisonous.

Charlie heard the sound of Charlotte's stool legs scraping across the floor. His stepmother had taken a seat across from the boys. "So INK's finally here," she said with a sigh.

"You knew she'd come to Cypress Creek?" Jack asked.

"I had a hunch. Where else would she go now that she's stuck on this side?" Charlotte asked. "Her lighthouse in Maine burned down. And Kessog Castle in Orville Falls is being demolished. I saw it on the news this morning."

Charlie shouldn't have been so surprised to hear it. Over the summer, Kessog Castle had been home to the goblins that helped ICK and INK sell Tranquility Tonic. Once the tonic had turned the

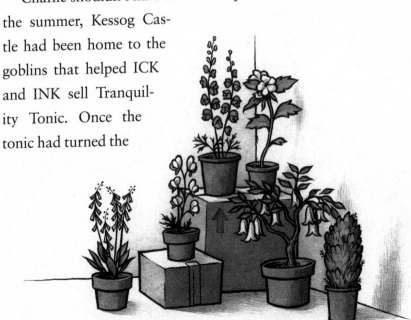

people of Orville Falls into Walkers, the goblins forced them to work at the castle as slaves. Charlie didn't blame the town's citizens for wanting to knock the whole place to the ground.

"INK told me today that the castle belonged to her uncle," Jack said. "And I don't think she liked him very much."

"So Alfred Kessog was ICK and INK's *uncle*. How interesting . . ." For several seconds, Charlotte seemed lost in thought. Her eyes darted from side to side, her eyebrows were knitted, and her lips formed silent words. She was on to something, Charlie could tell.

Finally he couldn't stand the suspense any longer. "Charlotte?" he said.

Hearing her name brought her out of her trance. "What?" She looked startled to find them still sitting across from her.

Jack giggled and Charlotte broke into a grin. "Sorry, boys. I was just thinking about Alfred Kessog. They were talking about him on the news this morning. It sounds like he was a really weird dude."

"Well, he sure did build a creepy-looking castle," Jack said.

"Yeah, and then he locked himself up inside it," Charlie added.

Charlotte nodded. "But the funny thing is, that's pretty

much all anyone seems to know about Alfred Kessog. The reporter said Kessog wasn't even from Orville Falls. He paid for the castle to be built, and then he showed up one day, closed the door behind him, and refused to come out. The people in the town rarely saw him. They say he had groceries and supplies delivered and left on the doorstep."

"He sounds a lot like . . . ," Charlie started.

"Silas DeChant," his stepmother finished the sentence for him. "I thought so too." One of Charlotte's ancestors, Silas DeChant, had built the purple mansion they lived in as a place to hide away from the world. Alone in the mansion, he'd allowed his fears to take over his life. Eventually his terror grew so powerful that it ripped a hole in the Waking World and created a portal to the land of Nightmares.

"Do you think Alfred Kessog opened a portal to the Netherworld inside the castle?" Jack asked.

Charlotte shook her head. "If every miserable old hermit were able to open a portal, the world would be filled with portals. No, I think Alfred Kessog may have allowed his fears to do something far worse."

"What could be worse than opening a portal and living with your nightmares?" Charlie wondered.

"Letting your fears hurt the people around you," Charlotte said. "I'm starting to think that's what Alfred Kessog might have done to his two young nieces. Why else would they try so hard to destroy Orville Falls? Do you remember when ICK and INK used to send messages to your mom and me?"

Charlie couldn't have forgotten if he'd tried. Charlotte and his mother, Veronica, had been friends when they were both Charlie's age, and they'd visited the Netherworld together. For a few frightening months, ICK and INK had sent them a series of notes, trying to lure Charlotte and Veronica into the Netherworld version of the lighthouse where the twins lived.

"The last time your mom and I dreamed about the lighthouse, we found a note written in sand on the ground outside. It said YOU'RE ALL THE SAME. YOU'RE JUST LIKE HIM. Back then, we had no idea what that meant. But now I wonder if they might have been talking about Alfred Kessog."

"But what does it mean, 'You're just like him'?" Charlie asked.

"I don't know," Charlotte admitted. "We didn't ask. Your mother wanted to, but I was dead set against it."

Jack leaned in. "Mom wanted to know?"

"Veronica had a very big heart. She thought we should leave them a note that asked, WHY? But I wouldn't let her. ICK and INK had been terrorizing us for months. I was exhausted, and I just wanted it to end. And after that dream, it did. We never heard from ICK and INK again."

WHY? The last time Charlie had visited his mom in

the Dream Realm, she had challenged him to ask the same question. WHY had two little girls tried to destroy three worlds? Did the answer have something to do with Alfred Kessog and his castle?

There was a knock at the front door, and Charlotte and the boys all jumped. A small figure in a long black cape was standing on the sidewalk outside the shop. The Closed sign hid most of her face, but her lips were visible, and there was only one person in Cypress Creek who wore lipstick in such a startling shade of red. Ms. Abbot from school had come to speak to Charlie's stepmom.

"Isn't that the teacher from the cafeteria?" Jack whispered. "Are we in trouble or something?"

"I don't know," Charlie replied, wishing the shop had a back entrance he could use as an escape route.

Charlotte unlocked the shop door and cheerfully ushered her visitor inside.

"Have you closed for the evening?" Ms. Abbot asked. "Am I too late?"

"Not at all! You're always welcome here, Samantha. Come in. Your order is packed up and ready to go."

Charlie and Jack glanced at each other in surprise. The science teacher wasn't there to talk about school. She was obviously the person who'd ordered the poisonous plants on the floor. And judging by the tone of their voices, Charlotte and Samantha Abbot were more than just shopkeeper and customer—the two women seemed to be quite friendly.

"Ah, so *these* are the stepsons I've heard so much about." Ms. Abbot was looking directly at them. "I believe I met them both in the school cafeteria today."

Charlie waited for her to tell the rest of the story. Surely the teacher would mention Ollie's nail polish mural or Rocco's lunchtime showdown. But as the seconds ticked past, Charlie realized Ms. Abbot wasn't going to say a word. It felt like she was trying to win him over with her silence, and that made Charlie uncomfortable. He wasn't cute or cuddly like Jack anymore. When you reached twelve years old, most adults were only this nice when they wanted something from you.

"I hope the boys weren't causing any trouble," Charlotte joked as she gathered up the plant-filled bags from the corner.

"Oh, I don't mind a *little* trouble," Ms. Abbot assured her, still staring at Charlie. "Trouble keeps life interesting, wouldn't you agree?"

Yes, Charlie thought. But it was a highly unusual philosophy for an elementary school teacher. Though most teachers didn't dress all in black—or purchase dozens of deadly plants either.

"I've had enough trouble for one lifetime, I think,"

Charlotte said with a chuckle. "I could stand to be bored for a while." She gestured to the clear plastic bags she now held in her hands. "Would you like these in the backseat of your car or the trunk?"

"The trunk, please," Ms. Abbot said. "By the way, Charlotte, didn't you tell me that your older boy is a marvelous gardener?"

"Oh yes, he's a natural," Charlotte confirmed, sounding completely phony. She and the teacher seemed to be reciting lines they'd practiced in advance. If Charlie hadn't been so unnerved by the performance, he would have rolled his eyes at the terrible acting. It was clear they'd made some sort of deal.

"His name is Charlie," Jack threw in.

Ms. Abbot's lips formed a sickle when she smiled. "Oh, I know *exactly* what your brother's name is," she said.

CHAPTER SIX

THE GHOST

Charlie grumbled all the way home. He was still miffed when Charlotte's ancient Range Rover pulled up in front of the purple mansion. She removed the keys from the ignition and then turned to face him.

"INK's in town, and we have work to do," she said. "There's no time for arguing, Charlie."

"And it's not the time to be hanging out with some weird science teacher either," Charlie replied.

"Since when do you have something against weird people?" Charlotte asked. "Has it ever occurred to you that you're weird too? The weirdos of the world need to stick together!"

"Hrumph!" Charlie said. Charlotte had never sent him to work for anyone else before.

"Awkward," Jack muttered in the backseat. "I'm out of here." He opened the door and slid out of the car.

"I still can't believe you farmed me out," Charlie huffed. "And you didn't even ask my permission!"

"I'm sorry! I really thought you'd be happy!" Charlotte exclaimed. "Samantha needs help planting her garden, and you're super good at that sort of thing. And did I happen to mention you're going to get paid?"

"Why should I be happy?" Charlie argued. "My bizarre new science teacher just bought a trunkload of the world's most dangerous plants, and I'm supposed to help her get them into the ground, and you won't even tell me why. Ms. Abbot—*Samantha,* if that's even her real name—isn't who she says she is, is she?"

Charlotte's face gave nothing away. It was a shame she didn't play more poker, Charlie thought. "I'm afraid it's all confidential," she said, making it perfectly clear that she wasn't going to spill any beans.

"So it's true! She *is* hiding something!" Charlie blurted out. "Of course she is! What kind of teacher wears black capes and lives in a shack in the middle of the woods? That sounds like a *witch* to me. And you know how I feel about witches, Charlotte. Don't you remember that I used to have nightmares about that sort of thing?"

"And you beat those nightmares ages ago! Plus, it's not a shack anymore," Charlotte countered. "Samantha's worked wonders on the old Livingston place!"

"Yeah, I'll believe it when I see it," Charlie mumbled. The old Livingston place was at the end of a dirt road that cut through the darkest part of the forest surrounding Cypress Creek. For most of Charlie's life, the house had been a total ruin. Teenagers dared one another to spend a night inside. Legend had it that no one had ever lasted more than an hour. It was the kind of house you'd buy if you wanted to scare visitors away.

"I'll tell you what I can't believe," Charlotte said. "I can't believe that a boy who's taken on a million Nightmares and a pair of evil twins could be so disturbed by a perfectly nice woman who teaches children for a living."

Charlie turned to Charlotte. "You think she's okay just because she's a *teacher*?" he asked. "I guess you're like all the other old people. You've forgotten what it's like to be a kid."

He jumped out of the car and slammed the door behind him.

Charlotte rolled down the window and leaned outside. "I'm not old yet, you little fart!" she shouted at his back.

Charlie said nothing in return. He and Charlotte hadn't had a fight in months. He couldn't understand how everything had gone so wrong so quickly. Why was his stepmother pressuring him to do something he didn't want to do?

Inside, he marched down the hall toward the kitchen at the back of the mansion. There, he found his father standing at the stove, stirring a pot of his famous spaghetti sauce—and sautéing a dozen intriguing little brown balls in a pan beside it.

Charlie's stomach rumbled, and hunger briefly triumphed over anger. He dumped his backpack on the kitchen table and went to investigate. "I can't believe it. Are those *meatballs*?" He hadn't seen real meatballs since his father had married a vegetarian.

"Yep," his father confirmed. "It's my new recipe. Made with beans, lentils, and a little bit of banana to hold it all together."

"Oh," Charlie said, losing interest fast. "So they're really bean balls. *Banana* bean balls. Great. They sound really . . . delicious."

"Jack says you and Charlotte are having an argument?"

That was fast, Charlie thought bitterly. "Jack needs to mind his own business," he grumbled.

"Yes, and that's exactly what I told him," Andrew Laird said. "But if there's anything I can do—"

Charlie didn't give his father a chance to finish the

sentence. Suddenly the words were rushing out of him like seltzer from a shaken bottle. He told his dad about Ms. Abbot, her crazy garden, and the shack in the woods.

He'd only just finished when Charlotte appeared in the kitchen and gave Charlie's father a kiss. "Charlie's annoyed with me."

Charlie crossed his arms and raised an eyebrow at his stepmother. She was using all the kissy-kissy stuff to win his father over to her side. She wasn't playing fair.

"So I've gathered," Charlie's father said. "You know, honey, if Charlie really doesn't want to work for this woman, maybe we shouldn't make him."

Charlie smirked, but Charlotte refused to give in. "But, Andy," she pleaded, catching her husband's eye, "Ms. Abbot's the one I told you about."

"Yes, I know," Andrew replied. "And I agree that it would be nice if Charlie offered to help her. But if forcing him to do it starts a family feud, I don't think it's worth it."

Charlie hated it when his parents spoke in grown-up code. It was clear that his father and stepmother both knew something about Ms. Abbot that he didn't. On another day it would have driven him crazy, but now Charlie could see that his father's words were working their magic on Charlotte. She was on the verge of surrender.

"Oh, all right," she finally sighed. "I'll call Samantha in the morning and tell her the deal is off."

Charlie exhaled and felt relief fill his body.

"Woo-hoo! Another problem solved by Andrew Laird!" his father announced, raising his greasy spatula in victory. "Now maybe one of you can help solve a little mystery for me. Where are the keys to the locks on the tower door?"

Just like that, Charlie's argument with Charlotte seemed like a distant memory, and the relief he'd briefly enjoyed was long gone. The tomato sauce in the pot was popping loudly and launching droplets into the air. When they hit the stove top, the splatter looked like blood from a crime scene.

"What?" Andrew Laird asked when he caught sight of the expression on his wife's face. "Did I just say something wrong?"

Charlie's father had no idea what the locks were really for. The night Charlotte and Charlie barricaded the tower door, a powerful thunderstorm had swept through Cypress Creek. And the next morning, Charlotte had come downstairs with the perfect excuse. She claimed the storm had damaged the tower. She'd been forced to lock the door to keep everyone out until it could be properly fixed. Never once did she or Charlie mention that an evil creature in the guise of a twelve-year-old girl might be lurking on the other side.

Charlotte cleared her throat nervously. "Of course you

didn't say anything wrong! I'm trying to remember where I last saw the keys. Why do you ask?"

Andrew Laird turned back to his spaghetti sauce. "No big deal. I just thought I heard something up there when I got home this afternoon. I was going to check it out, but I couldn't find the keys."

"You heard noises?" Charlie asked, struggling to sound perfectly casual when his heart was about to burst through his chest. "What did they sound like?"

"A ghost," Andrew replied bluntly.

Charlie gulped. There were no such things as ghosts in the Waking World. If his dad had heard noises in the tower, it meant that ICK had arrived. She'd come through the portal. She had been in their house.

"A *ghost*?" Charlotte asked.

"I'm kidding!" Andrew Laird exclaimed with a hearty laugh. "Actually, it sounded like an animal had gotten in up there. In my experience, squirrels are usually the culprits, but from the racket this one was making, I'd say it's a bit bigger. A raccoon, most likely."

If only it were a raccoon, Charlie thought. Even a rabid monster raccoon with a taste for human blood would have been better than ICK. "Do you think it's still up there?" he asked.

The three of them looked at the ceiling and listened.

"Hard to tell. I haven't heard any thumps in a while," Andrew said after a few seconds had passed. "It might have gone out the same way it came in. I'll take a look in a bit and make sure it isn't building a nest and making itself at home. One minute they're sleeping in our tower, the next they're eating our bean balls. And *nobody* steals our banana bean balls." He stopped and seemed to be waiting for the others to laugh. No one did.

Charlie caught his stepmother's eye. He knew Charlotte was thinking the same thing he was: if ICK had been in the house, there was no telling what Andrew Laird might find if he paid a visit to the tower.

"You know what?" Charlotte said. "My grandmother's desk is still in the tower, and she'd roll over in her grave if I let it get covered in raccoon poop. You just keep cooking, honey. I think I'll go run and have a peek right now."

Charlie's dad frowned. "You sure you want to go up there alone? Raccoons can get pretty ferocious. Back when I was in grad school, I once saw one leap out of a trash can and attack a mailman. Poor guy had to get a million rabies shots. In his *stomach*." Andrew Laird stabbed his belly with the handle of the spatula for emphasis.

"Don't worry. I'll go with her," Charlie announced. "That way it'll be two against one."

The grin on his father's face told Charlie he'd just said

the right thing. "How about that?" Andrew said. "I guess there's nothing like a furry little intruder to bring a family back together."

"Thanks for coming with me," Charlotte whispered on their way up the stairs.

"You're welcome," Charlie told her. "I may have been mad at you, but that doesn't mean I'd let you die alone at the hands of some killer kid."

"How *gallant*," Charlotte drawled.

When they reached the tower door, Charlie put his ear to the wood. A minute passed—then another. He couldn't hear a thing. "It's quiet," he informed Charlotte. "I think this one might have been a false alarm."

Charlie stood back while Charlotte removed the locks one by one. Then she took a deep breath and opened the door. The staircase on the other side was empty.

"I'll go first," Charlotte said. "You stay right behind me."

At the top of the stairs lay the little octagonal chamber that housed the mansion's portal. The room had once served as Charlotte's office, but they'd moved everything except her grandmother's desk downstairs when they'd realized ICK could get through the portal. Charlotte stood in the doorway, blocking Charlie's view. Her head swiveled from side to side as she scanned the space for intruders. Then she walked over to the giant oak desk and checked beneath it.

"I think you're right—false alarm," she said, breathing a sigh of relief. "It doesn't look like ICK's been in here."

Charlie stuck his head into the room and had a look for himself. All he saw was the desk and the piece of paper lying on top of it. The letter to ICK was right where they'd left it. And the portal was closed as well.

"But then what did Dad hear?" Charlie asked.

Charlotte shrugged. "Maybe there *was* a raccoon in here," she said.

Charlie wasn't convinced. He pointed at the windows, which they'd boarded up. "How did it get in? And how did it get back out?"

"Chimney?" Charlotte asked. There was a small fireplace along one wall of the room. They hadn't bothered to block it. There was no way for a human—even a small one—to squeeze past the flue.

"There's your answer right there," said a male voice from behind them.

Charlie turned around so quickly that he nearly spun right out of his skin. Charlotte teetered on her heels for a moment with her hand pressed against her heart.

"Andy!" she gasped. "You scared me to death."

Andrew Laird threw an arm around his wife and

laughed. "Sorry 'bout that. I guess you didn't hear me yelling from downstairs. Dinner's ready." Then he pointed to the corner of one of the tower's two windows, where a board had shifted to reveal a gap about five inches wide. "That's probably where the varmint got in. Looks like you guys didn't nail down the end of that board very well."

Charlie crossed the room and squatted in front of the window. The board had been pried loose from the wall. Behind it, the glass was open a crack, and he could see the purple mansion's roof just below. There was no doubt that a raccoon could have gotten up to the roof and squeezed through the hole. But it couldn't have opened the glass window—and Charlie was certain it had been closed and locked when they'd sealed off the room.

Andrew Laird bent down beside Charlie. "Ha!" he exclaimed, plucking something from one of the rough boards. "And here's the proof. Our visitor left evidence behind."

Charlie's dad held his evidence up to the light. It was a single black hair—and Charlie could tell it wasn't human. More importantly, it wasn't auburn.

The discovery should have made Charlie feel better. But it didn't. He was no forensic scientist, but to him the hair looked a lot like *wool*.

CHAPTER SEVEN

BLAH, BLAH, BLACK SHEEP

A moon hung in the sky, casting a pale silver light over the Netherworld. Wherever he looked, Charlie saw sheep. Fat, stinky, beady-eyed sheep. There had to be hundreds of them—all chewing and bleating and pooping. One brushed past Charlie without so much as a glance. Another nibbled at the grass between his toes. Since it wasn't Charlie's nightmare, they treated him as if he weren't even there.

Charlie figured he had to be inside some sort of sheep pen. What else would keep the animals from wandering off? But he'd been searching for what felt like hours and he still hadn't found a fence or a gate. His legs were exhausted from forging through the muck. In the distance, he could see the lights of a building perched on the side of a hill. It looked eerily familiar, but even if it turned out to be Dracula's lair, it had to be better than a field covered with sheep poop. Yet no matter how long Charlie walked toward the lights, he never seemed to get any closer.

At last he gave up. He searched for the cleanest patch of ground he could find and sat down with a thump. There was nothing to do, no one to talk to—and nothing to see besides sheep. After a while, Charlie began to worry that he might die of boredom. So he did the only thing he could think of to keep himself sane. He started to hum.

He'd barely made it past the third note of the lullaby when he was interrupted by a high-pitched screech. A glob of muck flew out of the darkness and splattered against the side of his face. Then a second slammed into the side of his head.

One of Charlie's ears was filled with mud, but he could still hear something running toward him, and he knew from the way it was growling and panting that it certainly wasn't a sheep.

"OUT!" it howled. "GET OUT!" The voice belonged to a girl.

Charlie sat straight up in bed, sweat dripping from his hair. The clock on his bedside table said 2:37 a.m. Charlie knew there would be no getting back to sleep that night. He lay awake with the sheets pulled up to his chin and the screech echoing in his head. He'd only heard two words, but the voice had clearly been young and female. A strange idea started to form in Charlie's head.

Then a noise outside put his thoughts on hold. It was a soft crunch, as if someone had stepped on the mulch-covered flower bed right under his window.

Charlie sat bolt upright. He'd never heard that particular sound before—and he'd spent enough time awake at night to be familiar with all the weird noises the purple mansion made. He knew it creaked and groaned in even the gentlest wind. The soft, stealthy footsteps that often passed outside his door belonged to Charlotte's cat, Aggie, who patrolled the halls while the Laird family slept. (Once bitter enemies, Charlie and the cat had finally declared a truce, and it had been over a month since Charlie had woken up with cat butt in his face.) Downstairs, the dishwasher would always beep as it switched itself off, and ominous gurgles would issue from the bathroom drains.

But Charlie had never heard anything like the sound he'd just heard. Listening closely, barely breathing, Charlie picked up the slap of the plastic dog door in the mansion's kitchen. Rufus, the family mutt, must have popped inside for a snack. Charlie waited for the familiar sound of Rufus's slurping and chomping. When the house stayed silent, he lay back down and let his thoughts return to the girl who'd kicked him out of the dream.

Could it be possible? he wondered as he stared at the ceiling. Could the sheep and the darkness belong to *ICK*? No, it didn't make sense. Why would a villain have nightmares about a flock of sheep? Why would a little humming drive her so insane? And why the heck was he in her dream?

Charlie hadn't even begun to consider the answers when his ears detected a new noise, and his heart stopped. This time, Charlie knew exactly what it was. There were fifteen stairs between the first and second floors of the purple mansion. If you stepped in the middle of the thirteenth stair, it squeaked like a rubber mouse.

Charlie rolled over to face the door. A faint golden light was leaking into his room. Someone was in the hall outside. Charlie slid his legs over the edge of the mattress until he felt the hard wooden floor beneath his toes. He tried to convince himself that it was just his little brother heading to the bathroom for a pee. But then the soft clunk of a chain against wood confirmed his worst fears. Someone was messing with the locks on the tower door. And Charlie knew it wasn't Jack.

He tiptoed to his bedroom door and slowly pulled it

open, trying his best not to make any noise. A girl was standing at the other end of the hall with one ear pressed against the tower door. In her hand she gripped what looked like a small blowtorch, lit with a bright blue flame.

"Izzie!" INK whispered at the door. "Izzie! Are you there? Can you hear me?"

There was no response. The hall was so silent that Charlie could hear tree branches swaying in the wind outside.

"Izzie, this is no time for jokes. I'm going to try to get you out, but I'll have to come back later with something that can crack these locks. I need to ask you a question first."

Once again, there was only silence. Then Charlie's dad started snoring in a nearby bedroom.

"Come on, Izzie!" INK pleaded. "It's very important! I need to know what you remember about Father's formula!"

Suddenly Charlie heard footsteps on the stairs behind the tower door. ICK was coming down for a chat with her sister. Charlie crept forward along the hall, hoping to eavesdrop on the conversation. Then his shoulder brushed against a portrait of one of Charlotte's weird redheaded ancestors and knocked it off the wall. The frame crashed to the ground, sending shards of glass flying in every direction.

INK spun around. In the light of the torch, her face was

horrible to behold. Her eyes were red and ringed with shadows, while her pale cheeks appeared swollen. She looked as though she might have been crying.

"It's you," she said. "The boy from school."

Charlie straightened his spine and did his best to look taller. "I live here," he told the girl. "And it's my job to keep you from opening that door."

"My sister is behind there," INK said. "You can't keep me out."

"We'll see about that." Charlie took one step in the girl's direction and shrieked with pain when his right big toe was speared by a shard of broken glass. The moment the scream left his lips, the light went on in the bedroom Charlie's dad shared with Charlotte. He heard the sound of bedsprings creaking and heavy feet hitting the floorboards. His dad was coming out to investigate.

INK must have heard it too. While Charlie was plucking the glass from his toe, she hit the stairs running. Charlie couldn't follow without cutting his feet to ribbons on the broken glass, so he ducked back into his room and grabbed some sneakers. He slid them onto his feet and made it as far as the doorway when he heard his father shout, "Charlotte, grab the bedspread!"

He found his dad at the top of the stairs, a golden light illuminating his face from below. For a moment, Charlie had no idea what was happening. And then he smelled the smoke and heard the crackling of flames. The purple mansion's stairway was on fire, and the blaze was already making its way toward the portrait of Silas DeChant on the landing. Charlotte ran from the master bedroom, her wild red curls springing in every direction. She tossed the bedspread to Charlie's father, and then sprinted into Jack's room for another. Andrew Laird threw the thick blanket over the flames and began to smother them as Charlotte arrived back on the scene with the second blanket. The fire was almost completely out before the alarms bothered to go off. Charlie knew what that meant. If he hadn't cut his foot and screamed, his father might not have been alerted in time. The thought nearly scared him to death. Another second or two and the fire could have raged out of control. The purple mansion could have burned down. And there was a good chance that his family wouldn't have made it out alive.

Charlie watched his dad examine the giant black burn mark on the wallpaper that lined the staircase. When Andrew Laird looked up, his eyes landed on his son and traveled down to the sneakers on his feet. "Why are you wearing shoes?" he asked. "What the heck just happened here?"

Jack came out of his bedroom, rubbing the sleep out of his eyes with his knuckles. "Did Charlie set the house on fire?"

"It wasn't me. It was *her*. She had some kind of blow-torch," Charlie said before he had a chance to think things through. "She must have set the wallpaper on fire as she went down the stairs."

Behind Andrew, Charlotte pressed a finger against her lips. She didn't want him to say any more.

"*Who* did?" Andrew demanded.

Charlie paused. He was close to breaking Charlotte's most important rule: no matter what happened, Andrew Laird couldn't find out about the portal. Knowledge of the Netherworld was as much a curse as it was a blessing, Charlotte always said. The portal chose who could see it. She didn't want her beloved husband burdened with pro-tecting another realm.

Usually Charlie agreed with his stepmom, but this time he was torn. She wasn't asking him to hide the source of a few mysterious noises. The fire INK set had nearly killed them all. Charlie couldn't lie to his dad about something so important. "It was a girl about my age," he told him. "I think her name is India."

Jack gasped at the name and looked at Charlotte.

"You're telling me some *kid* nearly burned down our house?" Andrew asked skeptically. "You've got to be jok-ing. What was she doing in here?"

Charlie shook his head. "I'm not sure, but I saw her. She was running down the stairs, and she had something that looked like a blowtorch in her hand. It must have set the wallpaper on fire."

"Charlie, are you sure about all this?" Charlotte asked nervously. "Is it possible that you might have been dreaming?"

"No," Charlie answered defiantly. "It wasn't a dream. And she wasn't a *ghost* either."

When Andrew Laird looked back at his son, Charlie could tell he believed him. "Where did the girl go?"

Charlie pointed down the stairs. "She ran out the front door."

Andrew Laird sighed. "Forget the wallpaper. There's a kid wandering around Cypress Creek by herself in the middle of the night with a blowtorch?" He stepped back into the bedroom and emerged again with his cell phone and a sweater. "Jack, go back to bed. Charlotte, call the police and tell them there's a little girl on the loose. I'm going to take a spin around the neighborhood and see if I can find her."

"And I'm going with you," Charlie told his father.

Charlie's dad drove slowly through the streets of Cypress Creek, searching for any sign of the girl who had nearly burned down his house. Charlie suspected that INK was long gone—and part of him was glad. There was so much his dad didn't know, and now wasn't the best time to tell him. Answering his questions about the fire had been tricky enough. Charlie had tried his best to be truthful without giving too much away, but it didn't feel good.

The car's headlights lit the way as Charlie's dad turned onto one of the wooded streets at the edge of town. While Andrew Laird kept his eyes on the road, Charlie watched the trees go by. The forest outside Cypress Creek was vast and wild. Bears and bobcats lived there. Some people claimed Bigfoot did too. Ms. Abbot's house was in there somewhere, which meant that the woods were home to at least one witch. The moon was out, and here and there, beams of silvery light broke through the trees and cast pale circles on the ground.

As Charlie was watching, he saw something dash through one of the moonbeams. He caught his breath and pressed his forehead to the window. His dad hit the brakes and the car skidded to a stop.

"What is it?" Andrew Laird asked. "Did you see something?"

"Yeah, I saw a white thing running through the woods," Charlie told him. It had been moving fast, as if desperate to avoid the car's headlights.

"In the woods?" his father asked. The woods were no place for a kid to be alone at night. "Do you think it could have been a deer?"

Charlie sighed. "I guess so," he told his dad.

It could have been, he thought, *but it wasn't.*

Andrew Laird yawned and mussed Charlie's hair. "What do you say we head back to the house? Both of us have school in the morning, and I think we've done all we can for one night. We'll let the police take over from here."

"Yeah," Charlie agreed with an exaggerated yawn. His nerves were on edge, and he wasn't sleepy at all.

"Then let's go," Andrew Laird said. "I'm sure the cops will find the girl." But the car wasn't moving, and he was still looking at his son. "You know, there may be a giant burn mark on our wall, but I'm glad I had a chance to spend time with you. Maybe we should chase delinquents together more often."

"You bet," Charlie answered with a wide grin.

But inside, he was miserable.

CHAPTER EIGHT

THE POISON GARDEN

By noon the following day, the police had already
performed a thorough search of Cypress Creek
Elementary—and found no trace of the twelve-year-old ar-
sonist who'd nearly burned down the purple mansion. On
his way to lunch, Charlie overheard two teachers questioning the very existence of the missing girl. Apparently, India
Kessog hadn't been officially enrolled in the school, and
her parents could not be identified. But Charlie knew INK
was real, and he wasn't taking any chances. He kept an
eye on the clock in the school cafeteria. At exactly twelve-
fifteen, Rocco, Paige, and Alfie marched through the door

like well-trained soldiers and claimed seats across from Charlie.

"The cafeteria and auditorium are clear," Charlie told his friends.

"So are the gym and the boys' locker room," Rocco said.

"And the girls' locker room and east wing classrooms," Paige added.

"There's no sign of any miniature villains in the west wing classrooms or administrative offices either," Alfie reported.

"So she's definitely not at school today," Charlie concluded.

"The building is completely INK free," Paige confirmed.

"What I don't understand is why none of the teachers figured out she didn't belong here *yesterday*," Alfie said.

"*Duh,*" Paige replied. "Nobody expects kids to lie their way *into* school."

"Good point," Alfie admitted.

"Okay, then," Charlie said, getting back to business. "After school, let's all meet on the front steps and get ready for a hike through the forest. The last place I spotted INK was in the woods around Freeman Road."

"Hey, would it be okay if Alfie and I caught up with you guys a little bit later in the afternoon?" Rocco asked. "We've got football practice right after school, and I need to be there. Jancy Dare got totally chewed out by the prin-

cipal yesterday, and I bet she'd love to pay me back by starting a mutiny."

"Fine," Charlie said. Though he wasn't thrilled to be
short two men, there wasn't much he could do. "But since
when did *Alfie* join the football team?" He looked over at
the boy, who was wearing a T-shirt that proclaimed I LOVE
PI. "I thought you'd sworn off exercise."

"Oh, I have," Alfie assured him. "But you don't really
work up a sweat when you're the water boy."

"Wait—you're the sucker who agreed to be water boy
this year?" Paige scoffed. Everyone in Cypress Creek knew
it was a thankless job. When Jancy couldn't find a quarterback to pummel, she'd often settle for the water boy.

"It's not very glamorous, I'll admit. But it's an important first step toward a Nobel Prize," Alfie said. "I've been
adding a few special ingredients to the water I serve. You
might say that I've turned the entire football team into
guinea pigs."

Rocco scowled. "*Don't* say that," he warned Alfie.
"*Ever.* You promised me that stuff was just vitamins and
electrolytes."

"It is, it is!" Alfie assured him.

"Well, *I'm* free to hunt for INK after school," Paige
piped up. "Charlie, do you mind if it's just you and me?"

"Nope," Charlie said with a smile. "Not at all."

The truth was, there was nothing he would have minded

less. In fact, fifteen minutes later, he was *still* smiling as he and Paige sat down at their lab table in science class.

"Good afternoon," said a voice at the front of the room, and Charlie's pleasant daydream came to an end. Ms. Abbot was wearing a stylish black dress, as if she were planning to go straight from class to a cocktail party in the teachers' lounge. She also seemed to be sporting a rather unusual piece of jewelry around her neck. Thin and black, with red and yellow stripes, it looked as though it was made out of rubber.

"Since this is our first *official* day of science class, I thought we'd kick off the school year by studying something fun," the teacher informed the students.

Charlie lurched forward in his seat. He was pretty sure he'd just seen Ms. Abbot's necklace *move*.

"I'd like you all to meet Darwin," the teacher said, twisting her necklace around to reveal a head and a tail. Several kids squealed, and a boy who'd been sitting in the first row bolted to the back of the room. "Can anyone tell me what kind of snake Darwin is?"

"It's a coral snake," Paige answered without bothering to raise her hand. She never really needed to. In the classes she and Charlie had without Alfie, Paige was the one who knew all the answers. "It's the only North American snake that belongs to the cobra family. And I'm really surprised that you brought one to class. Coral snakes are *super* dangerous."

Two more kids in the front row abandoned their seats and scrambled for safety.

"Oh, really?" Ms. Abbot replied nonchalantly. "Are they venomous or poisonous?"

"Venomous," Paige answered. "Things that bite or sting you are *venomous*. Things that make you sick if you eat them are *poisonous*."

"Very good, Miss Bretter," Ms. Abbot said. "I asked two tough questions and you got one of them right."

The smug grin that had been growing on Paige's face disappeared. "Which one did I miss?"

Ms. Abbot gave Darwin a little kiss. "This is not a coral snake," she said. "This is a scarlet king snake. They look nearly identical, but while the coral snake could kill us all with a single drop of its venom, Darwin here is perfectly harmless unless you're a cricket. Which brings us to the subject of today's lesson: *mimicry*. Who can tell me what that means?"

Charlie was surprised to feel his own hand rising. Charlotte had taught him all about mimicry during one of their weekend afternoons at Hazel's Herbarium. "It's when a species evolves to look like something else. There's a plant called the mimicry plant that looks exactly like a rock. And your snake is a mimic too. Darwin is harmless, but his stripes make him look like another species that no one would want to mess with. He's probably safer from predators that way."

"Yes, though Darwin might have more friends if he didn't resemble a killer," Ms. Abbot remarked. "Excellent answer, Charlie." Then she smiled at the kids who'd abandoned their seats at the front of the class. "Are you ladies and gentlemen ready to come back yet? You don't want to hurt Darwin's feelings, do you?"

While the kids slunk back to their seats, Paige leaned over to Charlie. "It works the other way around too, doesn't it?" she asked. "Sometimes dangerous creatures pretend to be harmless ones. Like ICK and INK. They get away with murder because they look like cute little dolls. INK practically burned down your house last night, and what did your dad do? He drove around all night trying to *save* her."

"Hmmm," Charlie said. "If I shouldn't trust cute girls, then maybe I should find a new best friend."

Paige batted her eyelids and grinned slyly. "You think I'm cute?"

Charlie felt his face flushing. That wasn't what he'd meant to say. He turned back to the front of the room, where Ms. Abbot was starting her lecture, and tried to ignore Paige's tittering.

Fortunately, Ms. Abbot's class turned out to be the perfect distraction. She kicked off the lecture with a slide show of fantastic creatures that were all in disguise. Bugs pretended to be sticks. Flowers took the shape of bees. Caterpillars slithered like snakes. And octopuses masqueraded as jellyfish. When her presentation was finished, Ms. Abbot handed out sheets of drawing paper and told Charlie and his classmates to design their own mimics.

Paige set to work immediately; Charlie had never seen her quite so inspired. For fifteen minutes, she remained hunched over her page with her arm hiding her art from view.

While the kids drew, Ms. Abbot walked around the classroom, peeking at all the works in progress. "So what kind of mimic are you designing?" she asked Paige when she finally stopped at their lab table.

Paige whipped her paper off the desk and proudly held up her drawing. The picture showed a lake with a creature lurking inside it. Above the surface, the animal appeared to have the head of a little boy. Below the water, however, a dozen deadly tentacles were treading the water. "It's an octopus that can mimic the appearance of a human child.

It waits in the water for people to try to rescue the kid. Then it eats them."

"Fabulous!" Ms. Abbot told her. "Brilliant and gruesome. I can't imagine a better combination. What about you, Charlie? What are you drawing?"

Charlie looked down at his own picture. It seemed dull in comparison to Paige's mimic, even though it was inspired by something he'd come across in the Netherworld. "It's a beetle that looks like a poisonous mushroom."

"How nice," Ms. Abbot said kindly. She tapped the paper with her fingertip. "As it happens, a species of mushroom that looks just like this one grows in the woods near my house."

"*Amanita muscaria?*" Charlie asked. They'd been a favorite of his mother's.

Ms. Abbot lifted a thin, black eyebrow. "*Very* impressive," she told him. "Have you ever seen one in person? If not, I can show you a few after school today."

It took a moment for the meaning of Ms. Abbot's words to make their way to Charlie's brain. As soon as it did, his stomach tied itself in a knot. Charlotte hadn't called Ms. Abbot like she'd promised. The science teacher still thought Charlie would be helping out at her house that afternoon. Maybe Charlotte had made a mistake. She'd probably claim she'd forgotten. But Charlie didn't buy it.

Charlotte had a sneaky side, and he had a hunch that his stepmother had never planned to phone Ms. Abbot at all.

"What's happening after school today?" Paige asked, looking back and forth between her lab partner and her teacher.

"Nothing too exciting, I assure you," Ms. Abbot said. She didn't sound eager to discuss their plans. "I've hired Charlie to help me with some gardening."

Paige began bouncing up and down with excitement. "Oh my gosh! Can I come? Can I come?"

Ms. Abbot frowned. She clearly wasn't thrilled by the idea. "It's going to be really hard work, Paige. And the plants we'll be working with can be pretty . . . tricky."

"That's okay, Ms. Abbot," Charlie jumped in. If he had to go to the woods with his strange science teacher, he'd rather not go alone. "Paige helps out around Hazel's Herbarium sometimes. She's a really hard worker. My stepmom thinks she's great."

"So she can be trusted?" Ms. Abbot asked. It was such a weird question that Charlie wondered if the teacher was joking.

"Of course. I've known Paige since kindergarten. I trust her with everything," Charlie said.

"It's true," Paige added enthusiastically. "I know all his secrets."

Most, Charlie thought. *But not* all. There was still one secret he hadn't shared.

"Okay, then," Ms. Abbot said, though she still didn't seem convinced. "I suppose we could use an extra set of hands. I'll meet you both outside the front door at two-fifty."

The teacher moved along to the next table, and as soon as she was out of earshot, Paige turned to Charlie with a hurt expression. "Why didn't you tell me you were going to Ms. Abbot's house today?"

"Because I didn't know! I thought we'd be looking for INK. Charlotte set the whole thing up with Ms. Abbot, and she promised me she'd cancel," Charlie said. "But it turns out my sneaky stepmother didn't keep her promise, so I guess I don't have any choice now. I have to help."

Paige looked completely flabbergasted. "I get that you want to go hunt for INK, but why don't you want to hang out with Ms. Abbot? After Charlotte and my aunt Josephine, she's the coolest lady I've ever met!"

Charlie searched for the words to explain why the teacher made him feel so uncomfortable. "She's weird, Paige, and the plants she wants to grow in her garden are all deadly. They could kill everyone in town."

"OMG, I can't wait to see them!" Paige was practically drooling with excitement, and Charlie felt his frustration growing.

"Yeah? Well, have you heard that Ms. Abbot lives in the old Livingston place? You know, that run-down old house in the middle of the woods? You really want to spend your afternoon there?"

"The old Livingston place? That's awesome! And wait— isn't that near the same spot in the woods where you saw INK last night?" Paige asked. "Now we can kill two birds with one stone!"

Paige had a point—and Charlie couldn't argue against it. He just wished he could find the words to explain why he didn't feel at ease around Ms. Abbot. She seemed perfectly nice. But there was something about her—something he couldn't put a finger on. Somehow Charlie knew in his gut that Ms. Abbot shouldn't be trusted.

That feeling grew worse as Charlie and Paige bounced in the backseat of Ms. Abbot's car as it sped down the bumpy dirt road to her house. He didn't know exactly who Fleetwood Mac was, but he thought the music Ms. Abbot played was pretty creepy. Along the way, Charlie tried to keep an eye out for INK, but he couldn't concentrate. Every few yards, the car zipped past another bright red No Trespassing sign Ms. Abbot had posted. She seemed eager to turn away guests. Which made Charlie wonder why she was so keen to make an exception for *him*.

By the time they reached the entrance to the long drive that led to the old Livingston house, Charlie was completely on edge. His palms were sweating, and his heart was pounding. He nearly bolted from the car when he saw that the narrow drive was lined with neatly trimmed oleander bushes covered in frilly white blooms.

"How pretty!" Paige marveled as they drove between the walls of flowers.

"Yup," Charlie agreed, wiping his palms on his pants and trying not to sound as uncomfortable as he felt. "That's oleander. It's one of the deadliest plants in North America."

"Cool," Paige responded appreciatively.

"You really know your stuff," Ms. Abbot praised Charlie from the front seat, just as the car emerged into a clearing with a house at its center.

Charlie couldn't believe his eyes. He and his mom had hiked past the old Livingston place several times. He hadn't been back in the years since she died, but he still remembered the dilapidated shack that had once stood on the very same spot. The building had been given a complete makeover. The windows had glass now, and the doorways had doors. Green moss still grew on the roof, but the walls were white and the shutters had been painted a cheerful blue. Yellow jessamine vines clung to trellises that ran alongside the house. Charlie might have found the blooms charming if he hadn't known that every leaf, seed, and petal of the plant was extremely toxic.

"Wow, this looks like something out of a fairy tale," Paige said.

"Yeah, 'Hansel and Gretel,' " Charlie blurted out before he could stop himself.

But Ms. Abbot didn't seem at all offended. "I'm afraid the house is made out of wood siding, not gingerbread," she said, turning off the car. "But if you want to give it a bite, I won't try to stop you."

"No offense," Charlie said. "But I wouldn't eat anything while I'm at this house. Everything you've got growing around here is poisonous."

"Charlie!" Paige whispered angrily. "What's wrong with you?"

"Nothing's wrong with him. It's true," Ms. Abbot said. Then she grabbed her bag off the passenger seat and got out.

Paige looked at Charlie, worry crossing her face. "Wait," she called through the backseat window. "What?"

Ms. Abbot opened Paige's door. "Don't worry. The plants in the front yard are harmless unless you get the urge to nibble on them," the teacher replied. "But I'm growing a proper poison garden behind the house, and I need some help with it. That's why you're here. Now come with me."

For once, even Paige didn't seem to know how to

respond. After a second's hesitation, she unfastened her seat belt and slid out. Charlie swore under his breath and followed.

They caught up with Ms. Abbot as she crossed the yard, making her way past several buzzing beehives toward the back of the house. There, they found a lovely glass greenhouse surrounded by a tall black cast-iron fence. The fence would have looked right at home surrounding a graveyard, and its pickets were topped with dangerously sharp spikes.

"This is where my little garden will be," Ms. Abbot announced. "The fence is probably overkill, but I can't risk anyone getting hurt."

"What are you going to plant in there?" Paige asked.

"Oh, all the classic killers. Angel's-trumpet, monkshood, stinking nightshade, dead man's bells, dogbane . . ."

"But *why?*" Charlie wondered.

"Why not?" Ms. Abbot asked. "You've got to remember—poisonous plants are not trying to hurt anyone. Their toxins are simply a form of self-defense—they're meant to keep insects and other pests away. For centuries, people thought plants like belladonna or dogsbane were wicked. But the very same chemicals that make my plants deadly can also be used to *heal*. That's why I chose them. You see, Charlie, the truth is, there's no such thing as pure good or pure evil in the world. Almost everything is a combination of both."

It was an interesting theory, Charlie thought. But Ms. Abbot was totally wrong. He knew from experience that there was indeed evil in the world. It went by the names ICK and INK, and every moment he spent in Ms. Abbot's garden was a moment he couldn't spend searching for the missing twin.

"So everything's a mixture of good and bad? Then what about ticks?" he heard Paige challenge the teacher. "There's nothing good about ticks."

Ms. Abbot grinned as if she were playing her favorite game. "What do you mean? Of course there is! What would you say if I told you that tick saliva contains a powerful drug that could one day be used to save people's lives during surgery?"

"I guess I'd say wow," Paige said, duly impressed. "But it wouldn't stop me from squishing them." Then her eyes rolled upward while she searched her brain for another example. "Okay, so maybe nothing's truly evil. But what about *good*? What about gerbils? Since when have gerbils ever done anything wrong?"

From the smile on Ms. Abbot's face, Charlie guessed Paige was in for another science smackdown. "Have you ever heard of the black death?" Ms. Abbot asked.

"Sure," Paige said. "It was a plague that killed millions of people around the world in the Middle Ages."

"Well, scientists used to blame rats for carrying the fleas

that spread the disease. But now they're pretty sure that gerbils were the original bad guys."

"*Gerbils?*" Paige couldn't believe it. "Cute, furry little gerbils?"

Ms. Abbot nodded. "So now do you understand why I feel the need to defend my plants? While most people see evil, I see *complicated*—and misunderstood."

"Okay, I get it," Paige said. "But we're going to be working with them, right? Is it dangerous to touch them?"

"It can be," Charlie answered. "*Extremely* dangerous."

"And that's why I brought in an expert," Ms. Abbot said, pointing at Charlie. "Charlotte told me you have experience working with unusual species."

"Sure, but . . ."

"But you need the right equipment?" Ms. Abbot finished for him. "You know I'm a science teacher, right? Safety is my middle name. Follow me."

She led them to a garden shed on the edge of the clearing. It was creaky and old and looked like it might have once served as the Livingston family's outhouse. Charlie heard its boards creaking in the breeze and guessed that a strong gust of wind would flatten it.

The shed's door was already open a crack when they arrived, and Ms. Abbot let out a sigh. "Looks like my raccoon is back," she said. "Nasty little creature keeps getting in here and messing up my organizational system."

She squatted down and began picking out supplies from a pile of items that had fallen off the shelves and onto the dirt floor. Charlie and Paige were each given spades, garden claws, face masks, goggles, and gloves. When Ms. Abbot stood back up, Charlie could see that she'd gathered a set of supplies for herself as well.

She laughed at the surprise that Charlie knew was written all over his face. "You thought I was going to let you guys have all the fun?" she asked as she pulled on a pair of green gardening gloves over the sleeves of her chic black dress. "By the way, look what I just found on the floor."

She was holding a small metal figurine. The paint had worn away in places, but it seemed to be a toy soldier. Charlie took the figurine, and when he held it up for a closer look, he nearly dropped it back down to the ground. The soldier's face appeared horribly deformed. Then Charlie realized it was wearing a gas mask.

"I'd bet that's a genuine antique, kid," Ms. Abbot said. "Must have belonged to one of the people who lived here way back when. Consider it your bonus."

"Gee, thanks," Charlie said, tucking the creepy toy into his pocket.

Inside the greenhouse, it was warm and damp. Charlie breathed in the smell of the soil and began to relax. Even in an eerie greenhouse filled with poisonous plants, Charlie felt at home. He'd started gardening with his mother when he was just a little boy. Charlotte said he had a gift for horticulture—a real green thumb. Maybe it was true, he thought as he took a spot at Paige's side and began to get to work. It didn't matter if he was wearing gloves and a mask. The feel of the earth in his hands comforted him. Charlie always seemed to know which plants needed water and which could use a fresh covering of manure. It was almost as if they spoke to him.

While Charlie worked quietly, Paige and Ms. Abbot chattered away. Paige seemed to have a million questions for their new science teacher. She'd started off by digging for personal details, but Ms. Abbot gave almost nothing away. The only information Paige and Charlie were able to glean was that Samantha Abbot came from New York, had no family, had gone to Harvard, liked cheese in a can, and had once grown a six-foot-long zucchini.

Then Paige turned the conversation to the subject of plants, and Ms. Abbot came alive. She knew dozens of stories about each plant they were potting. Some of the tales were pure fiction. Wolfsbane, for instance, was believed to act as a defense against werewolves, while henbane was said to help witches fly. But most of Ms. Abbot's stories were taken straight from the pages of history. Poisonous belladonna berries had been used to murder a Roman emperor.

And Russian spies had once used toxin that comes from castor beans to do away with a famous journalist.

"So what are you going to do with all these crazy plants?" Paige joked once Ms. Abbot's misunderstood plants were all in their brand-new pots. "You could make one heck of a witch's brew if you wanted to."

"Why, that's exactly what I plan to do," Ms. Abbot said, and Charlie's eyes flew up from his work. "But I'm not the kind of witch who poisons or curses," she continued. "I'm the kind of witch who tries to cure."

There was something in her voice that told Charlie the teacher wasn't kidding around. He set his spade aside and looked over at Paige.

"Wait," Paige said. "Are you saying you're a witch?"

"I don't ride a broomstick, and I don't have any supernatural powers," said Ms. Abbot. "I don't like cats, and I don't believe in magic. But I believe in the power of nature. And I believe that if you learn how to make use of it, you can do things that seem magical."

"Like what?" Charlie demanded. He'd never been very fond of witches, good or bad.

"Well, for instance, each of these plants contains powerful substances. For centuries, they've been used to kill. I believe they can be used to make drugs that save lives instead," said Ms. Abbot.

"So you're kind of like Charlotte," Paige said. "She uses plants to treat people too."

"Charlotte is an herbalist. She uses plants to make remedies and ointments," Ms. Abbot said. "I'm a chemist. I work with chemicals I extract from plants. They're two different jobs, but I suppose back in the old days, Charlie's stepmom and I could both have been burned as witches."

"Really?" Paige gasped.

"Absolutely," Ms. Abbot said. "Even today, it can be hard for people to understand that plants they think of as evil can have a good side too. So I need to keep my poison garden a secret. Charlie, I asked you to help because your stepmother said I could trust you. Paige, I let you come because you have Charlie's trust. I hope I can rely on you both not to talk about the things you've seen here today."

"Never!" Paige said. "Our lips are sealed!"

Charlie was careful not to make any promises.

Ms. Abbot smiled, her face lit by the golden sun, which was already sinking toward the horizon. "Good work today, guys," she said. "Looks like we finished just in time for me to get you home for dinner. Come inside and I'll pour you some lemonade and pay you for your fine services."

Charlie and Paige followed Ms. Abbot through the back door of the house and into the kitchen.

"Sorry for the mess," she said, gesturing to the kitchen table, which was covered with glass beakers, tubes, and various lab tools. "That's tomorrow's science class."

Charlie gazed at the mess and froze at the sight of a startlingly familiar piece of equipment.

"What are you making?" Paige asked.

"Well, until tomorrow at nine a.m., it's a secret," Ms. Abbot joked as she rummaged through her refrigerator in search of the lemonade.

"And what's this?" Charlie picked up the object he'd been eyeing. It was a blue can with a long metal nozzle that rose from the top. At the base of the nozzle was a plastic knob that twisted from side to side.

Ms. Abbot stuck her head around the fridge door for a look. "You know what a Bunsen burner is?" she asked.

"Yeah," Paige replied. "It's a piece of chemistry equipment. It produces a flame that you can use in experiments."

"Exactly," Ms. Abbot said. "That's a portable Bunsen burner. If you turn that nozzle, gas comes out of the can and you can set it on fire."

"Is this the only one you have?" Charlie asked.

"Nope," Ms. Abbot said, reaching for the glasses stacked up on one of her kitchen shelves. "I got a bunch of those things lying around. They're great for warming up leftover pizza and roasting marshmallows."

Charlie grabbed Paige's arm and pulled her close enough

to whisper in her ear. "This is what INK was using when she nearly burned down my house. She must have gotten it from here."

Paige sighed. "Or she could have gotten it from our school. Or a store. Or the Internet. Or the college—you know, the one where your *dad* works?"

But Charlie wasn't buying it. As far as he was concerned, the Bunsen burner was proof that INK had been inside Ms. Abbot's house.

The question was—had she been *invited*?

CHAPTER NINE

IT CAN ALWAYS GET WORSE

Ms. Abbot dropped Charlie off in front of the purple mansion just as a van emblazoned with a logo for Cypress Creek Security Systems pulled out of the driveway. Jack was playing with Rufus in the yard, and he stopped when he caught sight of his brother.

"Was that your weird teacher?" Jack asked. "Charlotte said you went to her house after school. How did it go?"

"It was educational," Charlie said, walking past Jack and stomping up the stairs to the porch.

Charlotte peeked out of the drawing room as Charlie went past, but she didn't stop him or say a word. The look on Charlie's face must have told her it was best to let him go. He made his way to the library, where his dad was sitting at his desk, reading through the manual for the mansion's new security system. Charlie reached into his pocket, pulled out a small item, and placed it in front of his father. Andrew Laird was a professor of history at the local university, and he was the only person Charlie knew who might be able to identify it.

His dad adjusted his glasses and his eyes lit up. "Whoa! Where did you get this?" He snatched the figurine off his desk, held it up to the light, and examined it as if it were a rare gem.

"You know what that is?" Charlie asked.

"Sure," his dad said. "It's a toy soldier. And a really cool one too. The uniform is English. It and the gas mask tell me this is from World War One. It was probably made around 1917 or so. Where on earth did you find it?"

"A garden shed," Charlie said. And he had a hunch he knew how a hundred-year-old English toy could have gotten there.

"Did you just get back from Samantha Abbot's house?" Charlotte had come into the room behind him. Charlie snatched the toy and shoved it into his pocket.

"Yep," Charlie said without turning around to look at his stepmother. "By the way, someone forgot to call her and tell her I wasn't coming. You tricked me."

"*Charlotte,*" Andrew Laird groaned.

"Sorry, guys," said Charlotte, though she clearly wasn't. "Was it as terrible as you were expecting, Charlie?"

"It was fine," Charlie said curtly. And that was all he planned to say. "Hey, Dad, do you mind if I grab some food and take it upstairs? I'm really tired after all that work, and I want to go right to sleep."

Charlotte and his dad traded looks. "Sure, Charlie," his father said. "Go ahead."

Charlie sat at his desk and ate a ham sandwich and pretzels in silence. As soon as he'd finished, he peeled off his dirty clothes and climbed into bed. He knew he couldn't stay annoyed at Charlotte forever. In the morning, he'd have to tell her what he'd discovered. But he was hoping to talk to someone else first. He was due a trip to the Dream Realm. He missed his real mother—and he desperately needed her help.

But once again, that wasn't where sleep took him.

The moment he closed his eyes, he was back in the same old dream. It wasn't completely dark this time, but it was far colder than it had been before. The sheep didn't seem to mind. They were huddled together in their thick black coats. Charlie watched his fingertips turn blue. It was only a dream, so he knew he wouldn't die. But that didn't mean that the next eight hours couldn't be *extremely* unpleasant. So he pinched his nose and began to squeeze in between two smelly sheep sitting side by side in the muck.

"A bit nippy, isn't it?"

Charlie's head snapped up at the sound of the voice. There, standing in front of him, was a girl in an old-fashioned uniform, her auburn hair parted primly on the side. She'd had time to calm down since Charlie's last visit to the dream. While she didn't exactly look thrilled to see him, at least she'd stopped flinging poo.

Charlie tried to respond, but his teeth were chattering too hard. All he managed was a single grunt. "ICK."

"I prefer Isabel, if you don't mind." The girl crossed her arms and glared at him. "And your name is Charlie Laird. You live in the purple mansion."

Charlie stared right back at her, clenching his teeth so they wouldn't rattle.

ICK walked in his direction. With each step, she sank halfway to her knees in muck, yet she didn't seem to care—or even really notice.

"Well, Charlie Laird, welcome back to my world. I imagine you're thinking that things couldn't possibly get any worse than they are right now," the girl told him. "But you're wrong. Take it from me. Things can *always* get worse. And after what you did to my tonic, I'm going to make sure things get *much* worse for you."

With his body wedged between the two sheep, Charlie was finally warming up enough to speak—just in time to give ICK a taste of her own medicine. "So I guess this is your nightmare? Funny, I never took you for the kind of girl who'd be scared of a bunch of sheep."

"Do I look scared to you?" she snarled. ICK and INK may have been twins, but ICK didn't sound like her sister at all. "The Netherworld is my home. I've been to your home too. Do you really imagine that a few little locks are going to keep me out of the Waking World?"

"Yep," Charlie said. "Because your sister isn't going to be able to break into our house anymore. My parents have installed a security system."

Isabel's lip curled into a snarl. "I don't know what a security system is, but it won't stop India. She'll never give up. She'll never leave me behind."

"Maybe not," Charlie said casually. "But are you sure you want INK to come to your rescue? The last time she tried, she almost burned my whole house down. And do you know what would happen if the purple mansion ever burned down? The portal would be destroyed and you'd be stuck here with these sheep forever."

"India made a mistake," ICK growled. "She won't make the same one again."

"You sure it was a mistake?" Charlie asked. "I think INK may be a bit of a pyromaniac. She torched your lighthouse, after all."

For a fleeting moment, Charlie saw something remarkable on ICK's face—surprise. She obviously didn't know that her sister had burned down the lighthouse. Maybe it *hadn't* been part of their plan. Maybe INK had acted on her own for some reason. But *why?*

"The lighthouse fire was an accident. You're lying," ICK said. "That's what people like you do. They *lie.*"

"Nope," Charlie said. He saw a chance to make trouble for the twins and he couldn't resist it. "If you don't believe me, go find a Nightmare named Ava. She was watching your lighthouse in Maine when the building went up in flames. She told me your sister walked out and just let the place burn. It was like she *wanted* to destroy the lighthouse's portal. So who's to say INK won't try to destroy the portal in the purple mansion too? Maybe after eighty years, she just doesn't want to hang out with you anymore."

ICK didn't say a word. She just stood in the muck, staring at Charlie. He'd gone too far. He'd said something cruel. It was a feeling he knew well—and one he hated.

Finally her cold blue lips parted and she spoke. "Get out of my nightmare, you horrid little boy," she ordered.

"Believe me, I'd love to," Charlie told her. "But I can't.

You keep dragging me here, and I haven't found a way out yet."

"I didn't bring you to the Netherworld!" ICK shouted. Her pale face began to burn bright red. "I don't want you here! I want to be by myself!"

"But you're not here by yourself," Charlie said, remembering his first visit to the dream. "There's someone else too. She hums. I've heard her! It sounds like . . ."

ICK's entire body seemed to freeze. *"No,"* she whispered.

But Charlie's lips were already pressed together, and the first three notes were on their way out.

ICK screamed—but not in anger. Her scream of sheer terror was so awful that Charlie almost began to scream too. He'd found the source of ICK's worst fear. It wasn't the sheep, he realized. It was the *lullaby.*

Charlie woke up in the dark. Sweat was pouring from his body, and he heard the sound of bare feet on the floorboards as Charlotte raced toward his room.

CHAPTER TEN

NIGHT RAIDER

Charlotte was sitting at the kitchen island with a cup of coffee when Charlie came downstairs the next morning with the toy soldier hidden in his fist.

"You okay?" she asked, eyeing him warily.

"Yep," he said.

"Good," Charlotte said. "Are you ready to talk about your dream yet?"

"Nope," Charlie replied. He wasn't going to say anything about the dream until he knew how he kept ending up in ICK's nightmare. It wasn't an accident; he knew that much for certain. It meant something—and he needed to figure out what. "But there is something I've got to tell you. INK was at Ms. Abbot's house. I have proof."

Charlotte looked startled. "What?"

"Remember I told you guys that INK was carrying some kind of little torch when she nearly burned down our house? It was a portable Bunsen burner. I saw one just like it in Ms. Abbot's kitchen. And this was in Ms. Abbot's garden shed." He showed Charlotte the toy soldier. "Dad says it's from England. From *1917*."

"No." Charlotte shook her head, refusing to believe it. "There can't be any connection between INK and Samantha Abbot. This is all just a coincidence."

"Hasn't this family been through enough to prove that *nothing* is 'just a coincidence'? How well do you know Ms. Abbot?" Charlie asked.

Charlotte seemed to bristle at the question. "Samantha's spent a lot of time in my shop. I'd say I know her well enough to be pretty darn confident that she's not in league with two evil twins from the Netherworld," she replied.

"Has she told you her secret?" Charlie asked. He was just fishing, but from the look on Charlotte's face, he'd caught something big.

"No," Charlotte said, clamming up.

"But you know something, don't you?" Charlie said.

Charlotte's lips didn't budge.

"Okay, fine," Charlie said. "Don't tell me. But I have proof that INK has been hanging out at Ms. Abbot's house. The same house that's completely surrounded by poisonous plants. Come on, Charlotte! You know what she has in her greenhouse! You sold most of it to her! She's growing stuff like white snakeroot and monkshood. And she's got enough of it to kill the whole town. Do you want INK getting her hands on plants like that?"

Charlotte leaned forward and looked her stepson in the eye. "Charlie," she said. "Do you trust me?"

Charlie huffed and crossed his arms. It was clear that he wasn't going to get a straight answer from her.

"Do you?" Charlotte asked.

"Yes," he admitted.

"Then trust me when I tell you that Samantha Abbot isn't helping INK, and she's not planning to kill the whole town. Got it?"

"Got it," Charlie said, though he wasn't sure he be-lieved it.

That afternoon, Charlie took his seat beside Paige at the lab table they shared in science class. At the front of the room, Ms. Abbot was busy putting together the glass bea-kers and tubes that had been lying on her kitchen table the previous evening. When clamped together, they formed a tall apparatus with a round beaker at the bottom and several long glass cylinders on top with plastic tubes sprouting from the sides.

As soon as she'd finished assembling the equipment, Ms. Abbot straightened and addressed the class.

"We'll get back to our study of mimicry tomorrow, but I'm having a little problem at my house, and I'm hoping you guys can help me out," she said. "A raccoon has been breaking into my garden shed and going through my trash cans for food. And he's a smart little thing too. I can't seem to keep him out. So today we're going to make raccoon repellent. But here's the tricky part: it needs to work on raccoons, but I don't want the stuff to keep birds away too. My garden needs birds. So what do you guys think I should use?"

"A BB gun," a kid on the far side of Paige called out.

Ms. Abbot frowned. "I suppose that might work, but I'm not a very good shot. Anyone else have a suggestion?"

"Poison," another kid suggested.

Charlie saw Ms. Abbot's worried eyes dart in his direction for a second, as if he'd let her secret slip.

"Well, there are two big problems with using poison as a repellent," she continued nervously. "First of all, I don't want to hurt the raccoon; I just want to keep him away. Second of all, if I poison the raccoon, I could end up poisoning the birds that come to my garden, and the soil that my garden grows in, and then maybe even myself."

"Perhaps you should try capsaicin." The voice was muffled and seemed to be coming from the closet at the back of the room.

"Excuse me?" Ms. Abbot called. "Would the gentleman hiding inside the supply closet mind stepping out?"

Charlie spun around in his seat in time to see Alfie emerge, looking simultaneously sheepish and thrilled.

"Well, hello there," Ms. Abbot said. "Are you in my class? Or were you sent here as a spy?" She may have been smiling, but there was an edge in her voice that Charlie hadn't heard before.

"He's not a *spy*," a girl said with a smirk. "He's a *geek*. Only a geek sneaks *into* a science class."

"Frankie!" Ms. Abbot admonished the girl.

"No, ma'am, she's right," said Alfie. "My name is Alfie Bluenthal, and I'm proud to be a geek. I was walking past your classroom this morning, and I saw you unpacking that *sweet* Soxhlet extractor, and I wondered what you were doing, so I thought I'd hang around and find out. I have PE this period, and now that I'm the football team's water boy, the coach lets me do whatever I like."

Charlie saw Ms. Abbot's guard come down in an instant. "How did you learn about Soxhlet extractors?" she asked in amazement. "Are you really a kid—or are you some kind of chemistry whiz in disguise?"

"What if I told you that I happen to be both?" Alfie asked.

Ms. Abbot grinned. "Then I'd say come on up to the front of the class," she told him. "It sounds like you know what's in store for my raccoon. Would you like to help me prepare it?"

"But he's not even part of our class!" Charlie heard Paige complain bitterly. Everyone else ignored her.

"I'd love to help!" Alfie replied. "I never get to do stuff this fun in *my* science classes. I have to wait until I'm at home in my private lab."

"You have a private lab?" Ms. Abbot asked.

"Sure!" Alfie said as he strapped on a pair of eye-protecting goggles and pulled on gloves. "Don't you?"

"Yes, but do your parents really let you—" Ms. Abbot began.

"Excuse me!" Paige shouted. She clearly couldn't contain herself any longer. "Now that you've taken over our science class, Alfie, do you mind telling us poor non-geniuses what you'll be making?"

Alfie adjusted his goggles nervously. Charlie could hear the jealousy in Paige's voice, and he was sure Alfie heard it too.

"My apologies, Paige," Ms. Abbot said. "Today we're going to be studying one of the wonders of the natural world. You've all experienced it, but who besides Alfie has ever heard of capsaicin?"

Charlie had, but he didn't think it was wise to raise his hand. He glanced over at Paige, who looked totally stumped—and completely furious.

"Capsaicin is a chemical that produces a burning sensation. It isn't poisonous, and doesn't bother birds at all, but just a teensy little bit of it can drive pests like raccoons away. And fortunately for us, capsaicin comes from one of the most common plants around." Ms. Abbot reached into her lab coat and pulled out a handful of bright red seedpods. "Today we're going to make a raccoon repellent spray by extracting capsaicin from these—ordinary chili peppers."

Alfie put his lunch tray down across from Charlie. "Your teacher is *amazing*," he said, still swooning from his encounter with Ms. Abbot. "Beautiful, brilliant, totally unafraid of raccoons."

Charlie watched Paige pop a tater tot into her mouth. He could have been wrong, but he was pretty sure her lips formed the word *show-off* as she chewed.

"Hey, guys!" Rocco dropped into a seat beside Charlie. "You never called me after football practice. What's the latest on INK?"

"Still missing," Charlie said. "Paige and I found a couple of clues, but we didn't get a chance to search for her. How was practice with the Quarterback Killer?"

"Jancy?" Rocco asked. "She left early yesterday. Said she wasn't feeling well—and right after she said it, she proved it by vomiting all over the coach." Rocco used a sweet potato fry to point to a table on the other side of the cafeteria where a miserable-looking boy was eating soup. "Lester's eating alone. Jancy's parents must have kept her home from school today."

Charlie put down his sloppy joe. He'd just lost his appetite. INK was at large; she'd been to Ms. Abbot's house, where every plant was poisonous; and now her sworn enemy, Jancy Dare, was sick. He hoped there wasn't a connection.

"Maybe the stuff Alfie's been putting in the football team's water made Jancy sick," Paige said, taking a slurp of tomato soup.

Alfie gasped. Paige's words must have felt like a sucker punch.

Charlie couldn't believe what he'd heard. "Paige!" he exclaimed. "You shouldn't even say stuff like that."

"I swear! It's just vitamins and electrolytes!" Alfie added.

"I guess we'll just have to take your word for it, won't we?" Paige replied, raising an eyebrow as if to suggest that she wasn't at all convinced. "You're so much smarter than the rest of us. If you swear there's nothing bad in your secret recipe, what choice do we have but to trust you?"

"I drink the stuff too," Rocco spoke in Alfie's defense. "And I feel perfectly fine."

"Sure, *for now*," Paige said. She picked up her tray and left the table.

"Wow, what was that about?" Rocco said as Paige walked away.

"You guys, I cross my heart and hope to die! There's nothing in the water that would make anyone sick!" Alfie said, looking a little nauseous himself.

"We know," Charlie said. "Paige is just mad that you took over our science class. Ms. Abbot's her idol. Don't worry. I'll go talk to her."

But Paige wouldn't listen to a word of reason. No matter what Charlie said, she refused to forgive Alfie, and her terrible mood wouldn't go away. At the end of the day, Charlie was relieved when he spotted his dad waiting for him outside the school. Even though he desperately needed to search for INK, he was eager for a break from his feuding friends. He left Paige, Alfie, and Rocco on the steps and ran to greet his father.

"Hi, Dad. What's up?"

"Thought I'd drop by and give Jack a ride to Hazel's Herbarium," his dad said. "Then you and I are going to take a little trip to Orville Falls."

Charlie perked up. "Really?"

"Yep, got a call this afternoon from a newspaper reporter who works up there. She said some workmen found something while they were tearing down that weird old mansion on the hill. . . ."

"Kessog Castle?" Charlie asked.

"That's the one. They think the item they found might be some kind of antique, and they've asked me to come have a look at it. When I mentioned it to Charlotte, she insisted I take you with me. I think it's your stepmother's way of apologizing for not canceling your appointment with that science teacher yesterday. So how about it, kid? Want to come?"

"Are you kidding?" Charlie asked with a laugh. He couldn't turn down a chance to do some snooping at Kessog Castle, but that was only half the draw. The best part would be spending alone time with his father—while Jack was stuck at work.

CHAPTER ELEVEN

THE MYSTERY BOX

The last time Charlie had visited Orville Falls, the zombie-like Walkers had taken over the town. He could barely believe how much had changed in just a few short weeks. The stores were open again, there were cars on the road, and everyone they passed looked perfectly clean and drool-free.

Andrew Laird pulled up to a stoplight, and a boy in the car next to them began pointing at Charlie. Soon the kid's parents and siblings had recognized Charlie and were banging on the windows and waving at him as if he were their long-lost best friend.

"Do you know those people?" his dad asked warily. Such displays of enthusiasm were rare back in Cypress Creek.

Charlie shrugged. "Kind of, I guess. The man driving is the coach of the Orville Falls soccer team. I think his name is Winston Lindsay, but I've never really spoken to him," he said. It was the truth—but not the *whole* truth. Charlie and the soccer coach had never had a conversation, but Winston Lindsay had certainly heard *Charlie* speak. After all, Charlie had given the speech that had saved the Lindsays' entire town.

"Hmmmm," Charlie's dad replied. "I always thought Orville Falls was a little weird."

"Really?" Charlie said nervously. "I don't know, Dad. It seems perfectly normal to me."

They drove through Orville Falls. At the far edge of town, the wilderness began again. Andrew Laird slowed down and squinted at the side of a mountain that lay dead ahead of them. Men and machinery covered the space, hard at work. "So you think that's the place? If so, it's changed so much that I barely recognize it."

For a moment, Charlie couldn't have said for sure if they were looking at the remains of Kessog Castle. There wasn't much of a building left. Crews of workmen had taken most of it apart board by board. Even the tall wall that had once surrounded the building had been reduced to a pile of stone. Everything the goblins had added over the summer was already on top of a rubbish heap. Only the oldest part of the castle was left. As they drove through the field that lay below the castle, something in the distance caught Charlie's eye. It was large and brown and almost perfectly round.

"Can you slow down for a second?" he asked his dad. "What's that over there?"

Andrew Laird squinted. Then he laughed. "I think it's a sheep," he said.

"A brown sheep," Charlie muttered.

"Sheep come in a variety of colors," Andrew joked. "That one looks like it hasn't been sheared in a while. Maybe he's an ancestor of one of the famous escapees."

"Escapees?" Charlie asked.

Andrew Laird stepped on the gas and steered the car up the drive toward the building on the hill. "There used to be a big wool mill here in Orville Falls, and the owner kept a flock of sheep in the fields out here by the castle. From what I've heard, the animals weren't treated very nicely. Then one day, someone snuck into the pen and set them all free. The townsfolk tried to round them up, but most of the sheep escaped into the forest and were never seen again. Now they're a local legend. Every few years, there will be a story in the papers about someone who claims to have stumbled across a rogue sheep in the woods."

Were the escaped sheep the ones from ICK's dream?

Charlie wondered as the car came to a stop. He looked out the windshield and realized that they'd reached their destination. A pretty blond woman was waiting for them outside. She looked exactly like her niece.

"Charlie! I didn't know you'd be coming too! Welcome back to Orville Falls!" Josephine said, wrapping Charlie in a hug and planting a peck on the top of his head. Then she held out a hand to Andrew Laird. "I'm Josephine, Paige Bretter's aunt and your son's biggest fan."

"Wow, Charlie, you sure are popular in this town," his dad marveled. "I wouldn't be surprised to find out there's a statue of you downtown."

"Not yet," Josephine chirped. "The sculptor's still working on it."

"Can we go inside?" Charlie asked, desperate to change the subject before his dad realized that Josephine wasn't kidding.

"Sure," said Josephine. "Follow me!"

She guided them into the last remaining section of Kessog Castle. It was just as dreary as Charlie remembered it. The walls were made of damp, rough stone, and the blackened windows were a haunting reminder of the goblins who'd recently lived there. As Charlie and his dad trailed behind Josephine, he tried to imagine what it would be like to live in a place like the castle. It must have felt like being cast into a dungeon.

After a short walk, the trio arrived at a room at the end of a hall. It was small and bare, and part of the floor was missing. Josephine told them that the workmen had been ripping up the floorboards when they'd come upon the box that was now sitting in the center of a workman's tarp.

"This it?" Andrew Laird asked, kneeling down beside the strange container. It was roughly two feet wide, two and a half feet long, and two feet deep, Charlie figured. It was made completely of wood, and the name Kessog was printed in black on a little metal tag that was screwed into the top.

"Sure is," Josephine confirmed. "They found it hidden in a secret compartment beneath the floorboards. One of the men told me it had about an inch of dust on it when they pulled it out. It must have been down there for a very long time."

"Well, let's see what we've got," Charlie's dad said. He flipped the clasp on one side of the box and it opened like a book into two parts that were joined together by a hinge. Andrew Laird sat back on his haunches and gazed in wonder at the contents of the box. The only thing he seemed able to say was "Oh *wow*!"

Inside the box were rows and rows of little glass bottles, all neatly labeled by hand. There must have been at least a hundred of them. Andrew Laird picked one up and gave it a little shake, stirring the white powder inside.

" 'Sodium cyanide,' " he read off the label.

"Cyanide," Josephine gasped. "The poison?"

"Yep," Andrew Laird confirmed. He picked up another bottle of white powder. This one he didn't shake. " 'Ammonium nitrate,' " he read. "It's the main ingredient in certain kinds of bombs. And look—this is amazing." He pointed to yet another bottle of seemingly boring white powder. "Here's sodium azide. I've heard of people accidentally pouring this stuff down their drains. It reacts with the metal pipes and makes them explode. I'd say most of the chemicals in these bottles are pretty ordinary. But there are about a dozen extremely dangerous substances here."

"Why would someone hide a box full of chemicals under the floorboards?" Josephine asked.

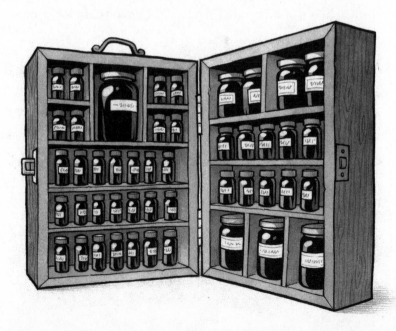

"And since when do you know so much about chemistry?" Charlie added. "You're a *history* professor."

"Well, to answer the less insulting question first, I suppose there are a million reasons someone might have hidden something like this under the floorboards," Andrew Laird said. "If I owned it, I wouldn't want anyone to touch it either. And to be perfectly honest, my dear boy, I don't really know anything about chemistry. But I know exactly what this is because my grandfather had one. He used to take it out and show me when I visited his house. It's a chemistry set. This is a really nice one—and there's a stamp on the inside that says it was made in London. Sometime in the 1930s, I believe."

"So Alfred Kessog liked to do chemistry experiments in his spare time?" Charlie asked. It didn't make sense.

"It didn't belong to Alfred Kessog." The voice came from the doorway. Behind them stood a very old man.

"Oh, hello, Mr. Pike," Josephine said. "Allow me to introduce you to Professor Andrew Laird and his son Charlie. Andrew works at the university in Cypress Creek. He kindly drove up here this afternoon to help us identify the contents of the box. Andrew and Charlie, this is Mr. Pike. He owns a farm just down the road."

"Thought I'd drop by and say farewell to this old eyesore before it's nothing more than a mound of rubble," Mr. Pike explained as he shook hands with Charlie's dad.

"Place is full of memories. I wouldn't say they're *fond* memories, but they're still memories, and at my age, I suppose I'm lucky to have them."

"Does that mean you knew Alfred Kessog?" Andrew Laird asked.

"Sure did," the man confirmed. "Most cantankerous old coot I've ever met."

"And you say this chemistry set they found here wasn't his?" Charlie asked, eager to solve the mystery. "His name is on the box, and I thought he was the only one who lived in the castle."

"Nope," said Mr. Pike. "Guess I'm the only one around here old enough to remember those days. Alfred Kessog was a miserable old hermit, and his only hobby was meeting with his lawyers and looking for ways to make other people's lives more difficult. No, that box didn't belong to him. It belonged to the girls."

CHAPTER TWELVE

THE LIMEYS

"They came to Orville Falls round about 1939," the old man said. "My brother and I called them the Limeys."

"That's a slang word Americans use for English people," Charlie's dad explained. "It's not very nice."

Mr. Pike snorted. "Maybe not, but everyone else in town called them *imps*. There were two of them—sweet-looking things, as I recall. Always nicely put together. You never saw a scuff on their shoes or a stain on their skirts. Which was pretty darned amazing when you consider how much trouble those two were always in."

Charlie's dad laughed, as though the thought of two

prim little girls wreaking havoc in Orville Falls was completely ridiculous. He didn't know ICK and INK.

"What kind of trouble?" Charlie asked, his tone perfectly serious.

"Any and all kinds," the old man responded. "Those
girls didn't have anyone looking after them, and that weird
old uncle of theirs wouldn't let them go to school or have
anyone come to visit. I don't think they liked Orville Falls
very much either. I figure their plan was to cause so much
trouble that they got sent back home."

"Where was home?" Josephine asked. "It looks like
that chemistry set was made in London. Is that where they
came from?"

The old man shrugged. "Can't remember," he said.
"They could have come from anywhere in Britain. It was
wartime, remember? World War Two. Britain's enemies
were dropping bombs all over their country, so a lot of
folks sent their kids this way. It was safer here in America
than back at home, with the sky exploding every time you
looked up."

Charlie remembered INK telling Jack that her old
school was destroyed by a bomb. He'd assumed she and
her sister were the bombers. Now Charlie realized that the
Germans must have been responsible.

"You said the girls were always in trouble. What did
they do that was so bad?" he asked.

"Well, it started off with pranks," the man said. "The kind of silly stuff that kids still do today. For instance, the spring they arrived, the Limeys were caught setting off stink bombs at the ladies' garden show. Didn't matter how many flowers there were in that building—whole place smelled like a giant fart for the rest of the year."

Charlie couldn't help but chuckle.

The old man grinned. "Yeah, I thought that one was pretty great too. They followed it up by adding baking soda to all the ketchup bottles at the diner down on Main Street. The stuff caused some kind of chemical reaction inside the bottles. Whenever anyone took a cap off, the ketchup would erupt like lava out of a volcano. The girls didn't get caught that time, but everyone in town knew it was them."

"Sounds like they must have been pretty good at chemistry," Andrew Laird remarked.

"Oh yes," the old man agreed. "Rumor had it that their dad was a famous chemist back in England—or maybe he was a pharmacist. Can't remember. Anyway, he worked with chemicals, and he taught his daughters how to use them. If I had to bet, I'd bet that he bought that box for them. And if the Limeys had stuck to harmless pranks, like stink bombs and disappearing ink, they would have been the heroes of every kid in town. But they didn't stop there." Mr. Pike's face had turned grim.

"What did they do?" Charlie was almost afraid to ask.

"I couldn't even begin to list everything," Mr. Pike replied. "For about six months, it felt like the whole town was under siege. Those girls must have been pretty desperate to go home, because they seemed prepared to do just about anything. I remember one of the first things they did was toss smoke bombs through the school's windows so we all had to evacuate."

That didn't seem so terrible, Charlie thought. But he could see Mr. Pike was just getting started.

"Then they spiked a punch bowl at the town fair with ipecac," he said. "Do you know what that is?"

Charlie shook his head.

"It's a syrup that makes you vomit," the man said. "They must have added the gunk right before the mayor made his big toast to celebrate the start of the festival. About two hundred people drank the punch. Now imagine all two hundred of those people throwing up at once."

Grimacing at the thought, Charlie glanced up at his dad, who looked like he might vomit too.

"Couple weeks later the Limeys snuck out at night and filled all the door locks downtown with something that looked like bubble gum but turned as hard as stone. Nobody could get inside their stores the next morning."

"Why didn't anyone try to stop them?" Josephine asked. "Weren't the girls ever punished?"

"Oh, I'm sure they were punished," the old man said. "Their uncle wasn't the kind of man who enjoyed practical jokes—even the safe kind. But in the end, the Limeys got exactly what they wanted. And they sure went out with a bang."

"Oh no," Charlie said. He had a hunch that he knew where the story was going.

"When you were driving through town on the way here, you must have passed our town square—with the fountain that stands in front of city hall," Mr. Pike said. "There's a little park around it."

"Sure," said Charlie. He remembered it well.

"That fountain may look like an antique, but we old folks know it's only a replica of the original. In the winter of 1940, the Limeys blew up the park. To this day, nobody's figured out how those girls did it, but one afternoon that whole square disappeared in a big ball of fire. Fortunately, the weather was terrible, and there weren't any people in the park that day. But the mayor's dog was relieving himself on the fountain when it happened. Poor little Gertie was never seen again."

"Two young girls blew up the town square?" Josephine marveled. "I've heard about the disaster, of course, but I never realized two kids were behind it."

"Yep," said Mr. Pike. "Hard to believe, but there's no other explanation. Maybe you never heard about the culprits because they never got caught. Of course, after it happened, everyone in town marched right up to Kessog Castle. The Limeys had been making us all miserable for months, but they'd never come close to killing anyone before. When the crowd got there, Alfred Kessog himself opened the door. He said it was *his* job to punish his nieces and he wasn't going to let a bunch of vigilantes do it for him."

"I bet everyone was happy to hear that," Charlie said sarcastically.

"They tried to bust down the door and get the two girls. But in case you haven't noticed, this place is a fortress. The door wouldn't give, and they couldn't find another way inside."

"So what happened?" Charlie asked.

Mr. Pike shrugged. "It got dark and cold, and everybody went back to town and planned to come back the next morning. But when morning came, they had bigger fish to fry. See, there used to be a huge flock of sheep in the field below the castle. That night, the Limeys set them all free. Hundreds of animals escaped, and everyone in Orville Falls had to help round them up."

That meant they were definitely the sheep from ICK's dream! Charlie thought. He was one step closer to solving the mystery.

"I was just telling Charlie that story on the drive here,"

Andrew Laird said. "But I didn't know the part about the girls."

"It was a nightmare, that's for sure," Mr. Pike said. "They never did find all the sheep. And by the time the townsfolk made it back to Kessog Castle, they were informed that the girls were gone."

"Gone? Where did they go?" Charlie's dad asked.

"Home to England, I suppose," said Mr. Pike. "It took them a year of terrible behavior, but they finally got their way."

"Well, good riddance!" Josephine said. "But I have to say, Mr. Pike, this is going to make an amazing story for the paper. I wonder if the Limeys are still alive. We might be able to find them in Britain."

There was no point in looking for the girls in Britain. Charlie knew the true end of the story—and it was much darker than anyone in the room suspected. Alfred Kessog hadn't shipped his nieces home. He'd sent them to a cold, dreary lighthouse on a desolate strip of coast in Maine. No wonder they hated him so much, Charlie thought. He would have despised Alfred Kessog too.

CHAPTER THIRTEEN

THE FIRESTARTER

Charlie went to bed early. For the first time in days, he was looking forward to going to sleep. He wanted to ask ICK about the chemistry set and Mr. Pike's tale. He believed the old man's account—apart from its conclusion. ICK and INK's chemistry crime spree hadn't ended with a trip home to Britain. Cruel Alfred Kessog had sent his naughty nieces away to live in a lighthouse instead. That was bad enough, but Charlie suspected he was still missing an important part of the twins' story. Something must have happened to the girls the night they set the sheep free—

something so terrible it had inspired a nightmare that had lasted for eighty years.

Charlie had just closed his eyes when a shrill scream rang through the night. In an instant, he was out of his bed and at the window. The scream seemed to have come from one of the houses below the purple mansion's hill, and it sounded like that of a very young girl.

Jack burst into Charlie's room. "Was that you?"

"Are you saying I scream like a five-year-old girl?" Charlie asked.

"No comment," Jack said, joining his brother at the window. "Is something going on down there?"

A second scream answered his question. This one clearly belonged to a woman. Charlie scanned the roofs of Cypress Creek for any sign of disturbance.

"Look," Jack said, pointing to a house less than a block away. A cloud of smoke was rising through the trees in the house's backyard. "That's the Hendersons' place. But their house looks fine, so what's burning?"

Voices were suddenly shouting, but Charlie couldn't make out any of the words. "Come on," he said, nudging his brother with his elbow. "Let's go check it out."

They charged down the stairs in their pajamas.

"Dad! Charlotte! Dad!" yelled Jack as they raced toward the front door.

Andrew Laird stepped out of the library. "What the heck is going on?" he asked.

"The Hendersons' house!" Jack shouted over his shoulder. "Call nine one one! Their backyard is on fire!"

Within seconds, Charlie and Jack were standing at a picket fence, their excited faces lit by the glow of flames. Eight-year-old Olivia Henderson's incredible playhouse— the envy of Cypress Creek elementary—was in flames. Designed to resemble a palace—complete with turrets, towers, and spikes on which to mount the heads of Olivia's enemies—the playhouse was far fancier than the house the Hendersons called home. Now flames were dancing in the playhouse's windows and pouring out the doors. Little Olivia, dressed in the frilly black dress of an evil queen, watched the disaster from her parents' porch. Her arms were crossed and her jaw was clenched, and—knowing Olivia—she was probably imagining terrible punishments for the person responsible. Charlie rested his chin on the fence and gazed at the fire. He couldn't put a finger on it, but there was something about the blaze that wasn't quite right.

"It's been burning for a while now. Why hasn't the playhouse turned black and fallen down?" Jack asked, hitting the nail on its head. There were flames, but the wood didn't seem to be burning.

"Maybe it was treated with a fireproofing chemical," said Andrew Laird.

Charlie spun around to see his dad and stepmom standing behind them. "What are you doing here?" he demanded.

His dad looked bemused. "We came to see the fire. Is that all right with you, Mr. Laird?"

"What about the security system?" Charlie asked. "Did you turn it on before you left?"

Andrew Laird glanced over at his wife and shook his head. "It's eight o'clock at night," he told Charlie. "No one's going to—"

Charlie didn't let his dad finish the sentence. He was already sprinting back up the hill to the mansion, where he found the front door standing open. Charlie crept into the house and up the stairs to the second floor, taking special care to avoid all the squeaky steps. By the time he'd reached the landing, he heard two soft voices with familiar English accents. Charlie could have kicked himself. After everything he'd heard in Orville Falls that afternoon, he should have known that the playhouse was just a ruse to draw the Lairds out of the purple mansion so INK could get inside without activating the security system.

"Are you messing about with a bobby pin?" asked a muffled voice. It was clearly ICK's, coming from behind the closed door. Charlie stopped and crouched on the stairs.

"Certainly not! I'm using acid," replied INK. "Do you think I'm an idiot?"

ICK grunted. "So why is it taking so long?" she demanded skeptically. "Are you certain you're really trying?"

"Of course I'm trying!" INK scolded. "There are quite a few locks here!" Charlie peeked around the corner and saw INK using a dropper to fill a lock's keyhole with a clear liquid. A puff of smoke emerged from the hole, and the lock popped open. "While I'm working, I have a question to ask you. When Father made the formula, he used a Soxhlet extractor, didn't he?"

"I'm not interested in talking about Father's formula, India" was her sister's reply. "If we must make pleasant chitchat, I'd rather discuss our lighthouse, my dear. And why you chose to burn it down."

For a few seconds, all noises stopped. Then Charlie heard INK take a deep breath. "How do you know about that?"

But the answer was drowned out.

"CHARLIE! WHERE ARE YOU? WHAT'S GOING ON?" It was Jack, shouting into the house from the front door. His cover blown, Charlie sprang to his feet. But as soon as he took his first step, he was knocked over by a girl barreling down the stairs.

Charlie followed her, but he knew there was no time to catch her. "It's INK, and she's heading your way!" Charlie shouted down at Jack, who was still standing in the doorway. "Stop her!"

The girl was rushing toward Jack at an impressive speed, and Charlie prayed she wouldn't ram straight into him. But as it turned out, there was no cause for worry—because as INK rushed at him, Jack simply stepped to the side and let her go past. Within seconds, the twin had vanished into the night.

"What are you doing?" Charlie shouted at his brother as he stormed down the stairs. "You just let that pyromaniac get away!"

"Indy's not a pyro . . ." Jack got stuck in the middle of the word. "What is that, anyway?"

Charlie shook his head at his brother's ignorance. "It's someone who likes to set fires," he growled. "Like the one we were just watching."

"Indy's not a pyro-whatchamacallit. And that wasn't even a real fire," Jack told him. "It was some sort of chemistry experiment. No one got hurt. The playhouse didn't even burn down. The fire department said it was all just a prank."

"Just a *prank*?" Charlie was fuming. "Do you know what kind of pranks ICK and INK used to pull? The kind that get people killed."

Jack crossed his arms and rolled his eyes. "Oh yeah? Like *what*?" Jack demanded.

"Like destroying the town square in Orville Falls! Ever wonder why the girls got sent to that lighthouse in Maine?" Charlie snarled. "Dad and I met an old man today. He said he knew ICK and INK when they were real kids. He told us the twins thought it would be a hoot to bomb the fountain in front of the courthouse. They killed the mayor's dog!"

"Maybe ICK bombed the fountain," Jack said stubbornly, though he looked a little less certain. "Indy would never do something like that."

"How do you know?" Charlie spat.

"Because she's my friend," Jack said. "And I trust her."

"Just like you trusted those ogres who all turned against you a few months ago?" Charlie asked. "When are you going to learn your lesson, Jack?"

Jack shrugged. "Probably never," he said. And walked away.

CHAPTER FOURTEEN

WHAT HAPPENED IN BROOKLYN

The next morning, Cypress Creek Elementary was abuzz. A crowd had gathered outside the cafeteria doors, and Charlie was pretty sure it wasn't for a taste of the scrambled "eggs" the cafeteria ladies whipped up from powder. At first he thought everyone might be talking about the fire at the Hendersons' house. But then he pushed his way through the mob of students. As an eighth grader, he was taller than most of the kids, and he could see what had drawn the spectators before he made his way inside. And Charlie had to admit—it was truly *spectacular.*

The walls of the cafeteria had become the canvas for a remarkable mural. Likenesses of each of Cypress Creek's lunchroom ladies graced the walls. Dressed as goddesses, they represented four of the food groups. There was Dairy in a snow-white apron, sitting astride a lovely cow and pouring fresh milk from a jug into a bucket held by a plump little cherub. Meat (standing at a respectful distance from Dairy's cow) wore a necklace of sausages, a crown of meatballs, and a belt that looked like it might be made of bologna. The raven-haired goddess of Grains, meanwhile, was nuzzling two big bunches of wheat and wearing bagels as bracelets. And last but not least was the elderly goddess of Fruits and Vegetables, skipping across a wall with a rainbow of tomatoes, mangoes, lemons, artichokes, blueberries, and eggplants trailing behind her.

Charlie watched in amusement as the furious principal of Cypress Creek Elementary burst from the kitchen, flanked by four very happy employees. "Who is responsible for this . . . this . . . ?"

"Masterpiece?" asked one of the cafeteria ladies.

"Tour de force?" offered another.

"Act of vandalism!" the principal corrected them. "Who did this?"

Everyone in the school under the age of thirteen knew exactly who the artist was, but no one was prepared to name names.

Charlie heard someone snickering beside him. He looked over to see Ollie Tobias enjoying the chaos he'd created.

"Nice work," Charlie whispered.

"Thanks," said Ollie. "I'm proud of this one. I even signed it—though it may take them a few days to find my signature." He leaned toward Charlie and whispered, "It's inside Dairy's left nostril."

Charlie chuckled as the principal shouted in the background. "As impressive as these paintings may be, the walls of this cafeteria are the property of the state! I demand to know who's responsible!"

"Let's see if she figures it out," said Ollie. "If not, I'll come clean tomorrow."

"You'll be expelled," Charlie warned him.

"Doubt it," said Ollie. "My mom has a black belt in check writing."

Suddenly Charlie felt fingers grip his forearm. "Come with me," ordered a familiar voice, and Charlie found himself being dragged down the hall and into Ms. Abbot's classroom. The door slammed behind them, the lock was flipped, and Charlie was suddenly released.

"What was *that* for?" he asked, massaging his arm where Ms. Abbot's fingers had squeezed it.

She stood before him now, hands on her hips. Dirt was caked under her fingernails, her lipstick was smeared, and Charlie was pretty sure she was wearing the same dress she'd had on the day before.

"I thought I could trust you!" she hissed, keeping her voice low. Charlie couldn't be sure, but Ms. Abbot sounded as if she might burst into tears.

"I have no idea what—"

"Charlotte knew how important this was. She said you were good at keeping secrets."

"I *am*," Charlie told the teacher. "Is this about your poison garden? Because I swear, I never whispered a single word to anyone."

Ms. Abbot must have seen he was telling the truth. "Then Paige must have."

"No," Charlie said. "I don't know what's going on, but Paige wouldn't have said anything either. She thinks you're the coolest lady on earth. She would never do anything to upset you."

Ms. Abbot collapsed into her desk chair, dropped her head into her hands, and groaned miserably.

"What happened?" Charlie asked.

"It's gone," Ms. Abbot said, choking back a sob. "The belladonna we planted. It's gone. Someone broke into my garden and took it. Ripped it right out by the roots. I went out to the greenhouse last night and found the door open. The thief had melted the lock off with some kind of acid."

And Charlie knew exactly who the thief was. "She took the *Atropa belladonna*? You mean deadly nightshade?" Ms. Abbot nodded, and Charlie had to reach for a seat too. "So she only stole a single plant? She didn't take anything else?"

It seemed a little weird that INK would go through the trouble of breaking into the greenhouse only to remove one plant. But then again, deadly nightshade was no ordinary plant. Just one black belladonna berry could kill a full-grown human, and now INK had *dozens*.

Ms. Abbot's head snapped up. "Wait a second—you keep calling the thief 'she.' So you think it *was* Paige?"

"Of course it wasn't!" Charlie said. "For your information, it was India Kessog."

"The girl who disappeared after the first day of school?" Ms. Abbot asked, seeming completely confused.

"India's not really a girl," Charlie said.

"What are you talking about?" Ms. Abbot asked as if she were questioning his sanity. "If she's not a girl, then what is she?"

"Do you remember when Charlotte told you I was good at keeping secrets?" Charlie asked. "Well, India's true identity is one of them. I can't tell you any more right now, but you need to trust me. Did she take anything else from your house?"

"Yes," Ms. Abbot admitted. "Chemistry equipment."

INK was planning to make something. Her father's formula—wasn't that what she'd mentioned to her sister? If it was anything like ICK and INK's last creation, Cypress Creek could be in terrible trouble. "And now she has all the poison and equipment she needs," Charlie muttered to himself. What was Ms. Abbot thinking keeping all that stuff around anyway?

"You think she's going to do something awful?" Ms. Abbot asked weakly.

"Not if I can stop her," Charlie said. "But I need you to do me a favor. I need you to have me kicked out of school. Along with Paige Bretter, Rocco Marquez, and Alfie Bluenthal."

Thirty minutes later, Alfie was down on his knees on the sidewalk in front of Cypress Creek Elementary, his arms wrapped around Ms. Abbot's shins. "I thought we were friends! How could you say that I vandalized the cafeteria? I swear I had nothing to do with that graffiti! I don't even know how to draw! I'm all left brain! LEFT BRAIN, I TELL YOU!"

Paige seemed torn as she watched Alfie grovel. She didn't look like she was enjoying it—but she wasn't exactly jumping in to help either.

"Alfie, Ms. Abbot knows you're innocent!" Charlie whispered between clenched teeth. "Everything's going to be fine."

Charlotte's Range Rover pulled up in front of school. She rolled down her window. "Get inside," she ordered.

"All of us?" Rocco asked skeptically. "What about my mom and dad?"

"I didn't call them," Ms. Abbot said. Four kids had been

suspended from school, but the teacher had only phoned one parent.

"Get in!" Charlotte repeated. "All of you! And make it quick."

"Mrs. Laird! We've been wrongfully accused!" Alfie cried as the kids piled into the car. "We must fight this injustice! My parents will disown me if I don't get accepted to Harvard."

"Close the door, Alfie!" Charlie ordered, and Charlotte sped off. Charlie watched out the rear window. As soon as he could no longer see the school, he turned back to face his friends. "I asked Ms. Abbot to suspend us."

"You did what?" Alfie yelped.

"Charlie!" Rocco shouted. "They'll kick me off the football team!"

"No, they won't," Charlie assured his friends. "Ms. Abbot accused us of painting the cafeteria mural, but Ollie's planning to take credit for his artwork tomorrow, which means we'll all be proven innocent. So relax! Until then, we have a free day."

Alfie gaped as if Charlie had lost his marbles. "School just started four days ago, and you already want to play hooky?" he asked.

"Yeah, what's this all about, Charlie?" Charlotte asked from the front seat. "You owe me an explanation too."

"We're going back to the purple mansion to make plans.

We need to find INK," Charlie said. "Before she poisons the entire town."

He told them everything he knew about the missing belladonna.

"Oh no. Poor Samantha," Charlotte groaned. "She's been through so much. This is the last thing she needs."

Charlie could hardly believe it. He'd just said that everyone in Cypress Creek could be murdered—and Charlotte was worried about Samantha Abbot.

"What exactly has poor Ms. Abbot been through?" he asked. "Don't you think it's time for you to tell us the whole story?"

"I promised I wouldn't," Charlotte said. "But I suppose I can't stop you from Googling Beatrice Swanson."

"Who's *that*?" Rocco asked.

The answer came to Charlie in a flash of inspiration. "I'd bet you anything that's Ms. Abbot's real name," he said. "How did you figure it out, Charlotte?"

"I recognized her the first time I saw her," Charlotte said. "I think I must have been the only one in Cypress Creek who did. To be honest, I'm something of a fan of hers."

Paige typed the name into her phone. Dozens of articles came up in the search, most from New York newspapers.

BROOKLYN TEACHER ADMITS
SHE'S THE SCIENCE WITCH

RUMORS SWIRL AROUND THE
"WITCH OF BROOKLYN HEIGHTS"

PARENTS PROTEST AT "WITCH" SCHOOL

The photos that accompanied the headlines were just as shocking. Before she'd moved to Cypress Creek, Ms. Abbot had been blond and blue-eyed, with a fondness for flowery sundresses.

"So she *is* in disguise! I knew it!" Charlie said.

"You would be too," Rocco replied. "Look at all those articles!"

Paige had settled on a story in the *New York Times*. A teacher at a fancy school in Brooklyn had been exposed as the author of *The Science Witch,* a popular website devoted to the magic of nature and science.

Charlie felt his stomach churning. He knew that a discovery like that could lead some people to think that the pretty blond teacher might be hiding a sinister side. And according to the newspaper, that seemed to be the case. Rumors about Beatrice Swanson had spread quickly through Brooklyn. People said that she grew deadly plants on her apartment's rooftop terrace. Some claimed that she kept venomous snakes and a Gila monster as pets. Children reported that she refused to kill spiders—no matter how large or hairy. And teachers whispered that Beatrice was always cooking up foul-smelling goop with equipment that looked like it came right out of a mad scientist's lab.

And all of it was true.

The *Times* reported that when the principal of the Brooklyn school confronted Beatrice Swanson, the teacher immediately confessed to keeping snakes and sparing spiders. But when a committee investigated, they found no cause for Ms. Swanson to be fired or arrested. Instead, they recommended that the brilliant and dedicated science teacher receive a promotion.

A few parents complained, but for a while it seemed as if the scandal would go away. And then a new round of rumors began on the Internet, and the second batch was far more potent. They each took a little speck of truth and wove a thick web of lies around it.

An anonymous neighbor said her baby had been sickened when a bird dropped a poisonous seed from the teacher's garden into the child's mashed potatoes and peas. A parent writing under the name WITCHHUNTER said that the students in one of Beatrice Swanson's classes had all come down with a mysterious illness the day she brought a plate of homemade cookies to class—and that lab tests on the baked goods had confirmed the presence of Gila monster venom. An anonymous school employee wrote that security cameras inside the school had filmed the teacher placing dangerous spiders in the lockers of the students who'd exposed her as a witch. He even included a picture of a plastic baggie filled with spider corpses that he claimed to have plucked from the students' belongings.

And worst of all, someone who claimed to have grown up with Beatrice Swanson said she had been practicing witchcraft since the age of fifteen, and there was evidence to suggest that one of her first victims had been her own twelve-year-old brother.

Charlie gasped when he read that part. Paige scrolled down, and a photo appeared. Charlie should have been shocked, but he'd half known what was coming. The picture showed the street outside a beautiful brick school somewhere in Brooklyn. It was packed with angry parents who, according to the caption, were demanding that Beatrice Swanson be permanently removed from the building and arrested. The *Times* had interviewed a few of them. One claimed that his little boy had developed a strange and horrifying rash in Ms. Swanson's class. (When the *Times* checked back in with the father a week later, he admitted that the boy was just allergic to their new laundry detergent.) Another parent said she'd overheard her daughter casting a spell while she was taking a shower. (The girl in question insisted she'd been singing a popular rap song.)

In the end, Beatrice Swanson had fled New York. But she was still being hounded. The papers continued to write about her. Websites were full of posts from people who claimed to have seen her taking part in New Orleans voo-doo ceremonies, dressed like a Celtic priestess in Ireland, or wearing a Maleficent costume at a comic-book conven-tion.

Meanwhile, Beatrice Swanson had been in Cypress Creek the whole time.

"Wow," Charlie said. "And I thought witch-hunts ended hundreds of years ago. Who would make up that kind of stuff just to get back at someone?"

"Me," Paige said. Her face was as white as a sheet and her lips were trembling. "I would."

"What are you *talking* about?" Rocco asked. "You are definitely not that kind of person."

"Yes, I am," Paige insisted. "Yesterday I was mad at Alfie for stealing the show in Ms. Abbot's class. So I accused him of making Jancy Dare sick with his special water recipe."

"That's okay," Alfie said with a shrug. "I can be a bit of a show-off, and I know you didn't really mean it."

"No," Paige said. "I didn't really mean it. I was just mad and feeling mean. I didn't want to hurt you. But I could have ended up doing something unforgivable. By saying what I did, I could have accidentally started a hor-rible rumor about you. I bet that's exactly how the stories started about Ms. Abbot in Brooklyn."

"Hey, Paige!" Alfie put his arm around her. "Really, it's okay! I forgive you!"

"Thanks, but I don't deserve it," Paige said, hugging him back.

"It's just proof that what happened in Brooklyn could happen here too," Charlie said. "And no one deserves to be treated the way Ms. Abbot was."

"That's right," Rocco said. "We've got to help her."

"Then we need to find INK," Charlie said. "If anyone in this town gets poisoned, Ms. Abbot will be the first person people blame."

CHAPTER FIFTEEN

THE SECRET RENDEZVOUS

Inside the purple mansion, the four kids and Charlotte huddled around the breakfast table with a map of Cypress Creek laid out in front of them.

"Charlotte, you should take downtown Cypress Creek," Charlie said. "Whatever INK's making, she may need more supplies. You should go door to door and ask all the shop people if they've seen any weird kids wearing old-fashioned uniforms.

"Alfie and Rocco, you guys split up and check as many backyards as you can. INK seems to have a thing for playhouses and garden sheds."

"Wait a sec," said Rocco. "I'm happy to look, but what am I supposed to do if I catch her?"

"Text the rest of us," Charlie said.

"And then?" Alfie asked.

Charlie frowned. "I haven't gotten that far yet," he admitted. "First we find her; then we figure out what to do with her. Paige and I are going to go back to search through the woods around Ms. Abbot's house."

"Why do both of you need to go to the woods?" Alfie asked. "Why doesn't one of you go check out the library or something?"

Neither Charlie nor Paige had a response ready. Charlie saw Charlotte struggling to hold back a smile and Rocco shaking his head at Alfie's cluelessness.

"Am I missing something?" Alfie asked. Charlie felt his face burning red.

Rocco rolled his eyes. "And I thought you were a genius," he said. "Come on, let's hit the road."

"I still don't understand!" Alfie hurried after Rocco as the taller boy headed for the front door. "Seriously, Rocco, what is it?"

Finally Rocco took pity on Alfie, stopped, and bent down to whisper something in his ear. By the time he'd finished, Alfie's mouth was hanging open in shock.

"You're joking!" he said, running to catch up with

Rocco, who was already halfway out the door. "Wait, Rocco—are you pulling my leg?"

As the door swung shut, Charlie found himself staring at the exit and wishing he too could make a mad dash for it.

He heard Charlotte grabbing her handbag and keys off the kitchen counter. "I'm off too," she announced. "Unless somebody finds INK earlier, I'll see you guys this evening."

"Bye, Charlotte," Paige said. "You ready, Charlie?"

He couldn't find the guts to turn and face her. So instead, Charlie offered a hearty grunt.

"I guess I should take that as a yes," Paige said. "But if you're planning to act weird all afternoon, maybe I'll head to the library by myself."

Charlie cleared his throat and forced himself to look Paige in the eye. "Act like *what*? I don't know what you're talking about," he said.

Paige laughed. "Whatever you say," she told him.

It was a warm fall day in Cypress Creek—until they turned down Freeman Road. The trees overhead blocked out the sunlight, and the temperature dropped twenty degrees in the shade. Charlie shivered and wished he'd taken a jacket from the coatrack by the purple mansion's front door. If he had, he would have offered it to Paige. In the forest, the leaves were already falling, and their brittle brown carcasses littered the ground, sometimes piling so high they hid the road from view.

Riding side by side on their bikes, Charlie and Paige moved cautiously as they searched for signs of life between the trees. Charlie spotted four deer, a rabbit, a raccoon, and something he hoped might be Bigfoot but turned out to be the blackened stump of a tree that had recently been struck by lightning. While there was no sign of INK, he had a hunch that they'd find her when they reached Ms. Abbot's house. With the teacher at school, it was the perfect time for a thief to break into a house and stock up on supplies.

Charlie glanced over at Paige. Her hair was blowing in the wind, and she looked like a girl from a television commercial. They hadn't spoken much since they'd hopped on their bikes, but somehow the awkwardness was totally gone, and Charlie was just glad to be hunting for villains with one of his best friends since kindergarten.

When they reached Ms. Abbot's house, they parked their bikes out of sight and scouted the property. The garden shed was empty, and there were no signs that anyone had been inside for a while. Several new locks had been added to the greenhouse door. When Charlie and Paige peered through the glass, they could see the empty space where the belladonna had once been, though it didn't seem like any of the other plants had disappeared. The house was locked up tight as well, but Paige insisted they have a look inside. She located a window that was open a crack. Standing on Charlie's shoulders like an acrobat, she was able to slip inside.

"Whoa, you've got to see this place," she whispered when she unlocked the back door for Charlie.

The living room was one giant laboratory. There was very little furniture, just several tables that seemed to be devoted to different experiments. There were so many beakers, tubes, coils, and extractors clamped together that Charlie could barely make sense of it all. Corked flasks of strange liquids waited their turn to be studied, along with bowls filled with poisonous berries and toxic leaves.

"What has Ms. Abbot been doing?" Paige asked, just as Charlie caught sight of a black car pulling up in front of the house. Without pausing to think, he grabbed his friend and pulled her into a closet in the hall.

"Why are we hiding?" Paige whispered. "It's probably Ms. Abbot, and she knows we skipped school to look for INK."

"Yeah, but we forgot to mention we'd be snooping around her house," Charlie said. "It's lunchtime. She's probably just stopping by to get something. We won't have to hide for long." Though Charlie had to admit—he was perfectly content to share a closet with Paige for as long as possible. The smell of her shampoo always made him giddy.

They heard the front door open. There were light footsteps on the floor. And then came the sound of shattering glass.

"What's happening?" Paige whispered. It sounded like someone was taking a hammer to the laboratory.

The ruckus lasted a full minute. Then the shattering ended, something heavy fell with a thump on the floor, and the footsteps walked away. Terrible fumes began to fill the closet. Charlie opened the door and peeked outside. All that was left of the laboratory was broken glass. Chemicals of all colors had splattered the ceiling, and acid had burned holes the size of tangerines in the plaster. Blobs of goo left trails of slime as they oozed down the walls toward the floor. Smoke rose from the remains of the destroyed equipment.

Someone had destroyed Ms. Abbot's lab, as if in a fit of rage.

The house was silent, aside from a few rumblings coming from the bedroom. Together, Charlie and Paige tiptoed toward the door. They found Ms. Abbot inside, yanking clothing off hangers in her closet. She tossed an armful of dresses onto a suitcase lying open on the bed. She looked at the suitcase for a moment, then burst into tears and collapsed into a miserable heap on a nearby chair.

"I give up," Charlie heard her say between sobs.

Paige's phone buzzed in her pocket. She pulled it out and they checked the screen. The text was from Rocco. FOUND INK AT PARK NEAR LIBRARY. GET HERE FAST. Charlie glanced back up at Ms. Abbot. Something was terribly wrong with her, and he hated to leave anyone alone in such a state, but there was nothing else to be done. India Kessog had to be caught.

Rocco was crouched behind some bushes at the edge of the park when Charlie and Paige sped up on their bikes.

"Where is she?" Charlie asked.

Rocco stood up and pointed to the opposite side of the park. INK was there, all right, sitting primly on a bench with a basket in her lap and her legs crossed at the ankles. "She's been there for the last thirty minutes."

"You've been watching her for that long? Why didn't you grab her?" Alfie had arrived.

"What for?" Rocco asked. "She hasn't been bothering anyone."

"Rocco," Charlie huffed. "Do I need to remind you that INK stole a deadly plant? She could poison the entire town and ruin our science teacher's life."

"Maybe," Rocco said, being unusually stubborn. "But she hasn't."

The argument stopped as the four of them ducked down behind the bushes. Someone was wading through dried leaves a few yards away. Then a small figure walked out into the park.

"Jack!" Charlie groaned. "What's he doing here? Why isn't he in class?"

Paige checked her watch. It was three o'clock. "School just got out," she announced.

Charlie's little brother waved to INK from across the park. When he reached the bench, he took a seat beside the girl. They chatted like best friends for a few minutes, and then INK reached into the basket on her lap and pulled out a small bottle.

"Oh no!" Paige whispered.

INK handed the bottle to Jack. And he took it.

"What's he doing?" squealed Alfie.

Jack examined the contents, then uncorked the bottle . . .

"Ummm, Charlie?" Rocco said nervously.

. . . and lifted it toward his face . . .

"STOP!" Charlie shouted, bolting from his hiding spot. "JACK, DON'T DRINK THAT!"

The bottle slipped out of Jack's hands, and INK leaped up from the bench. Before Charlie could reach them, she'd disappeared between the trees. Jack dropped to his knees and grabbed the bottle off the ground. Most of its contents had spilled, but there were still a few drops of a milky-white liquid left at the bottom.

"Look what you did!" Jack shouted at his brother.

"Look what I did? Are you kidding?" Charlie yelled back. "I just saved your sneaky little butt!"

"I wasn't going to drink the stuff, you doofus," Jack growled. "I was just smelling it! Indy said I could!"

Charlie snorted bitterly. "Don't you know smelling stuff can be dangerous too? Besides, what were you doing taking *anything* INK handed you? And why were you meeting with her in the first place?"

Jack didn't answer right away. And when his lips stayed shut for longer than they should have, Charlie knew something was up.

"What is it?" he demanded.

"She asked me not to tell you," Jack said.

For a minute, the shouting had seemed to be over, and Charlie's friends had started making their way toward the brothers. Now they stopped in their tracks again as Charlie let loose on Jack. "ARE YOU COMPLETELY INSANE?" He could barely believe what he'd heard. "A creature who nearly destroyed three worlds wants you to keep something a secret from your own brother and you *agree*?"

Jack narrowed his eyes. "Indy is not a *creature*. And she only asked me to keep the secret because she's scared of you."

"SHE *SHOULD* BE SCARED OF ME!" Charlie shouted. "I'M TRYING TO *CATCH* HER."

He felt a hand on his shoulder and looked to his left to see Paige, with Rocco and Alfie standing beside her.

"Okay, okay." It was Rocco. "Calm down, Charlie. What's going on, Jack?"

Charlie almost told his friend not to waste his time. But Jack seemed perfectly happy to talk to Rocco.

"You know how I always climb the oak tree at recess?" he said.

"Sure," Rocco said gamely, though Charlie doubted Rocco paid much attention to his nine-year-old brother's recess routine.

"Well, today when I got to the second branch, I found a note from Indy," Jack continued. "It said, 'I have something to show you.' And it asked me to come here after school. Indy's my friend, so I came."

Charlie shook his head. "INK turned everyone in Orville Falls into sleepwalking zombies, and then she nearly burned down our house, and my brother says she's his *friend*," he grumbled.

"That's enough, Charlie," Paige said.

"This is what she wanted to show me," Jack told Rocco. He handed the older boy the little bottle.

"What is it?" Rocco asked.

"I don't know!" Jack said. "Indy called it her father's formula. I figure it's got to be something important, but Charlie scared her away before she could tell me."

"Oh, come on!" Charlie cried. "We all know it's the poison she made from the belladonna! She was probably trying to test it on Jack."

He expected to hear Jack say it wasn't true, but it was Rocco who came to INK's defense. "We don't know what she was planning to do with it," he said. He gave the contents of the bottle a sniff and his nose wrinkled in disgust. "It's not perfume, but we don't know for sure that it's poison either." He passed the bottle to Alfie. "Do you think you can do some tests and find out what's in this stuff?"

"Sure," said Alfie. "I can give it a shot."

Charlie could barely believe his ears. Two of his best friends in the whole wide world seemed to be siding with *Jack*.

CHAPTER SIXTEEN

A DREAM WITH NO MONSTERS

Neither of the Laird boys had taken a single bite of their tofu surprise. Jack was constructing a fortress with the white cubes, while Charlie was mashing his tofu into a nasty white paste.

"Traitor," Charlie mumbled under his breath.

"Jerk," Jack replied under his.

Andrew Laird put down his fork. "Okay, that's enough. You guys want to tell me what the heck is going on?" he demanded.

"They're just having a spat," said Charlotte, who knew

the whole story and had refused to take sides, much to Charlie's frustration. "Something about a girl at school."

"The argument needs to end now," Andrew Laird said. "We don't call each other names like that in this house."

Just then the phone rang and the lecture ended as Charlie's dad stood up to answer it. "Hello?" he said. "Yes, this is he." For the next thirty seconds, Charlie watched the expression on his father's face change from confusion to surprise and then finally settle on anger.

"That was interesting," he told his family as he took his seat at the table. "Your principal just called, Charlie. She wanted to apologize for suspending you this morning. Seems the teacher who accused you and your friends of vandalism confessed that she hadn't actually caught any of you in the act. She's resigned from her position."

Charlie sat up straight in his chair. That wasn't what they'd planned at all. Ms. Abbot wasn't supposed to *resign*. Ollie was going to take credit for his artwork, his mom would probably pay to have the school repainted, and everything would be perfectly fine.

"And while I'm glad to hear that you aren't a vandal," Andrew Laird continued, "I do have one question for you: where exactly did you go when you were sent home at eight-thirty this morning?"

Charlie couldn't help it. He glanced at Charlotte.

"I picked Charlie up from school," she confessed.

"That's what I thought," Andrew Laird said. "And you didn't bother to tell me because . . . ?"

Charlie could tell Charlotte was nervous. The fork in her hand was shaking so hard that a lump of tofu fell off it. "Because I knew Charlie was innocent, and I didn't want to upset you," she said, sticking fairly close to the truth.

"Well, it didn't work. I am upset," Andrew said as Charlie watched in horror. He'd never seen his father and stepmother argue like this before. "I don't like being excluded from important family business as if my opinion doesn't matter."

"I'm sorry, Andy," Charlotte said. Charlie wished she could sound a little more convincing. "I should have called you."

"He's my son," Andrew told her. "I'm glad you two have gotten so close, but the secrets have to stop. If Charlie's suspended from school, I need to know."

Charlie stood up from the dinner table and dropped his napkin on his plate. "Don't get mad at her. It was all my fault," he said. "I'll punish myself. I'm going to my room."

"Charlie!" his dad called as Charlie rushed up the stairs. "Come back and eat your dinner!"

But Charlie couldn't face it. In a single day, his best friends had turned against him and he'd started his whole family fighting. It was better for everyone if Charlie locked himself away alone in his bedroom.

When he got there, he lay down face-first and fully clothed on his bed. A split second later, he was knocked to the ground by a fat, smelly sheep. When Charlie stood up again, he was dripping with foul-smelling muck and on the verge of tears.

Why was he back in ICK's dream? Why was he being forced to spend his nights in a sheep pen? And what did it say about *him* that he shared a dream with a villain?

He heard someone humming in the distance. But this time the sound of the lullaby wasn't comforting. Instead, it reminded Charlie that he was completely alone, and he found himself doing something he never would have expected.

"ICK!" he shouted. "I mean, *Isabel*! Isabel Kessog! Are you out there?"

There was no answer aside from the whistling wind.

"I'm not here to fight you! I just want to talk!"

Charlie gave up and took a look around. The moon was out for once, and he could see that he was in the field outside Orville Falls, just below Kessog Castle. And the sheep that surrounded him were the ones that had escaped right before ICK and INK were sent to the lighthouse in Maine.

Something had happened here, Charlie knew. That was why it had become the scene of ICK's never-ending nightmare—a dream so bad that she always came back to it. It had something to do with the lullaby that seemed to scare ICK to death. But no matter how hard he tried, Charlie couldn't figure out what it could be.

CHAPTER SEVENTEEN

DINGLEBERRY

Andrew Laird stopped the car in front of Cypress Creek Elementary. Charlie pulled the door handle, gave the door a light nudge with his shoulder—and tumbled out onto the sidewalk.

"Sorry!" Ollie Tobias had pulled the door open at the very worst moment. It was eight in the morning, but Ollie was buzzing with so much energy that Charlie half expected him to explode. "I didn't mean to make you fall, but I gotta talk to you right away."

"Ollie Tobias, just the person I wanted to see." Charlie's books had spilled out of his backpack and he was cramming them back inside. "You said you were going to take credit for all your art yesterday. Why didn't you?"

"I was busy with a new project! When the muse calls, I gotta listen," Ollie said. Then he looked up to see Charlie's dad watching them. "Have a nice day, Mr. Laird!" he called cheerfully, shutting the car door.

"So what do you want now, Ollie?" Charlie demanded.

"Not here," the boy told him. "In private." He guided Charlie into the school, toward a room that had recently served as a broom closet. When Ollie opened the door, Charlie saw that it was now painted to resemble a small Italian grotto.

"Step inside my office," Ollie said.

Charlie complied, and Ollie closed the door behind them.

Out in the hallway, the first warning bell rang. "Okay, what is it?" Charlie asked.

"Did I ever tell you about my pet monkey?"

Charlie groaned. "Oh, come on! You've got to be kidding, Ollie. I don't have time for this. I've gotta get to class."

"No," Ollie insisted. "I'm not kidding. He was a capuchin monkey, and his name was Dingleberry, and he was totally evil."

"Yeah, probably because you gave him a name like *Dingleberry*."

"Give me a break!" Ollie said. "I was five! Dingleberry

was the coolest name I could think of. But listen, Charlie! He really was a horrible monkey. He used to yank my hair when my parents weren't looking. And he'd do stuff around the house like paint pictures on the walls with grape jelly or poop in a corner. Whatever he did, I'd always end up getting blamed for it."

"A monkey painted pictures on your walls with grape jelly?" Charlie asked skeptically.

"All right, all right, that was me," Ollie admitted. "But I swear I never pooped in a corner or put bugs in my mom's face cream or covered the neighbor's cat with maple syrup. It was all Dingleberry. You've got to believe me, Charlie."

Charlie put one hand on the door handle and the other on Ollie's shoulder. "I believe you. But as much as I've enjoyed this trip back to your extremely strange youth, I really have to get to class. Big things are happening, Ollie, and I can't be stuck in a broom closet all day."

"I know big things are happening!" Ollie practically screamed. "That's what I'm trying to tell you! Just wait for one second. I'm getting to the point!"

"Fine," Charlie said with a sigh. "But let's get there faster."

"Okay, okay! My mom gave Dingleberry to a rescue center when I was six, after she caught him cutting my dad's hair with pruning shears at three o'clock in the morning, but I had bad dreams about that monkey for years. And last night I had another."

"Ollie, you read Charlotte's book. You know what you have to do to beat your nightmares . . . ," Charlie began.

"Of course I do! I memorized that book from cover to cover. So last night when I saw Dingleberry, I didn't run away. I stood right there, and I told that monkey I wasn't scared of him anymore. And guess what, Charlie. He wouldn't leave. He told me—"

"Your monkey could talk?" Charlie said, trying not to laugh.

"It was a nightmare!" Ollie cried. "Dingleberry told me he had something to show me. He said something bad was about to happen in the Netherworld. I didn't really understand everything, 'cause he was speaking with a Portuguese accent. But he mentioned some kind of prophecy, and he made it pretty clear that he wasn't going to let me wake up until I went with him."

"What did you do?" Charlie asked.

Ollie scrunched up his face. "I didn't have much of a choice, did I? When a monkey appears in your nightmare and tells you there's trouble brewing, you let him show you what he needs to show you! And oh, man, Charlie, am I glad I did."

Charlie felt dread settle over him like a cold, wet blanket.

"Dingleberry took me to a house in the Netherworld. It

was in a town that kind of looked like Cypress Creek, and it was a little white house. . . ."

"A little white house?" Charlie repeated incredulously. "You don't see many of those in the Netherworld."

"Yeah, I know!" Ollie said. "This place looked totally normal. I'm tellin' you, Charlie, it was *super* creepy. When you find a regular-looking house in the Netherworld, you know there's gotta be something really awful and disgusting inside."

"And?" Charlie asked. "Was there?"

Ollie took a deep breath. "I'm getting to that part. So anyways, we get there, and Dingleberry tells me to be really quiet, and he took me up to one of the windows and made me look inside. And guess who I saw in there, Charlie. That horrible girl! The same one who was here—the one we all saw in our dreams."

"There are two girls, remember?" Charlie asked. "The one in Cypress Creek is INK. If you saw one in the Netherworld last night, it was probably her sister, ICK."

"Whoever it was, she wasn't alone. The whole house was filled with Nightmares. And I'm talking about some of the scariest Nightmares I've ever seen! You'd have to be a real sicko to dream about some of that stuff. And the Nightmares were all gathered around ICK. I couldn't hear what she was saying to them, but it looked like she was giving them orders. ICK's planning something, Charlie. I swear it."

Ollie paused to catch his breath. Then he looked at Charlie as if searching for some kind of reaction. "Well? What do you think?"

Charlie felt sick. "I think it sounds like ICK has been making some new friends," he said.

CHAPTER EIGHTEEN

ICK'S ARMY

That night, after school was out, dinner was eaten, homework was finished, and most normal people had gone to bed, Charlie was preparing for his latest trip to the Netherworld. Unfortunately, so was Jack.

"I told you, you're *not* coming with me!" Charlie hissed loudly. "I need to find out what ICK is up to. And bringing you on a surveillance mission is like walking around with a giant sign that says LOOK AT ME. You're practically a celebrity—like Justin Bieber. Everyone in the Netherworld knows you, and they all either love you or want to kill you."

"Sorry. You can't stop me from coming," Jack replied

defiantly, looking as serious as anyone wearing Captain America pajamas with a giant white star on the belly could possibly look.

"Oh yes, I can," Charlie growled.

It was midnight, and the boys and their stepmom were standing right outside the bedroom where Andrew Laird was blissfully dozing. So when Charlie and Jack started to squabble, Charlotte quickly herded them back downstairs to the landing, where a portrait of Silas DeChant peered at them from the wall.

"Boys!" she whispered frantically. "Keep it down! If your father hears any of this and thinks we're keeping secrets again, we're all going to be in big trouble. He's still furious that I didn't tell him about Charlie's suspension from school."

"Fine," Charlie said, keeping his voice low. "But I'm not taking Jack to the Netherworld. He's not even on our side anymore."

"What are you *talking* about?" Jack said. "Just because I met Indy in the park, I'm suddenly Benedict Cumberbatch?"

"It's Benedict *Arnold,* you moron," Charlie replied.

"That's enough!" Charlotte hissed.

"ICK is up to something," Charlie said. "We need to find out what it is, and we can't risk Benedict here blabbing all about it to ICK's sister."

Charlotte turned to Jack. "Are you going to tell INK about anything you see in the Netherworld tonight?" she asked.

"No!" Jack cried.

"Then that's that!" Charlotte told Charlie. "If your brother promises he won't tell INK, he won't."

"But—" Charlie started to protest.

"Stop it right now! Your brother is not a traitor!" Charlotte said, a little too loudly. Her head swiveled toward the second floor, and she waited for a moment, as if worried she'd woken her husband. Then she continued in a whisper. "I don't know why Jack feels the need to hang around with that weird little girl-creature, but I do know that he's not going to do anything that puts us at risk. He's just like your mom."

It felt like a punch in the gut. "What do you mean?" Charlie asked.

"Veronica used to give everyone the benefit of the doubt," Charlotte said. "I was the skeptic. I never believed anything unless I had proof. But that's why your mom and I always made a good team—and that's why you and Jack do too. You're all head, Charlie—and Jack's all heart. If you put the two together, you can't be beat."

Charlie looked down at Jack, trying not to feel jealous that his brother was the one who'd ended up just like their mom. "ICK and INK made the Tranquility Tonic, remember? Have you forgotten what it did to the people who drank it? Have you forgotten that it nearly destroyed three worlds? Why do you still talk to INK when you know what she's done?"

"Correction," Jack said. "I've *tried* talking to India, but you always show up and butt in before I can ask her about the tonic."

"Then maybe you should spend less time chitchatting and get right to the point," Charlie spat.

"You want me to sit down and say 'So tell me, Indy, why did you and your sister decide to turn everyone in Orville Falls into Walkers'? You really think that would work? Besides, I was planning to ask Indy about the Tranquility Tonic that day at lunch, but then *you* came over and interrupted us. Who knows? Maybe INK had a good reason for making it that we just haven't thought of."

The idea was completely ridiculous. "You think there could be a good reason for creating something as evil as the Tranquility Tonic?" Charlie asked his brother.

Jack shrugged.

"See what I mean?" Charlie asked Charlotte with a sigh.

"I know," his stepmother agreed. "It seems nuts to me too. But you know what? Your mom would have said the very same thing. Now, do you boys think you can be quiet long enough to go back upstairs? It's getting late, and I still have locks to open."

"Yep," Jack whispered, and Charlie nodded reluctantly. Then they both followed Charlotte to the second floor.

When the final lock was removed, Charlotte stood back and held the tower door open for the boys.

"Please be careful, and please be quiet!" she whispered, pointing to the bedroom where the boys' dad lay sleeping. "And please, please, please try to be nice to each other!"

She stayed behind on the second floor while Charlie and Jack climbed up to the octagonal room that held the entrance to the Netherworld. The portal opened the second they passed over the threshold.

"Show-off," Charlie grumbled. It had always bugged him that his little brother could open the portal faster than anyone else.

"I thought you were supposed to be nice tonight," Jack observed.

"Whatever," Charlie replied with a huff.

They crossed through the portal and into the black Netherworld mansion—which was identical to the Waking World purple mansion in every way but its color. Looking out the tower's window, they saw the nightmare version of Cypress Creek below them. Charlie spotted a giant, bloodthirsty hound chasing a screaming little girl. A sea monster emerged from a nearby koi pond and wrapped its tentacles around a man on a riding mower. Pterodactyls had cornered several people in the ATM kiosk at the local bank and were attempting to break through the glass with their beaks.

"Another night in paradise," Jack said. "Look over there. That one seems pretty interesting." He pointed to a street in the distance where a giant crowd with torches and pitchforks was chasing someone the boys couldn't see.

"Meh," said Charlie, unimpressed. He pointed in the other direction, where an enormous blob was attempting to swallow an elderly gardener. "I'm more of a giant slug man myself."

The people of Cypress Creek could be quite creative when it came to the Nightmares they conjured in their sleep. But as far as Charlie was concerned, nothing he'd seen was as disturbing as ICK's dream.

"I've been having ICK's nightmare," Charlie told his brother. He hadn't meant to confess. It had just come out.

Jack's reaction was lighting fast. "What?"

"Every night when I go to sleep, I don't have my own nightmares or dreams. I visit ICK's nightmare instead," Charlie explained.

"You do?" Jack said. "That's crazy! Why didn't you say anything?"

Charlie knew he should have come clean sooner, but he'd been too ashamed to admit that he and ICK shared something in common. "Because I don't know why I keep having it," he admitted. "She doesn't want me there, and I don't want to go, but I keep ending up in it anyway."

"Maybe you're there because you might understand it," Jack replied sensibly. "What's it about?"

"Sheep," Charlie said.

He expected Jack to laugh or say something like "That's not so *baaaaaad*," but his brother didn't even grin. It made Charlie feel better that someone was taking it seriously. "What kind?" Jack asked.

"Black sheep," Charlie said. "Like the ones from the lullaby."

"Do they bite or something?" Jack asked.

"Nope," Charlie said. "They don't do anything except eat and poop."

"Oh," Jack said. He looked stumped.

"I visited the dream again last night. I was going to ask ICK what scared her so much," Charlie said. "I guess I was feeling a bit sorry for her. But she wasn't in her nightmare. She was hanging out with a bunch of other Nightmares instead. Ollie Tobias said they were the scariest he'd ever seen."

"Maybe ICK just wanted some company," Jack said.

"I don't think ICK's interested in making friends," Charlie said. "There's gotta be another reason she's suddenly so social. And that's why we're here. We need to find out what it is."

Ollie's description of the house from his nightmare had been very clear. It was a small white house on a street in the Netherworld's Cypress Creek. Ollie said the buildings around it were run-down and abandoned, but the house where he'd seen ICK was one of the weirdest nightmare houses he'd ever encountered. What made it so unusual was that it didn't look scary at all.

Charlie had expected to find the house right away, but he and Jack had been searching for hours, and they still hadn't come across anything that matched Ollie's description.

"It has to be around here somewhere," Charlie groaned miserably. He and Jack had been down a dozen streets, past more graveyards, swamps, and haunted mansions than either of them could count.

Then they turned a corner and Jack stopped in his tracks. "Charlie," he said, "I think we just found it."

Charlie looked in the direction his brother was pointing. Sure enough, there was a pleasant-looking house about half a block away. Charlie felt his knees buckle.

"No," he muttered. "That can't be it."

But it was, and Charlie knew it. The little white house was the only normal-looking building they'd passed all evening. And it just happened to be an exact copy of the one Charlie and Jack had lived in when their mother was still alive.

"I don't get it," Jack said. "Why is our old house here in the Netherworld?"

"Because I built it here," Charlie admitted. The little white cottage was the scene of the worst nightmare he'd ever had. And now he was back. "This is where I said goodbye to Mom."

"That was months ago, wasn't it?" Jack asked. "I thought you beat that nightmare. So why is the house still here?"

When a Netherworld nightmare was over, its set was either reused or disappeared. No one else would have any use for Charlie's old house. So if the little white building was still standing, there could be only one reason, and Charlie and Jack both knew what it was. Charlie's nightmare wasn't quite over yet. There was something inside the house that he still hadn't faced. And now ICK was part of it.

Charlie felt the anger burning inside him. It had been ages since he'd been so furious. "Let's go," he told his brother. He couldn't wait to get in there and drag ICK out of his dream.

"Charlie!" Jack rushed after him. "Wait just a minute! You've got to calm down!"

But Charlie didn't want to calm down. He wanted ICK

to leave his house. A horrible creature like her didn't deserve to set foot in a place where his mother had lived. Charlie barged through the front door and came to a halt. Inside, the house was nothing but an empty shell. The furniture and decorations were all gone. There weren't even any walls. But there was a door—right where the entrance to the cellar had been.

Before his mother got sick, that cellar had been home to Charlie's worst nightmares. He still remembered how dark it had seemed from the top of the stairs. He'd been sure there were monsters down there that would snatch kids away and hide them from their families forever. Charlie had always sped up when he'd walked past its door.

"ICK's got to be down there," he told his brother.

Charlie opened the door to reveal a rectangular patch of pitch-blackness. The air that escaped from below smelled rank and rotten.

"Are you sure about this?" said Jack.

"Yes." Charlie was terrified, but he couldn't turn back. He reached out with his right foot and located the first step. "Take my hand," he told his brother—for his own comfort as much as Jack's. Together they were swallowed by the darkness as they climbed down the stairs.

"Where are we?" Jack asked.

"This is the cellar," Charlie told him. "It used to scare

me to death when I was little." With every step, he felt as if another large weight had been placed around his neck. It wasn't just fear that was dragging Charlie down, though. It was sadness as well. He'd thought it was gone, but some of it had been buried. Everything Charlie didn't like about himself—the stuff he used to call the darkness—seemed to be there in the cellar. "I built this too."

When they reached the bottom of the stairs, Charlie was almost relieved to hear a voice in the distance and see a dim glow ahead at the end of a tunnel. As they walked toward it, the light became brighter and an enormous cavern appeared. And to Charlie's horror, it was completely filled with monsters.

There were enormous yeti whose heads scraped the roof of the cavern—and tiny winged gargoyles that buzzed in circles around them. There were ghouls with no eyes and beasts that were almost entirely teeth. Charlie saw a wolf the size of a small car hungrily eyeing a beast with a man's body and a deer's head and antlers. In all his trips to the Netherworld, Charlie had never encountered such horrifying creatures. And while the sight was shocking, the smell was far worse.

As Charlie did his best to avoid breathing through his nose, one of the smallest creatures climbed up onto a rock in the center of the cavern. It was ICK, still wearing her schoolgirl uniform. Standing among the monsters, she looked like she was there not to lead the beasts, but to be sacrificed to them.

Yet when she spoke, the vast room immediately fell silent.

"You're here because you've all heard of the prophecy," ICK proclaimed in her lovely accent. "They say that the Netherworld will one day be visited by a human child with the strength to destroy it."

She paused, as if to let the information sink in. When she spoke next, ICK's voice had become far more sinister.

"I am the prophecy," she announced.

The monsters began to murmur among themselves. Some seemed awestruck, while others didn't appear to believe her. Then a Nightmare with the head of a squid shot a long tentacle in ICK's direction and wrapped it around one of her wrists. ICK grabbed the tentacle with her free hand and, in a remarkable show of strength, dragged its disrespectful owner to the front of the group. "Tell them how I taste," she demanded.

The squid monster gagged. "Like human!" it managed to cry.

"Did you hear that?" ICK asked the crowd as she ripped the tentacle off her wrist and let the humiliated Nightmare collapse to the ground. "I taste human because I am here in the flesh. Just as the prophecy foretold! So believe me when

I tell you now that the Netherworld's days are numbered! This world will soon be reaching its end!" She paused, and the anger on her face was replaced with a sinister smile. "However . . . I am willing to spare everyone in this room. Those who swear their allegiance to me will live. I will guide you to safety. The rest of you will be left here in the land of Nightmares to perish."

A Cyclops stepped forward to volunteer. "I will come with you," he said. Then the brow over his single eye furrowed. "Umm . . . where are we going?"

"To the Waking World," ICK said, speaking loud enough for everyone in the cavern to hear. "I can open the portal."

Charlie felt his little brother grasp his wrist. "Holy moly, Charlie! She's starting an army! She's going to invade the Waking World," Jack whispered.

But Charlie didn't dare answer. A three-headed dog near the cavern's entrance had just lifted its snouts and sniffed the air. The beast must have caught the scent of more humans. Before it had a chance to locate the source of the odor, Charlie quietly took Jack's arm and pulled him back into the darkness of the tunnel.

CHAPTER NINETEEN

THE WITCH-HUNT

The president of the Netherworld rolled down the window of her black limousine, and a demented-looking clown stuck his head inside.

"There's no one left in the cavern, Madam President," Dabney reported with a giggle. "I checked every nook and cranny myself."

Medusa's snakes slithered around her face. "And the mansion?" she asked.

"It's safe and under surveillance," the clown told her. "We sent Jack Laird back through the portal, and now we have two of our best Nightmares watching the building. They'll make sure no one gets inside."

"Are you sure two are enough?" Charlie asked. He was sitting beside Medusa in the plush backseat of her limo, which was parked in front of the old Laird family house. "It seems like a lot of Nightmares have joined ICK's army."

"Yes, and we know who they are," Medusa told him. "Most of them are outlaws who used to work for the villain they called President Fear. If any of them show their faces, they'll be arrested immediately and turned to stone." She looked back at the clown. "Good work, Dabney. We'll stop the prophecy from happening."

But after she rolled up her window, Medusa didn't seem quite so confident.

"I'm sorry it took us so long to get the news to you," Charlie said. "Jack and I got lost in the dark down there. We must have wandered those tunnels for hours before we found the way out. It was one of the worst nights of my life."

Medusa rapped on the window that separated the limo's driver from its passengers. The engine started and the vehicle began to move. Then the gorgon reached over and took Charlie's hand, careful not to scratch him with her blood-red fingernails, which she'd filed to dagger-sharp points. "You did the best you could, Charlie, and I am very grateful. But there is something that we must discuss, and

I sent your little brother back to the Waking World so we could talk in private," she said. "Can you tell me why ICK was inside your nightmare? How did she find out about the cellar?"

Charlie shook his head in shame. "You knew the cellar was part of my old nightmare? You knew it wasn't over?"

"Of course I did," Medusa told him, squeezing his hand. "Don't be embarrassed. You left a few fears buried beneath the surface. It happens to people all the time. The biggest fears often take a lifetime to conquer. I've been hoping you'd realize and come back to deal with yours. But it seems ICK discovered your nightmare first. Do you have any idea how she managed to get inside it?"

"No," Charlie said. "But I've been in her nightmare too. It's all about sheep."

"Man-eating sheep?" Medusa asked.

"No," Charlie was embarrassed to tell her. "Just the regular kind."

"You don't say!" Medusa exclaimed. "How *unusual*."

"What does it mean?" Charlie asked.

"I haven't a clue," Medusa admitted. "I may be president of the Netherworld, but I've never been able to interpret human dreams. Your kind comes up with some very strange things. Just look over there, for example! What do you suppose *that* means?"

She tapped the window beside her with one of her nails. Outside, a giant red spider was climbing the side of a building toward a window with Hello Kitty curtains.

"Yeah, I know everyone has weird dreams. That wasn't what I was trying to ask," Charlie said. "What do you think it means that ICK and I can share each other's dreams?"

"Ah," said Medusa. "Well, that's exactly what I wanted to discuss with you. It doesn't happen very often. And when two people end up sharing dreams, it usually means that they're either related—or extremely close friends."

"My mother and stepmother used to share nightmares," Charlie said. "But they were best friends. I don't know ICK at all. I've only spoken to her once—and we're *definitely* not related!"

"That may be so," said Medusa. "But there must be something that connects the two of you."

"There can't be. . . ."

Medusa stopped him before he could argue. "I'm sorry, Charlie, but it's true. You and Isabel Kessog are linked together, and you have to figure out how. The answer you find may help us stop her."

Charlie turned and rested his forehead against the window. His fears had just been confirmed. He didn't want to have anything in common with ICK. As the limo drove through the Netherworld's Cypress Creek, Charlie watched ordinary people fighting off trolls or running from ghosts and desperately wished he could be one of them.

Soon the limo slowed and pulled up outside the Netherworld courthouse, where Medusa spent most of her nights hard at work.

The president of the Netherworld gave Charlie a hug. "I know that what I've asked you to do will be difficult, but I also know I can depend on you," she said. "Now, would you like my driver to take you to the mansion?"

"No thanks," Charlie said, sliding out of the car. "I could use a walk."

He wasn't ready to go back just yet. Charlotte and Jack would probably want to know what Medusa had said to him, and Charlie needed some time on his own to think. Wandering along the dark streets of the Netherworld, he could tell that the sun was rising in his world. As people woke up on the other side, there were fewer and fewer Nightmares left on the streets. But the sound of chanting in the distance told him there was at least one terrible dream that wasn't quite over. Curious, Charlie jogged toward the sound until he found himself in a schoolyard where hundreds of people holding torches had gathered. The tines of metal pitchforks gleamed in the flames.

"GET THE WITCH!" the furious crowd was chanting. "GET THE WITCH!"

"Hey, what's going on here?" Charlie asked a woman

at the edge of the mob, but she didn't respond. He tried once more before he reached out a hand. Sure enough, his fingers passed right through the lady. Charlie did the same to a burly man standing beside her, with the same result. They were figments, he realized. There wasn't a real creature among them. They were all the product of some terrified dreamer's imagination.

Charlie walked to the entrance of the school. Along the way, he passed straight through figments, but none of them seemed to notice. When he reached the front doors, Charlie found them unlocked. Inside, the school looked perfectly normal—with no monsters in sight. Charlie's footsteps echoed in the empty hallway, and he wondered if the dreamer had woken up from her nightmare. Then he heard glass shattering in a nearby room.

Charlie rushed toward the ruckus and found a woman in a science classroom hurling beakers and flasks to the floor. It took him a moment to recognize her without her black wig and red lipstick.

"Ms. Abbot?" Charlie asked.

The woman cringed like a hunted animal. Her eyes were wild and her muscles tensed. "Charlie," she panted. "Are you with *them* now?"

"No," he told her. "I'm real, but those people out there aren't. They're just figments of your imagination."

The words seemed to mean nothing to the teacher.

"You've got to go, Charlie," she urged him. "They'll be in here soon. If they find us, they'll destroy us both."

"No, they won't!" Charlie said. "I promise, Ms. Abbot. It's just a nightmare. Those people aren't real. You can stop them!"

Suddenly they heard pounding on the front doors of the school. The mob was on the move. Ms. Abbot rushed to a window and threw it open. "They'll be breaking down the doors any minute. Come with me! We might be able to make it!"

"Please don't run, Ms. Abbot!" Charlie told her. "Stay here and face them. You can't hide forever. You'll have to fight them eventually."

"Not if I keep on running," Ms. Abbot said, slipping out the window. Charlie watched her drop to the ground and sprint across the schoolyard, a crowd of figments racing behind her.

When Charlie crossed back through the portal, he didn't say a word to Charlotte or Jack about Ms. Abbot's dream. What he'd witnessed was far too private to share. But he knew he needed to act fast, and he was glad the next day was a Saturday. When morning arrived, Charlie was up and dressed before the rest of the family opened their eyes. By the time his dad came down to make breakfast, he was already halfway out the door.

"Where you going?" Andrew Laird asked. "I'm about to make waffles."

There were few things on earth for which Charlie would have missed his dad's waffles. The task before him just happened to be one of them. Charlie pulled his backpack on and adjusted the straps. The pack was unusually heavy. "I have to make a quick delivery," he told his dad. "I'll be back in an hour."

Charlie didn't wait around for a response. He hurried outside, grabbed his bike, and was off before anyone in the purple mansion could stop him.

He rode his bicycle all the way up to Ms. Abbot's front door; then he dropped it beside a yellow jessamine bush. Standing next to a small brown box that someone had left on Ms. Abbot's doorstep, Charlie pressed the doorbell. He pressed a second time when he got tired of waiting for an answer. And again and again. Until, at last, he heard her shuffling toward the door.

"Charlie." Ms. Abbot looked terrible. There were streaks of mascara running down her face, and her eyes were tomato red. "That's so weird. I just—"

"—had a dream about me," Charlie finished the thought for her. "Yeah, I know. Can I come in?"

The teacher hesitated. "I don't think so. It's a bit of a mess in here," she said.

"I know that too," Charlie said as he squeezed past her.

The house was even more of a disaster than the last time he'd seen it. Half-filled cardboard boxes cluttered every room.

"What's with all the boxes?" Charlie asked.

"I'm moving," Ms. Abbot explained with a sigh. "Cypress Creek just isn't for me."

"That's what I thought you'd say," Charlie said. "But tell me the truth, Ms. Abbot. The problem isn't really Cypress Creek, is it? Someone stole the belladonna, and now you think your cover is about to be blown. You're running away again, aren't you? How long are you going to keep doing that?"

"Pardon me?" Ms. Abbot asked. She looked astonished to find herself being lectured by a kid.

Charlie wasn't going to back down. "I was in your nightmare last night. I saw the people chasing you with torches and pitchforks. It was a witch-hunt, and I know what that means. You're worried that the same thing that happened to you in Brooklyn is going to happen here in Cypress Creek. Am I right?"

Ms. Abbot gasped. "Charlotte told you about Brooklyn!"

"My friends and I read about it online," Charlie said,

managing to tell the truth without getting his stepmother in trouble. "I know people up there said some terrible things about you. They even claimed you killed your brother. I bet you don't even have one, do you?"

"Actually, I did," Ms. Abbot said sadly. "My brother Joseph died when he was your age after he ate some yew-berries and swallowed the poisonous seeds."

Charlie let the information sink in. "So your brother really was poisoned?" he finally asked. He didn't think it would be polite to ask Ms. Abbot where her brother had gotten the berries that killed him. Fortunately, he didn't have to.

"Yes," said Ms. Abbot. "Joe and his friend were camping and they found the berries in the woods. It happened almost twenty years ago, and ever since that day, I've been trying to turn Joe's death into something good. I've been experimenting on my own, trying to find ways to use chemicals like the one that killed my brother to save people's lives. But now it looks like it's over."

"Maybe not. Maybe I can help you."

Ms. Abbot shook her head. "No, Charlie," she said. "You can't. You're only twelve years old. You can't get involved in my grown-up problems."

"I'm already involved," Charlie told her, remembering Medusa's words. "I'm supposed to help you. I think that's why I was able to visit your nightmare last night."

Ms. Abbot rubbed her face with her hands. "This is all so strange," she said.

"You've got a garden filled with poisonous plants," Charlie pointed out. "And you think what I just told you is strange? Here." He shrugged off his backpack and unzipped the top. "I brought you something to look at."

Charlie pulled out a large black binder with the word *Nightmares* painted on the front in gold. Inside were illustrations of monsters of every imaginable variety—and all the information you'd need to conquer them if you happened to meet them in your dreams. "Charlotte wrote this," he told Ms. Abbot. "I helped her with some of it."

Ms. Abbot sank down on a sofa covered with trash. "This is remarkable," she said as she flipped through the pages. "What a wonderful imagination Charlotte must have."

"She does have a great imagination," Charlie agreed. "But this book isn't fiction."

Ms. Abbot looked up at Charlie with an indulgent grin. "You're kidding."

Charlie shook his head solemnly. "You might want to put on a pot of coffee, Ms. Abbot. I'm about to let you in on the truth about Nightmares. I know your secret. Now I'm going to tell you *mine*."

CHAPTER TWENTY

THE QUARTERBACK KILLER KILLER

An hour later, when Charlie stepped out of Ms. Abbot's house, he noticed there was still a little brown box sitting on the doorstep.

"The mailman must have left this for you," he said, picking it up and handing it to Ms. Abbot.

"Thank you," she said as she took the box. "And thank you for sharing Charlotte's book with me." When she'd first opened *Nightmares* and began to read about the Netherworld, it had been clear to Charlie that Ms. Abbot found it all hard to believe. But he'd patiently answered her questions and taught her everything he knew about battling Nightmares. Now hope seemed to be spreading through her, and the color was finally returning to his teacher's pale face.

Then Ms. Abbot glanced down at the box in her hands. "That's odd. There's no address on this package. Someone must have delivered it by hand. But why didn't they ring the bell? I've been here at home all day."

Ms. Abbot ripped apart the brown paper wrapping and tore into the cardboard. She pulled out a little bottle filled with a milky white liquid. The teacher's eyes slowly left the bottle and rose to meet Charlie's. The fear was back again. It was written all over her face.

"Do you think this could be from India Kessog?" she asked. Charlie had told Ms. Abbot about ICK and INK. He'd also warned her that INK had created a poisonous potion from the belladonna she'd stolen and had tried to give a bottle of it to Jack. It seemed likely that she'd attempt to poison other people as well.

"I don't know, but I wouldn't drink it if I were you," Charlie told the teacher.

He took the box out of Ms. Abbot's hand. When he checked inside, he found a folded note written in neat cursive handwriting.

"*Thank you very much for the* Atropa belladonna," the note read. "*I used it to make this elixir for a girl I met*

at the local school. As a fellow scientist, you might like a sample of it for your studies." It was signed *India Kessog.*

Charlie's head was spinning, but he did his best to stay calm. "May I use your phone?" he asked Ms. Abbot.

She reached a trembling hand into the pocket of her robe and passed her phone to Charlie. He quickly punched in Rocco's phone number.

"Hello?" Rocco answered grumpily. It was early in the

morning, and he wouldn't have recognized Ms. Abbot's number.

"Rocco, it's Charlie. Do you know where Jancy Dare lives?"

"Huh?" Rocco replied. "Sorry, I mean, sure. The Quarterback Killer's house is a few blocks from mine."

"Great. Head over there right away," Charlie told him. "Don't let Jancy eat or drink *anything*. After you get to her house, call Alfie and Paige and tell them to meet us there as soon as possible. INK's finally made her move."

Even in an emergency situation, with a classmate's life on the line, it was impossible to ignore the fact that Jancy Dare's family had the perfect lawn. The front part alone was almost as big as a football field, and the grass was a carpet of rich, dark green. The blades appeared to be about an inch tall, which the football team's new water boy had once informed Charlie was the ideal height for sports.

Charlie also noticed that the Dare family yard appeared particularly stunning when compared to the neighbors' lawns. Those on either side of the Dare residence were brittle and brown, with large patches of bare dirt where the grass had died. Charlie had cared for enough sickly plants to know exactly what the problem was: something was eating the grass's roots. But whatever was destroying the neighbors' lawns had somehow steered clear of the Dares' property.

From the car, Charlie spotted Rocco's bike lying on its side near the sidewalk, where the boy must have dumped it in a hurry. As Ms. Abbot slowed to a stop, Paige rode up beside them and a wailing ambulance rounded the corner and screeched to a halt.

"What happened?" Charlie heard Paige call out to the two EMTs who leaped from the front of the ambulance and began grabbing equipment from the back.

"Report of a possible poisoning," one told her.

Charlie's heart sank. "I guess it's too late," he told Ms. Abbot. "Jancy must have taken the stuff in the bottle."

With a groan of defeat, Ms. Abbot rested her forehead against the steering wheel just as Paige knocked on the passenger-side window. "Are you coming or what?" she yelled through the glass.

Charlie put a finger to his lips to politely shush Paige and then turned to the teacher. "Ms. Abbot?" Her knuckles were white from gripping the wheel. "Please don't drive away when I get out of the car. I know you're scared. But if you run this time, you might not be able to stop."

The teacher lifted her head, took a deep breath, and threw the car into park. "You're right," she said, unbuckling her seat belt. "I have to tell Jancy's parents what happened. It might be the only way to save her."

As Charlie, Paige, and Ms. Abbot hurried across the lawn to the house, Charlie couldn't help but marvel at the soft cushion of grass beneath his feet. He'd never encountered a lawn like the Dares'. Under other circumstances he would have asked what their secret was, but this clearly wasn't the time to talk fertilizer. He shouldn't have even been thinking about it. The front door of the house was wide-open, and Charlie could see several large and worried people gathered in the living room on the other side.

Jancy's dad was as big as any ogre Charlie had ever encountered, and her mom wasn't much smaller. A beefy body builder EMT was interviewing them while Rocco sat quietly in a leather recliner. Looking around, Charlie noticed that the entire living room was devoted to football. There were football trophies, framed jerseys, balls covered with signatures, and even an athletic supporter displayed in a special glass case. Every spare inch of wall space held a photo of Jancy playing football—either on the school field or in front of her house.

"Jancy's been sick since Monday," her father was telling the EMT. "By the time she got to football practice that afternoon, she was already feeling dizzy and weak. Then she threw up all over the coach and got sent home. The

doctor thought it was just a regular bug. But our daughter's been in bed for the last two days and she hasn't gotten any better."

"We spoke to the doctor again last night," Jancy's mother said. "So when the package arrived on our doorstep this morning, we figured it must be from her. There was a little bottle inside. We gave Jancy some of the stuff because we thought it was medicine." She paused to wipe away the tears that were streaming down her face. "And then the Cypress Creek Elementary quarterback showed up and told us it was poison and said we needed to call an ambulance right away."

"What kind of poison do you think it was?" the EMT asked Rocco.

Ms. Abbot stepped forward. "It was extract of belladonna," she said. "Also known as deadly nightshade. I'm afraid the plant used to make it came from my garden."

For the first time, the Dares seemed to realize that a new group of people had entered the room.

"Who are you?" Jancy's mom asked.

The teacher looked pale, and there was still mascara smeared all over her face, but her feet were firmly planted. Charlie could tell she wasn't going to run away. "My name is Beatrice Swanson, though I also go by Samantha Abbot. I'm a science teacher at your daughter's school. And I need to tell you something important about your daughter's condition."

Jancy Dare's parents waited nervously for Ms. Abbot to begin. The teacher had opened her mouth to speak again when the second EMT appeared in the living room with his medical kit in his hand. He'd just come from Jancy's bedroom, and his face was a picture of grief.

"What's wrong?" Jancy's father jumped up.

"Is our daughter . . ." Jancy's mother clapped a hand over her mouth.

"What happened back there, Fred?" his partner asked.

"It's terrible," the EMT responded miserably.

"Tell us!" Charlie shouted, unable to stand the suspense.

"I just got my butt kicked by a twelve-year-old girl," the EMT said. "The kid challenged me to an arm-wrestling match and pinned me in about ten seconds flat."

Paige laughed out loud, and Charlie gave a giant sigh of relief.

"She beat you at arm wrestling?" Jancy's dad asked in astonishment. "But she hasn't been able to sit up for the last two days!"

"Well, your daughter's sitting up just fine right now," the EMT told Mr. Dare. "She's got a pretty impressive arm—and quite a lip on her too. Told me my triceps are puny and my biceps are underdeveloped."

Jancy's parents both looked like they might explode with happiness. Mrs. Dare was on her way to check on her daughter when Alfie finally arrived. His latest science T-shirt was soaked with sweat, and he was panting so hard that he could barely speak. He must have biked at full speed all the way across town.

"Hhhis not hhhoyshhhun," Alfie said, clutching Mrs. Dare's arm to hold himself up.

"Excuse me?" Jancy's mom asked. "Where are all these children coming from? Who are *you*?"

"Well, look at that—it's the water boy!" Jancy's dad

exclaimed. "Kid's supposed to be some kind of genius." He bent down next to Alfie and studied him. "Is he speaking a foreign language or something? What's he trying to say?"

"I'm trying to tell you that the stuff Jancy took wasn't poison!" Alfie managed to blurt out. He stopped to catch his breath again; then he found Charlie in the crowd. "I ran some tests on the liquid that was in the bottle INK dropped in the park. It wasn't poison, Charlie. It was *atropine*."

The only person who understood appeared to be Ms. Abbot, and she couldn't have seemed more surprised. "Atropine?" the teacher marveled. "India Kessog extracted atropine from the belladonna? That's *amazing*!"

"I know, right?" Alfie agreed. "I mean, it's not like INK's a real twelve-year-old or anything, so it's not as impressive as it seems. But still! I can't wait to find out how she did it."

"Whoa, whoa, whoa." Paige stepped between the two scientists with her hands raised. "Why don't we all stop right here for one teensy little moment. What the heck is *atropine*?"

Ms. Abbot smiled broadly. "It's a chemical found in belladonna. Remember when I told you that sometimes the same plants that can make people sick can also be used to make sick people better? Atropine comes from belladonna, but it isn't poison. It's *medicine*."

"Medicine for what?" Charlie asked.

"Organophosphate and muscarine poisoning, primarily," Alfie told him.

"Excuse me?" Rocco asked.

"English translation, please?" Paige asked with an annoyed huff.

"Emergency rooms keep atropine on hand to treat people who've accidentally eaten certain kinds of toxic mushrooms," Ms. Abbot said.

"Oh, that wouldn't be Jancy," Mrs. Dare chimed in, shaking her big blond head. "Our daughter never touches vegetables."

"Yeah, but mushrooms aren't . . . ," Alfie started to say, until Charlie shot him a warning look and he sealed his lips.

"All right, so I guess Jancy wasn't poisoned by mushrooms," said Ms. Abbot, staring at the floor as she rubbed her temples. "Well then, let's see. What else does atropine treat? Oh!" She looked up. "Sometimes soldiers carry syringes of atropine so they can give themselves an injection if they're exposed to chemical weapons."

Mr. Dare chuckled. "I'd say it's highly unlikely that Jancy got caught up in anything like that here in Cypress Creek," he said. "We're a peace-loving town."

"Oooh, oooh, oooh!" It was the familiar sound of a

lightbulb going on in Alfie's head. Charlie turned to see him hopping up and down like an excited toad. "What about pesticide poisoning?" Alfie asked Ms. Abbot.

"Pesticides?" said Mr. Dare. "You mean the chemicals some farmers put on their crops?"

"Exactly. They're meant to keep bugs from eating plants, but some of them can make people quite sick," the teacher explained.

"Well, I don't know where Jancy could have gotten into any pesticides. We haven't been to a farm in years," said Mrs. Dare.

Ms. Abbot looked stumped. "Well, then I guess I'll need to do a little more research. Right now I have no idea what made Jancy ill—or why the atropine seems to have made her better."

That was when Charlie recalled the conversation he'd overheard between Jancy and INK in the school cafeteria.

"INK definitely figured out what was wrong with Jancy the day they met. I remember she said something about Jancy sweating a lot and asked Jancy if she had been near a war. I thought INK was just poking fun at her."

"Did you notice that Jancy was perspiring heavily?" Alfie asked the Dares.

"As a matter of fact, I did. It started Sunday night," said Mr. Dare. "Jancy and I played a game of ball out in the yard, and even after we came inside she never stopped sweating."

They were playing a game out on the yard. The words bounced around in Charlie's head, and suddenly he knew what it all meant. "Something's been eating your neighbors' yards," he said to the Dares.

"Yep, lawn grubs," Mr. Dare confirmed. "Little white monsters chew up the roots. Whole neighborhood's infested with them."

"Except your lawn," Charlie said. "*Your* yard is still perfect."

Mr. Dare nodded proudly. "That's because I'm the only one willing to put in the time and do the research. I found this new kinda spray called Grasstastic. It sets up a defensive perimeter around the whole yard and body checks any grub that comes within five feet of my grass. It's expensive stuff, 'cause it comes all the way from China, but I figure it's worth it. Jancy and I spend a lot of time out there. That girl's gonna be the first female linebacker in the NFL someday."

"Not if she's sick from pesticide poisoning," Charlie told him.

"Pardon me?" Mr. Dare asked with a horrified look on his face.

Then Ms. Abbot gasped and Alfie began hopping up and down again.

"Charlie! That's it!" Alfie cried. "You figured it out! You cracked the case!"

Mrs. Dare looked at her husband. "We still don't understand," she admitted.

"The spray you've been putting on your lawn to kill grubs is making your daughter sick," Charlie explained.

Mr. Dare shook his head. "But it says on the bottle that Grasstastic is perfectly safe for mammals over fifteen pounds," he argued. "Jancy weighed more than that the day she was born."

Mrs. Dare suddenly gasped. "Honey, does it say what happens to the ones that weigh under fifteen pounds?" she asked. "'Cause I can't remember the last time I saw a squirrel in the yard. And remember what happened to the neighbors' schnauzer?"

"There's no doubt that Grasstastic is a pesticide, and atropine is a proven treatment for pesticide poisoning," Ms. Abbot chimed in. "That's why it cured Jancy."

"And you say you *made* this atropine stuff out of a plant from your garden?" Mrs. Dare asked the teacher. "That means you saved our daughter!"

"Well, actually . . ." Ms. Abbot started to disagree. But with both giant Dares wrapping her up in a bear hug, the teacher could no longer speak.

It was INK, Charlie marveled. *She'd* cured Jancy Dare. Did that mean India Kessog was a good guy, like Jack had always claimed? Or was she just a mimic—a killer who wanted them to think she was harmless while she patiently waited for the perfect chance to attack?

Charlie didn't have the answer. But he wasn't going to take any chances.

CHAPTER TWENTY-ONE

STORMING THE TOWER

Andrew Laird was pulling out of the purple mansion's driveway when Charlie arrived back at home.

Charlie's dad rolled down the car window.

"Where you going?" Charlie asked.

"Just running some errands. You know, it's almost eleven. You sure were gone for an awful long time. Your stepmother was getting worried," he told his son. "Mission accomplished?"

"Mission accomplished," Charlie reported happily. Ms. Abbot had faced her fears—and Jancy Dare was recovering from pesticide poisoning. Things couldn't have gone better.

"Glad to hear it," Andrew Laird said. "I guess you've earned the stack of waffles I left in the kitchen for you. Better find them before Jack figures out there were leftovers."

"Jack's still here?" Charlie asked. Usually Charlotte and the boys were at Hazel's Herbarium by ten on Saturdays, while Andrew Laird seized the opportunity to sleep in.

"Charlotte's opening the store late today," his dad informed him. "She said she wanted to wait for you to get back."

Of course she did, Charlie thought. She knew there was bound to be news.

He found Charlotte and Jack in the kitchen as usual. When he told them about INK and the atropine, Jack began doing a victory dance.

"I told you so! I told you so!" he sang.

"Yeah, yeah, yeah," Charlie replied. "You might have been right just this once." He grabbed his little brother and gave him a noogie.

Charlotte was sitting in her favorite spot at the kitchen island. She'd been cooking up a batch of her popular body odor reducer. The ingredients were organized in piles on the counter, and scraps covered the floor. "That's all really great, Charlie. But here's what I don't understand," she said. "How would INK recognize the symptoms of pesticide poisoning? She's been hiding away in a lighthouse for eight decades. The stuff Jancy's dad was spraying on the lawn was probably invented in the last year or two—in *China*."

"I don't know how she figured out what was making Jancy sick," Charlie said, setting his little brother free. "But I think I know how she came up with the cure. She told Jack the stuff was her father's formula. And the old man Dad and I met in Orville Falls told us that ICK and INK's father was some sort of chemist in England."

"Why are we guessing about all this?" Jack asked. "Let's just ask her when we find her! Hey, Charlotte, now that we know she's not some crazy killer, can India come stay with us?"

Charlie saw his stepmother chew on her lower lip the way she did whenever she got nervous. She seemed to be undecided on the subject of INK—but Charlie wasn't.

"No," Charlie told his brother. "INK still isn't allowed in this house."

"Why not?" Jack asked.

"Because even if it turns out that she really is some kind of saint, her crazy sister is on the other side of the portal recruiting Nightmares to help her take over the Waking World," Charlie explained. "Come on, Jack! You were there! You saw ICK's army! We can't run the risk. If INK helps her sister escape from the tower, we'll all be dead meat."

But Jack refused to listen to reason. "What if India is the one who can stop Isabel from doing bad things? Remember what the prophecy says, Charlie? It says there will be one child with the power to destroy the Netherworld— and one with the power to save it. If Isabel is the first one, maybe India is the second!"

"Or maybe it's all a big trick," Charlie replied. "What if INK saved Jancy so that we'd let down our guard and invite her into the mansion?"

Jack stared at Charlie as if he barely knew him. "Wow, that's cold! You really think India would do something like that?" He turned to appeal to his stepmom. "Charlotte!"

"I'm afraid Charlie's right, Jack," Charlotte said, finally choosing a side. "It's too big a risk."

Jack was shocked. "So you guys are going to let India keep sleeping in garden sheds or out in the woods?"

Charlotte winced. "Well, when you put it that way . . . ," she started.

"India Kessog is not a real girl!" Charlie shouted. "Maybe she doesn't have anything to do with ICK's army, but she's not an innocent kid, either! She's almost a hundred years old, and she helped invent a tonic that turned people into zombies. We are not letting her into this house!"

Charlotte sighed. "I've got to agree with Charlie on this. For now, keeping INK out of the mansion is the only logical thing to do," she told the younger boy.

Jack's shoulders sagged. "Maybe. But it's not the right one," he answered. His voice was small and he sounded disappointed, as if his brother and stepmother had failed some sort of test. "If you need me, I'll be in my room."

"Hey, now," Charlotte said, rushing to catch up with the boy as he made his way to the stairs. "Don't be like that, Jack."

"You're wasting your time, Charlotte. Let him go sulk if he wants to," Charlie said, stomping out of the kitchen after them both.

Jack had reached the landing between the first and second floors when they heard the first thump come from above. Charlie saw his brother pause in front of the portrait of Silas DeChant, cock his head, and listen. The second thump was louder, and the third shook the entire house.

"Oh no," Charlotte moaned.

"It's happening," Charlie said. "ICK is coming."

"What are we going to do?" Jack asked. None of them had expected ICK to launch an attack so quickly.

Charlotte ran back to the kitchen and returned with a hammer and a box of nails. "I bought these yesterday in case we needed them," she said. "All right, guys, come with me."

The pounding continued as they hurried toward the second floor. Something big was beating its fists (or paws or tentacles or flippers) against the tower door. Thankfully, the staircase on the other side of the door was too narrow to fit more than one large Nightmare at a time; otherwise, the barricade might have fallen in seconds. Even now the locks were rattling and plaster was raining down from the ceiling.

Charlotte seemed to have a plan. "Come with me," she ordered. "We need to get the headboard out from behind my bed."

Together, the three of them dragged the heavy oak piece out of the master bedroom and into the hall. They shoved it in front of the tower door just as the wood began to splinter. Charlotte quickly sank two nails into each side, and she'd begun to add more when they heard the Nightmare break through the tower door and hit the back of the headboard. A roar of rage filled the mansion.

"I bet that's the Cyclops," Jack said.

Charlie remembered the one-eyed monster they'd seen in the cavern with ICK. If that monster wanted to get through the tower door, there was no way the three of them were going to stop him.

"I'm going to need another headboard in a second,"

Charlotte said. "You guys go grab the one from Jack's room."

Charlie and Jack raced to Jack's bedroom. As they slid the wooden headboard out from behind the bed, they heard something crash outside. Boards were flying out of the tower windows and landing on the lawn.

"They opened a window," Jack said. "There's no way to stop them now."

"Actually, there is," Charlie told his brother. The idea had come to him in a flash.

He left Jack in his bedroom, sprinted past Charlotte, and headed down the stairs. "Where are you going?" his stepmother shrieked. "I need your help!" She had thrown her own weight against the barricade, as if her skinny body could keep a Cyclops from breaking through. With every thud from the other side, she shook like Jell-O.

"I'm going to put a stop to this," Charlie said.

In the kitchen, he pulled open a drawer and took out his weapon. Then he walked outside to the yard. The grass was already littered with debris, and a wooden board whizzed past his head.

"Isabel Kessog!" he shouted up at the tower. "ICK!"

The pounding suddenly stopped and all was quiet. A sweet-looking face appeared at one of the tower windows. Its skin was milky white and its cheeks were rosy pink. No one would have guessed it was the face of a monster.

"Charlie Laird," ICK called down. "Are you prepared to surrender?"

"No," Charlie said. "I'm ordering you to leave."

ICK cackled. "And why on earth would I do that? In a few seconds, we'll be through the door and the mansion will be mine."

"You won't leave the tower today, Isabel," Charlie told her as he pulled out the weapon he'd brought with him from the kitchen: a little box with a few tiny sticks inside. "And the mansion will never be yours. I'll do whatever it takes to protect it." He took out one of the little sticks and dragged its end against the side of the box. The match promptly burst into flames. "Even if protecting the mansion means burning it down."

ICK leaned out the window. "You wouldn't dare," she sneered.

"Oh yes, I would," Charlie told her truthfully. "I will do it right now unless you and those creatures return to the other side. We both know what will happen to you if the portal is destroyed. Being stuck in the Netherworld for eternity doesn't seem like a lot of fun to me. Especially when your twin sister is here in the Waking World."

ICK stared at Charlie. He could see the rage in her big brown eyes—and behind that, something else he recognized as well. Then she smiled at him. "Oh, well. If you insist," she said. "I wouldn't mind spending a little more time in your nightmare, anyway. There's something about it that makes me feel . . . *stronger.*"

Charlie grimaced. He hated the idea of ICK lurking inside his head. "Stay out of my dream," he growled.

"Or *what*?" ICK demanded. "What will you do about it, Charlie Laird? You see, if the portal is destroyed, your body will be stuck *here* in the Waking World. I'll be able to do whatever I want in that cellar where you hide your deepest, darkest fears—and you won't be able to come through the portal and stop me. So toodle-oo." She gave a sweet little wave. "My friends and I will be seeing you soon."

ICK stepped away from the window, leaving Charlie perplexed. The match between his fingers had gone out, so he dropped it to the ground. Maybe his threat really had done the trick, but he had a queasy feeling in his stomach. It had all been too easy. He looked up at the tower. It seemed to be quiet now, as if all the Nightmares had passed back over to the other side.

Then he noticed that ICK had left something behind on one of the windowsills—it looked like a small stone sculpture. It was a trick, Charlie realized at once. There was no way to get a good look at it without unsealing the tower door. And that was exactly what ICK wanted.

Charlie grinned. He'd show ICK what he thought of her

latest game. He searched the yard until he found an old tennis ball that Rufus had abandoned near the hoary mugwort bush. Then he took careful aim and hurled the ball at the sculpture. He hit it squarely, but the thing didn't fall off the sill as he'd hoped. Instead, it stretched out a pair of granite-colored wings and took flight. It was a small gargoyle, Charlie could see now, with the head of a frog and the body of a dragon. Tied to one of its legs was a little metal cylinder that glinted in the sunlight. Screeching like a demonic bird, the monster soared in circles above Charlie's head before launching a missile of its own. A squirt of gargoyle guano splattered the ground just to Charlie's right side. Then the little Nightmare flew off above the trees. It had a delivery to make, Charlie realized. Whatever was in the cylinder strapped to its leg was almost certainly meant for INK.

Charlie raced into the mansion to tell Charlotte and Jack what he'd seen. They'd need to catch the escaped Nightmare quickly. He found Charlotte on the floor in front of the tower door, so exhausted she couldn't stand up. Jack was squatting by her side.

"Is it over?" Jack asked Charlie.

"For now," Charlie said.

"She'll be back," Charlotte said. "We're just lucky we were here in the house when she tried to get through this time. She's been paying attention to our schedules. She knew the three of us are usually gone on Saturday mornings. On an ordinary weekend, your dad would have been here on his own."

Charlotte was right, Charlie realized with horror. ICK had scheduled her invasion for a time when his dad would be by himself in the mansion. Somehow she knew that Andrew Laird wouldn't be expecting her. If Charlie hadn't decided to ride out to Ms. Abbot's house—and if Charlotte hadn't decided to wait for him to come home—the Waking World would have been overrun by Nightmares.

"I guess we'll just have to make sure we never leave Dad alone in the house," Jack said.

"No," Charlotte told them. "That's not enough. We were foolish to think we could keep ICK out of the Waking World with locks and barricades. We're going to have to destroy the portal."

"We can't!" Jack cried. "Then ICK and INK will be trapped on different sides. They're sisters. They need to be together!"

"And that's the last thing any of us need," Charlotte said. "Jack, do you understand how much danger the Waking World is in right now? We can't risk it anymore. We need to burn the tower down."

"Please," Jack begged. "Just give me a chance to talk to Indy. If we're going to destroy the portal, we should let her choose which side she wants to be on."

Charlotte was about to tell him no again when Charlie cut in. "We need to burn down the tower as soon as possible—but we can't torch it right away," he informed his stepmother. "There's a flying gargoyle loose on our side. We have to catch it and send it home."

CHAPTER TWENTY-TWO

THE TRAITOR

"WHAT IN THE HECK IS GOING ON AROUND HERE?"

Charlie grimaced at the sound of Andrew Laird shouting in the hallway. He hadn't even heard his dad come in, and he and Jack had been hoping to get out of the house before they were forced to deal with him.

"CHARLIE AND JACK, COME OUT HERE THIS INSTANT!"

Charlie and Jack rushed out of their rooms at the very same time and almost slammed right into each other.

Their father was standing by the door to the tower. Charlie couldn't remember the last time he'd seen his dad so angry.

"What did you do to this headboard?" he demanded. "Why is it nailed to the wall?"

"Ummmm," said Jack. Usually he was the one with the clever excuses, but this time he'd apparently drawn a blank.

"Jack and I heard a ghost in the tower," Charlie said.

"And we got scared," Jack added quickly. "It sounded like a really big one."

"You heard a big *ghost*?" Andrew Laird scoffed. "So you decided to destroy an expensive piece of furniture? Haven't you guys ever watched a haunted-house movie? Ghosts can walk through walls! What makes you think they can't get past a headboard?"

It was an excellent question, Charlie had to admit.

"Where is your stepmother?" Andrew Laird demanded.

"She went out to pick up a few things in town," Charlie said. Those things were Alfie, Rocco, and Paige. The six of them were going on a gargoyle hunt.

"Do you have any idea what she's going to do to you when she sees what you've done?" Andrew Laird asked. "This headboard is a DeChant family heirloom. It belonged to Silas DeChant himself!"

"So are you going to punish us?" Jack asked meekly. "Please don't wait and let Charlotte do it!"

Andrew Laird crossed his arms and glared down at his sons.

"Now that you mention it, I think that's a great idea, Jack. I'll let Charlotte punish you when she gets home," he said, playing right into Jack's hand. The kid was a genius, Charlie thought. "In fact, I think I hear her pulling up in the drive right now."

Charlie's father stormed downstairs to greet his wife, with the two boys trailing behind him.

"They did *what* to my great-great-grandfather's headboard?" Charlotte yelped when her husband told her the news. She was a wonderful actress, Charlie thought.

"They nailed it to the tower door," Andrew Laird said. "I'm really sorry, honey."

"You two did all that while I was out picking up your friends?" Charlotte pretended to fume, pointing outside at the three kids sitting in the backseat of her Range Rover. She was overacting now, Charlie thought, but her performance was still passable.

"Sorry, Charlotte," Jack said. Charlie stayed quiet and let his brother do the acting.

"I'll remove the nails and see what I can do to fix it," Andrew Laird told his wife.

"No, just leave it for now, Andy," Charlotte said. "We'll hire an expert to remove it. And you two"—she pointed at

Charlie and Jack—"get in the car. I'm taking your friends home, and then you're both going straight to Hazel's Herbarium to work off the cost of the repairs."

"Come on, Charlotte," Jack groaned. "We weren't trying to be bad."

"Do what she tells you," their dad ordered. "I don't want to hear any complaining."

The boys obediently climbed into the car. Charlie took the front seat and Jack crammed into the extra seat in the very back.

As soon as they were out of sight of the purple mansion, Charlie turned to face his friends. Six long sticks with metal loops on the ends were lying across their laps.

"Butterfly nets," Alfie explained. "From my lepidoptera obsession in the third grade. I figure they'll be perfect for catching small flying Nightmares."

"Charlotte told you what happened?" Charlie asked.

"Yeah," Paige said. "The invasion must have been really scary."

"It was," Jack agreed. "I thought we were goners for sure."

"We're going to burn down the tower before they try to come back," Charlie said. "But first we need to locate the gargoyle that escaped."

"And INK," Jack added. "We need to find her too, remember."

The kid was way too nice for anyone's good. "Don't be so naïve," Charlie told his little brother. "When we find one, we'll find the other. Like I said, the gargoyle had a little metal cylinder strapped to its leg. I'm sure ICK was using it to send something to INK. Probably a message to let her sister know she's coming."

"Hold up, Charlie," said Rocco. "I thought we figured out that India Kessog is a good guy. She saved Jancy Dare's life this morning, didn't she?"

Charlie snorted. "Jancy's the school bully. Does saving a bully really make you a good guy? Besides, maybe INK just wants us to *think* she's good. Maybe it's all part of the twins' evil plan."

Rocco leaned forward in his seat. "Or maybe she wants us to think that because it's *true*," he said.

Charlie turned around to look at his friend and understood immediately. Rocco was now firmly on Jack's side. Charlie felt his heart sink even further. It was a massive betrayal. "Anyone else agree with Jack and Rocco?" he asked.

The car was silent, and then Alfie began to fidget. "Ummm . . . ," he said.

"Spit it out," Charlie demanded angrily. He could feel the darkness growing inside him. As hard as he'd tried to get rid of it, it had been there all along, hidden beneath the surface.

"INK made *atropine*," Alfie said. "That's really, really

hard to do. I think if she were out to trick us, she could have found an easier way."

"So the three of you are all against me," Charlie said, glad he was in the front seat and not stuck in the back with a bunch of traitors.

"What are you talking about?" Rocco said. "Don't make it sound like this is some kind of war. We're not *against* you. We just don't *agree* with you."

Charlie ignored him. "Paige?" he asked. He didn't know what he would do if she was on their side too.

"Sorry, guys, but I'm for playing it safe," Paige announced. "As soon as the tower is gone and the Waking World is no longer in danger, I'll be happy to have INK over for a tea party. Until then, I'm with Charlie."

"I am too," said Charlotte. "I know it's not fair, Jack, but there's too much at stake. If we find INK, we need to find a secure place to put her until the gargoyle is back in the Netherworld and we've burned the tower down."

"No!" Jack said defiantly. "That's what will happen if *you* find INK. That's not what I'll do if I find her first. Stop the car and let me out."

"You've got to be joking," Charlie said.

"Actually, I'd like to get out too," said Rocco. "Alfie?"

"Really, guys?" Alfie groaned. "Is this necessary? It's so comfy here in the car."

Rocco raised an eyebrow and Alfie gave in.

"Fine," he sighed. "I guess I'd like to get out too."

Charlotte pulled to the side of the road by the Cypress Creek library.

"What? I can't believe you're going to let them do this!" Charlie told his stepmother. "It's a mutiny!"

"A mutiny is when people stop taking orders from a leader. This isn't a mutiny, Charlie, because you were never in charge," Rocco said. "You're our friend and we like you, but you can't stop us from doing what we think is right."

"Charlotte!" Charlie yelped as the three boys slid out of the vehicle.

"Relax," Charlotte told him in a low voice. "We have the car."

"And the nets," Paige said, gesturing toward the butterfly nets that the boys had left behind. "Jack, Alfie, and Rocco are unarmed and on foot. There's no way they're going to capture that gargoyle."

As it turned out, having a car wasn't much of an advantage. Charlotte, Charlie, and Paige spent the rest of the day driving all around Cypress Creek. They checked every playhouse and garden shed in town—and then they drove into the woods to see if Ms. Abbot had received any unexpected guests. When they arrived at the cottage in the clearing, they found it empty. Charlie briefly worried that the teacher might have fled town after all, but a peek inside the teacher's house convinced him otherwise. She'd been home since the incident with Jancy Dare, and it looked as though she'd begun to unpack a few of the cardboard boxes that were scattered throughout the living room.

By six o'clock, the sun had started to set. The three of them were hungry and exhausted, and there was no point in continuing the search in the dark, so Charlotte dropped Paige off at her home. Then, on their way to the purple mansion, Charlotte's phone began to ring. It was Jack, calling from the other side of town. His search had been a bust too, and he needed a ride home. After Charlotte turned the Range Rover around, Charlie got out. Rather than sit in a car with Jack, Charlie walked the rest of the way to the mansion alone.

By the time Charlie arrived home, the smell of cauliflower casserole had filled the house. Charlie groaned when he first caught a whiff of it. While he had been out hunting gargoyles, his dad had been home alone for at least an hour. Charlie, Jack, and Charlotte had let down their guard again. Anything could have happened.

As famished as he was, Charlie headed straight for the stairs. He didn't have the strength left for a conversation with his father. So he flinched when he reached the landing and heard Andrew Laird's voice calling to him from below.

"Where are your brother and stepmother?" he asked.

"They should be home soon," Charlie said.

"Did Charlotte make you work hard at Hazel's Herbarium today?" his dad asked.

Charlie shrugged. He'd almost forgotten that he was supposed to be in trouble.

"I ask because I drove past the shop this afternoon and it was closed."

Charlie turned around and looked over the railing at his father.

"Charlie?" Andrew Laird asked. "Is there something going on that I don't know about?"

"Yes," Charlie told him. "There's a portal in the tower upstairs. A nightmare land lies on the other side. A villain who looks like a twelve-year-old girl has formed an army of monsters, and she's trying to get into our world. So far, we've managed to keep her locked in the tower, but she's trying to break free. That's why we had to nail the headboard to the door. If she reaches the Waking World, we're all in serious trouble."

Charlie's father regarded him with a mixture of disappointment and concern. "I was hoping you'd give me a straight answer for once," he told his son.

"I did," Charlie said. "You just don't believe it."

Charlie let out a deep breath and climbed the rest of the stairs. He walked down the hall to his room and closed the door behind him.

The sun was long gone and the moon was rising over the mountains. Charlie looked out the window at the wilderness beyond Cypress Creek. What had he been thinking? INK had been hiding out there for at least a week and they hadn't found her yet. And what hope did they have of locating a small flying creature that looked just like a rock?

Charlie was about to plop down on his bed when he heard a scratching sound inside the closet. He would have assumed it was mice if he hadn't lived in the same house as Charlotte's cat, Aggie, who was every rodent's worst nightmare. Charlie tiptoed quietly to the closet door and pulled it open in one swift movement. On the floor was a large object with a blanket thrown over it. Something under the blanket was moving.

Summoning his courage, Charlie reached down and snatched the blanket away. The thing on the floor was a metal cage, but the thing inside it definitely wasn't a bird. A tiny granite-colored gargoyle growled at him and flexed its wings. Tied to the top of the cage was a small metal canister with a stopper in the top.

Charlie removed the stopper and pulled out a scrap of paper.

I have an army.
Join it or fight it.
-IZZIE

Charlie flipped over the paper to find another message written on the back in a different hand. This one said:

No thank you.
-INDY
Charlie Laird, please send this
gargoyle back where it belongs.

The little creature in the cage reached through the bars and tried to snatch the message, but Charlie yanked it back just in time. So the gargoyle *had* been delivering something to INK. Charlie looked at the message again. She must have captured the Nightmare and brought it back to the purple mansion with her response. Charlie thought it over. INK didn't want to join ICK's army. Was it the truth, or just a trick to get access to the tower so she could set her sister loose in the Waking World?

Then he realized how wrong he'd been. If INK had brought the gargoyle back, that meant she'd been inside the purple mansion on her own. She'd had the chance to remove the locks and the barricades from the tower door— but she hadn't.

Charlie raced downstairs to where his father, now wearing a frilly apron, was taking a golden casserole out of the oven.

"Hungry?" he asked his son.

Charlie shook his head at the casserole. He'd eat kale pancakes and banana bean balls, but he drew the line at cauliflower. "Was the house's security system on today?" he asked.

"Umm, I'm pretty sure I locked all the doors," Andrew Laird said.

"But the *alarms*—were they on?" Charlie asked.

"Well . . . ," his dad said with an embarrassed grimace. "I'm afraid the security system isn't quite up and running yet."

"When did it stop working?" Charlie asked.

"It never started," his father said. "I couldn't figure out where the On button was. Someone from the company is coming out to show me in a couple of days."

Charlie couldn't believe it. INK could have set ICK free at any time.

CHAPTER TWENTY-THREE

THE HISS OF REASON

Charlie felt bright sunshine on his face, and when he opened his eyes he let loose a shout of pure joy. After more than a week of miserable, sheep-ridden dreams, he'd finally made it to the Dream Realm. There was warm white sand beneath his body, and he could hear the crash of waves in the distance. He sat up and looked around, expecting to see his mother lounging on a beach chair nearby. But there was no one in sight but a surfer riding a wave to the shore.

As the surfer came closer, Charlie could see that he was wearing a brightly colored Hawaiian shirt with an old fedora. Charlie got to his feet and waved with both arms.

"Meduso!" he shouted. The surfer looked in his direction—and took a brutal tumble into the surf.

When he rose from the ocean, the hat was off and the three snakes that grew out of his head were all coughing and sputtering. Fortunately, Meduso's sunglasses remained on. One look from the eyes behind them and Charlie would have been instantly turned to stone.

"Charlie Laird," said Basil Meduso as he hauled his board up onto the sand. "Still trying to murder me, I see."

"Sorry about that," Charlie told the gorgon. "I was just happy to see you guys." Not as happy as he would have been to see his mother, but happy all the same.

"Charlie!" the snake named Fernando cried as soon as he'd recovered enough to greet him. "You've returned victoriousss! Your triumph over ICK and INK isss already a legend here in the Dream Realm!"

It took Charlie a second to realize that Fernando was talking about the Tranquility Tonic.

"Yeah, well, turns out we just got rid of the tonic," Charlie admitted. "ICK and INK are still causing trouble. One of them has started a Nightmare army. She wants to take over the Waking World."

"You sssee, I told you it wouldn't lasssst," hissed a bitter brown snake in a nasal voice.

"Hi, Larry," Charlie said politely. "Good to see you too, Barry." He nodded to the emerald-green snake who never spoke, and it flicked the side of his face with its tongue in return.

"So I suppose you're here for some advice." Meduso sighed theatrically.

Though Meduso would never have admitted it, Charlie could tell that the gorgon was pleased to see him. He didn't think any good would come of informing Meduso he'd arrived at the beach by accident. So instead, Charlie nodded gamely.

Meduso lay down on a bright orange beach towel and Charlie gave the gorgon his side of the story. He and Jack had discovered ICK's army—and for a while Charlie had been convinced that INK was involved too. Maybe he'd been wrong about that. But Charlie was only trying to do what was best for everyone. It hurt that his brother, Alfie, and Rocco didn't support him.

"So Alfie and Rocco chose Jack's side, did they?" Meduso said.

"Shhhocking," sneered Larry.

"Indeed!" agreed Meduso. "How dare they have their own opinions after you went to such trouble to find weak-willed friends who would always do exactly what you tell them to do?"

Charlie was about to agree when he realized what was going on. "Wait, are you making fun of me?" he asked.

"No, I'm making a *point*," said Meduso. "Would you rather have smart friends who think for themselves—or lackeys who think only what you tell them to think?"

"My friends are smart," Charlie replied. "And I like them that way."

"Of course you do. That's what makes them interesting," said Meduso. "But if you like smart friends who think for themselves, why is it such a giant betrayal when a couple of them agree with Jack?"

"Sssnap!" hissed Larry.

Fernando slithered down far enough to look Charlie in the eye. "Larry, Barry, and I disssagree all the time," he said. "And we ssstill ssstick together."

"Yeah," Larry sneered. "'Causssse we're all ssstuck to thisss guy'sss head."

"Let your friends have their own opinions," Meduso counseled. "It seems to me that the disagreement between ICK and INK is far more important. One twin is starting a war. The other seems to be aiding the enemy. They appear to be on two different sides at the moment. If you want to put an end to this episode, I suggest you get to the bottom of the girls' little spat."

"So you think Jack is right too?" Charlie asked, though he already knew the answer. "INK really might be a good guy?"

"Absssolutely not!" said Larry emphatically.

"I'd sssay it'sss cccertainly posssible," Fernando disagreed.

"They may be on two different sides, but that doesn't mean one side is good and the other one evil," replied Meduso. "It's never quite as simple as that. Nobody's perfect— not even you, Charlie Laird. But if you want to know if INK is a good guy, I doubt you'll find the answer here in the Dream Realm. Why don't you wake up and *ask* her?"

CHAPTER TWENTY-FOUR

BAIT

The next morning, Charlie was spying on his little brother when Jack woke up to find a miniature gargoyle making faces at him from a cage resting beside his pillow. First the creature stuck its black tongue out of its mouth and up one of its nostrils. Then it filled its cheeks with air until its head was the size of a grapefruit and on the verge of bursting. And for an encore, it rolled its eyes back until only the whites were showing—and then spun its head around in a complete circle.

"What the *what*?" Jack yelped loudly, and tumbled out of bed.

Charlie snickered and snuck downstairs.

"Did you like your present?" Charlie asked when his brother took a seat at the breakfast table.

"So you found the gargoyle," Jack said miserably. "Did you find India too?"

"Nope," Charlie admitted. "She delivered the gargoyle and left without saying hello."

Jack looked back and forth between his brother and stepmother. "So *she* was the one who captured the creature?"

"Yep," Charlotte said. "And Charlie says she brought it here. Which means you might be right about INK being a good guy."

"It's *possible,*" Charlie said. "But I'm not ready to give her a medal. She hasn't explained why she made the Tranquility Tonic yet."

"Still! This is great news!" Jack said merrily, tucking into his breakfast. "Where's Dad?" he asked with his mouth full of food. It was a good question. As long as

Charlie had known his father, Andrew Laird had never missed a breakfast.

Charlotte shifted uncomfortably in her seat. "He had to get to work early," she told the boys.

They must have argued again when Charlotte got home, Charlie thought. Even if ICK didn't manage to destroy any worlds, she was definitely doing terrible things to his family. It had to end. And it had to end now.

At school, Charlie set out in search of his friends, and the first one he found was Paige. In fact, she was standing so close to his locker that Charlie almost wondered if she'd been hanging out there, waiting for him to arrive. After he told her the news, Paige joined the hunt for Alfie and Rocco. But they'd only made it a few steps down the hall when Paige threw out an arm, catching Charlie in the stomach and bringing him to a halt. Just ahead of them, a girl carrying a large cardboard box was walking into Ms. Abbot's classroom. She looked familiar, but Charlie couldn't figure out who she was. The girl was wearing a pair of acid-washed blue jeans, neon pink sneakers, and a bejeweled T-shirt with a fluffy black kitten on the front.

"Hold up, is that *INK*?" Paige gasped. "OMG, what is that poor girl *wearing*?"

Charlie shook his head in amazement. INK looked like

she'd traveled back in time to the 1980s and raided a third grader's closet. No wonder no one else in the hall seemed to recognize her. Charlie and Paige rushed toward Ms. Abbot's class and peeked inside. They watched INK pull pieces of chemistry equipment out of the box and arrange them carefully on a table at the front of the room.

"Do you need any help with the assembly, India?" Charlie couldn't see Ms. Abbot, but he recognized her voice at once. She was back on the job. Charlie and Paige traded an astonished look.

"Oh, I think I can manage," INK said. "I'm just waiting for Jancy to arrive with the other box."

"Move it or lose it, Laird," said a gruff but friendly female voice behind Charlie and Paige. It was Jancy Dare, carting an enormous box of beakers, flasks, and tubes. Not only was she the picture of health, she was sporting the same wide, toothy smile she usually wore after knocking a quarterback unconscious. "Hey, guys, looks like we have a couple of visitors," she announced, bodychecking Charlie as she entered the room. Jancy's boyfriend (or servant) followed in her wake, carrying a tiny box of pipettes. As soon as Lester saw Charlie, he tackled him with a fierce hug.

Just as Charlie managed to free himself from Lester's unexpected embrace, INK spun around to face her guests. She didn't say a word. It wasn't just her clothes that had changed, Charlie realized. INK didn't look like a doll anymore. She seemed far more human than she had before.

"Charlie! Paige! Welcome!" Ms. Abbot stepped into view. She was still dressed in black, but her dark wig was gone and her naturally blond hair was pulled back in a chic ponytail. She laughed out loud at the shock on their faces. "Looks like we've left you completely speechless. Come in and we'll explain what's going on."

Paige glanced around the room. Darwin the snake was in his cage, and Ms. Abbot's collection of animal brains was back on the shelf. "Does this mean you're staying in Cypress Creek?" Paige asked the teacher.

"I'll be staying in town for now," said the teacher. "And even if I do decide to leave, I promise, there won't be any more running."

"What about India?" Charlie asked, gesturing toward INK. "What's her story? Is she staying too?"

"I think I'll let her tell you," Ms. Abbot said. "She has a much nicer accent than I do."

India stepped toward them. "I'm staying in Cypress Creek because I want to go to school," she said politely.

"And I'm gonna make sure nobody bothers my friend while she gets an education," Jancy added with a menacing air as she pummeled her left palm with her right fist. Lester tittered.

India set her equipment down on the table and turned her attention to the football player. "You sounded quite aggressive just then, Jancy. Are you sure you're feeling well?" she asked with concern.

"Everything's peachy," Jancy said with a sinister laugh. "Messing with Laird always makes me feel awesome."

India offered Charlie an apologetic smile. "I suspect that Jancy has been suffering from pesticide poisoning for quite some time now," she explained. "It may have been responsible for some of her more unpleasant behavior over the past few months."

"Yeah, I'm not so sure about that," Charlie remarked. "Jancy's been the same way for as long as I've known her."

"Watch it, Laird!" Jancy barked.

"Don't make her angry," Lester warned ominously. "You know what happens when she gets angry."

"I think *unpleasant* may be part of Jancy's personality," Paige added.

"That is another possible explanation," India conceded.

"Hey!" Jancy shouted. "I'm serious! Stop talking about me like I'm not here!"

"Sorry," Charlie said. He hadn't come to start a fight. "Do you mind if we ask INK—I mean, *India*—about your miraculous recovery?"

Jancy fumed for a moment and then grunted her permission. "Lester and me are gonna go get the rest of the stuff out of your trunk, Ms. A," she told the teacher. "Laird and his girlfriend can talk about my health all they want, but my personality's off-limits."

"Of course," said Ms. Abbot. "There will be no gossiping while you're gone."

Paige turned to India, wasting no time once the linebacker and her boyfriend (or servant) were gone. "So how did you figure out that Jancy had been poisoned?" she asked.

"Yeah," Charlie said. "And how did you know what the treatment should be?"

A cloud passed over India's face. "My father, George Kessog, was a chemist . . . ," she started to say.

"And a hero," Ms. Abbot chimed in.

"Yes," India agreed, her sadness transforming into a proud smile. "He was a hero too. When he was a very young man, he was sent to the front lines in World War One. Britain's enemies were using poison gas on our troops. My father told Izzie and me about the horrifying symptoms of gas poisoning. And I remember he said that they usually began with very heavy perspiration."

"And Jancy was sweating a lot the day the two of you met," Charlie recalled.

"Yes. That's why I asked her if she'd been near a war," India said. "It was silly of me, I realize now. I hadn't left the lighthouse for quite some time, and I didn't know what was going on in the world. But as it turns out, I was on the right track. Pesticides and poison gas do similar things to the human body. Their symptoms and treatment are often the same. I knew how to treat Jancy because one hundred years ago, my father developed the treatment for gas poisoning."

"He saved thousands of lives," Ms. Abbot said.

"You will too," India told the teacher. "And you'll do it just as my father did, by using a chemical that came from one of the deadliest plants on earth."

"A plant that I just happened to have growing in my greenhouse," Ms. Abbot added, picking up the story where India had left off. It was almost as if they'd known each other for years.

"I stole Ms. Abbot's belladonna to make my father's formula," India explained. "I slept in her garden shed the first night I arrived in Cypress Creek, and I noticed she had some rather unusual plants growing around her house. After I met Jancy, I went back to see if there were any I could use to extract atropine. I was hiding in the woods when the three of you arrived that day to plant the poison garden. It was such good luck that belladonna was part of it!"

Paige crossed her arms and seemed to be letting it all

sink in. "So you're telling us you took the belladonna to save Jancy. You never wanted to hurt anyone?" she asked suspiciously.

"Certainly not!" India was aghast.

"Then how do you explain the Tranquility Tonic that you and your sister sold this summer?" Charlie blurted out, finally asking the question he'd been dying to have answered. If India couldn't explain the tonic, it would prove that her do-gooder disguise was nothing more than an act. "Your little potion turned everyone in Orville Falls into sleepwalking zombies, and you almost destroyed three worlds!"

Ms. Abbot's eyes flicked back and forth between the two of them as if she were watching a Ping-Pong game. "I don't understand," she said.

India sighed. "Unfortunately, I do," she said. "I invented a potion I called Tranquility Tonic. It was meant to help people by preventing bad dreams. In fact, I made the first batch for my sister. She suffers from terrible nightmares."

"Yeah, tell me about it," Charlie said with a snort. "I've been stuck in your sister's bad dream for the last week."

"*What?*" Paige yelped. "Why didn't you say anything?"

Charlie shrugged. "I was embarrassed. I don't know what it means."

India looked puzzled as well. "You've seen Izzie's nightmare? She never invited *me* to visit, and I'm her twin sister."

"Well, she didn't exactly *invite* me," Charlie said. "I just showed up unexpectedly. But you're right about one thing. Your sister's nightmare is pretty darn terrible."

"I don't doubt that it is," said India. "We'd been living in the lighthouse for less than a month when Izzie's fear opened a portal to the Netherworld. She passed over to the other side, and I followed. After that, she spent most of her time inside her nightmare while I waited for her in the Netherworld lighthouse. I suppose that's when time stopped for both of us. From that point on, we never got older, we never slept, and we no longer needed to eat.

"My sister and I lived like that for decades, and the entire time, I never gave up trying to save her. Tranquility Tonic was my last resort. I thought if I could find a way to destroy Izzie's nightmare, I might be able to set us both free. And for a while, Izzie let me believe that I'd finally succeeded. After I gave her the tonic, she said it worked so well that she wanted everyone in the Waking World to be able to buy it. So I wrote down the formula for her and she began to make more of it.

"But the truth was, Isabel never drank my tonic. She took my formula and added something awful to it instead."

"She added despair," said Charlie. That had been the tonic's secret ingredient—the one that turned people into Walkers. Its only antidote, Charlie had discovered, was *hope*.

India nodded solemnly. "That's correct. I had no idea that she was poisoning people in Orville Falls with it—or that she was planning to destroy the Netherworld—until the goblins arrived at the door of the Netherworld lighthouse. There were thousands upon thousands of them, and they were demanding I let them through the portal. My sister had promised them they could take over the Waking World as payment for helping her. I wasn't going to let that happen, so I did the only thing I could think of."

"You burned down the Waking World lighthouse," said Paige.

India nodded again. "Yes, I came back to this world and destroyed our portal," she said. "I knew there was another one in Cypress Creek, so I traveled all the way from Maine. I was hoping I could convince Izzie to come back to this side for good when I got here. But by the time I was able to talk to her, she was too mad at me to listen."

"That may have been my fault," Charlie admitted. "I made a real mess of things when I told her you started the fire in the lighthouse, didn't I?" He'd known he had made a mistake when he saw the look on ICK's face after he'd given her the news.

"It must have come as a shock to her. But don't worry," India tried to reassure him. "My sister may be angry at me, but she'll come around. We've been together for almost a century, and we've never been apart until now. It's been a month since I left the lighthouse. The second I set foot outside, it felt like a switch had flipped and I started getting older. I always wanted to grow up, but I don't want to leave Izzie—and she won't want to be left behind."

Charlie opened his mouth, but it took him a moment to find the guts to speak. He was about to take an enormous risk. But everything he'd heard so far made him think INK could be trusted. "There's something I need to tell you," Charlie blurted out at last. "You and your sister might not be apart much longer. ICK is planning a trip to the Waking World. Actually, it's more like an invasion."

India didn't seem terribly concerned. "Is Izzie talking about her so-called army again?" she asked. "You needn't worry. That's nothing but an empty threat. Isabel has been trying to build an army for years, but the Nightmares in the Netherworld never wanted anything to do with her plans. I suppose that's why she had to turn to the goblins for help with the tonic. But there's nothing those horrible little beasts can do for her now."

Charlie shook his head. "Maybe that's how things used to be, but something has changed," he said. "I saw your sister in the Netherworld two nights ago. She had a crowd of Nightmares around her, and they seemed willing to do whatever she asked. And yesterday, she tried to break out of the purple mansion's tower. I don't know how many Nightmares she brought with her. There was definitely at least one Cyclops up there—not to mention the gargoyle she sent to find you."

"I don't know what could have changed," INK told Charlie.

"I do," Paige told the girl. "Don't you see? Everything's changed because ICK doesn't have *you* anymore."

CHAPTER TWENTY-FIVE

THE SISTERS

There was a chance it would work, Charlie thought. A slim chance, but it was worth a shot. If India Kessog could bury the hatchet with Isabel and convince her sister to come to the Waking World for good, everyone's problems would be solved. The sisters would have each other, and Charlie might not need to destroy the tower and its portal. So that afternoon after school, he and Jack took India home with them to the purple mansion.

Charlotte was at the stove, mixing a batch of breath deodorizer. She was so absorbed in her work that she didn't hear the kids enter the kitchen. Charlie cleared his throat and his stepmother glanced over her shoulder.

"Hey there," she said. Then she dropped her spoon and did a double take.

"Charlotte, I'd like you to meet India Kessog," said Jack, performing the introductions. "Indy, this is my stepmother, Charlotte."

Charlotte wiped her hands on her apron and cautiously offered one of them to the girl. "Hello, India," she said. "I don't know if you remember me. You and your sister used to leave notes for me in the Netherworld."

India didn't even blink. "Yes, I remember you well," she said. "You grew up."

Charlotte looked down, as if surprised to find herself in an adult body. "I did," she said.

India smiled. "I'm looking forward to growing up too," she said. "Where is the other girl you used to bring to the Netherworld? Is she here?"

Charlotte cast a look at Charlie and Jack.

"That was our mom," Charlie explained. "She died a few years ago."

"My mother is dead too," India told him. "I'm terribly sorry to hear about yours. She always seemed quite nice. I would have liked very much to have known her." She turned to Charlotte. "I tried to introduce you and your friend to my sister, but I believe I may have scared you away instead."

"So the notes weren't a . . ." Charlotte paused, as if searching for the right word. "A trick?"

"A trick? Oh no," India answered. "My sister and I always thought we were the only humans who could enter the Netherworld. I was thrilled to discover there were two more girls like us. I thought Izzie might feel better if she had someone to talk to other than me."

"But I never accepted your invitations. Veronica and I hid from you instead." Charlotte was clearly aghast. "I'm so sorry."

India shook her head. "You shouldn't be. You were right to be cautious. The Netherworld is a very frightening place. When you're there in the flesh, you have to be very careful. It's a miracle none of us ever got eaten or trampled."

"That's true," Charlotte said. "I can't believe you survived all alone on the other side for so long."

"We were there for eighty years," India said, "but I don't recall ever feeling alone. I had Izzie to look after. As much as I despised that terrible place, I couldn't leave my sister, and she wouldn't come back to the Waking World."

"So you stayed to keep your sister company?" Jack asked.

"Of course," India answered. "Wouldn't you do the same for your brother?"

Jack shrugged. "Yeah, I guess so," he admitted.

"Jack loves the Netherworld," Charlie explained. "He'd go all the time if he could."

"It's fun to visit, but I wouldn't want to *live* there," Jack said. "Still, I definitely would if you needed me to."

Charlie didn't know how to respond, so he mussed his little brother's hair. "Why did your sister want to stay?" he asked India.

"I think this world scared her much more than the Netherworld," India said. "The things we saw here were worse than anything we saw there."

"What happened to you guys?" Jack asked.

India shook her head sadly. "That's a story for another time," she said. "You brought me here to talk to my sister. Perhaps we should find her?"

"Yes, of course," Charlotte said. "We're sorry for grilling you. Let's go ahead and get up to the tower."

"Not all of us," India said. "Izzie won't like seeing so many people around. I know you want someone to stay with me for safety, but I'm afraid only one other person can go."

"I can open the portal faster than anyone else," Jack said.

"Yeah, but the last time we saw ICK, she was hanging out in a cavern that belongs to *me*," Charlie countered.

"And I own the purple mansion *and* its tower," Charlotte said. "So I say we draw straws to see who gets to keep India company up there."

Charlie's stepmom pulled a matchbook out of a drawer, chose three matches, and ripped the end off of one. She held the three matches like a tiny bouquet and let Jack pick first. He drew a regular-sized match. Charlie chose next and got the short one.

"I thought *I* was supposed to be the lucky one," Jack grumbled.

Charlie decided it was best not to gloat. "Let's go," he told the others. "We've got a lot of work to do before India and I get anywhere near the portal."

It took almost an hour to remove all the nails from the headboard they'd used to barricade the tower door. Once it was off, they could see the damage ICK's army had done. A giant hole had been punched right though the center of the door. India bent down and studied the hole's ragged edges.

"We think that was the Cyclops," Jack explained.

"I still can't believe Izzie has a monster like that in her army," India marveled. "I suppose things really *have* changed. Those kinds of Nightmares would never give her the time of day while I was still living in the lighthouse. They used to call us stinky."

"Yeah, we got that too," Charlie told her.

They stood back and watched while Charlotte removed the locks that were still left on the door. Then Charlie retrieved ICK's gargoyle from Jack's room, and he and India climbed the stairs. The tower room at the top was empty. The boards Charlie and Charlotte had carefully nailed to one of the windows had been ripped off and thrown onto the lawn. And the desk that had once stood in the center of the room had been reduced to a pile of kindling. Some of the pieces were no bigger than toothpicks. Charlotte was going to be heartbroken when she saw what they'd done to her grandmother's desk.

The portal opened as Charlie approached, revealing the cavern beneath the old Laird family house. Somehow ICK had made it past Medusa's guards and back inside. India unlatched the door of the birdcage and set the gargoyle free. It took off at once, scraping against the walls a few times before it was able to fly straight.

A few minutes later, ICK appeared, making her way toward the portal. She was still angry, that much was clear. Her teeth were clenched, and her rosebud lips were scowling. Charlie stepped to the side so the sisters could speak.

"How delightful to see you, India. I'm so pleased that you finally made it into the tower. But why on earth did you have to bring *him*?" ICK sneered.

"Charlie and his family removed the barricades from

the tower door," India told her, "so that I could come see you."

ICK's grin was evil. "They're terrified of me, aren't they?" she said.

"Yes," India replied honestly. "I am too."

"You?" ICK asked, as if it were the most ludicrous thing she'd ever heard. "I've known you for almost one hundred years, and you've never been scared of anything."

"You're wrong, Izzie," India told her. "I was always scared, but I put on a brave face for you. I didn't want you to give up."

"Then why did you abandon me?" ICK demanded angrily. "You were all I had. Why did you set fire to the lighthouse and leave me alone?"

"What should I have done instead? You took my tonic and turned it into something terrible. And you were scheming to let goblins into the Waking World," India said. "I couldn't let that happen."

"Why not?" ICK asked. "Tell me those people in Orville Falls didn't deserve it after what they did to us!"

"They didn't deserve it," India said softly.

"So I'm the bad one, is that right? Is that why I deserve to be left all by myself?" ICK asked. For a moment, her tough exterior cracked just enough to give Charlie a glimpse of the sadness that lay beneath.

"I was never going to leave you alone," said India. "I

started walking toward Cypress Creek the night the light-house burned down. I always planned to find you."

"Well, now you have. Pass over to this side and help me lead our army," ICK ordered.

"No," India said. "I'm staying in the Waking World, and I want you here with me. I really think we could be happy in Cypress Creek. I've made friends, Izzie. They'll be your friends too."

"No, they won't!" ICK spat. "They're using you, India. You'll see. You're just bait. As soon as I set foot in the Waking World, they'll turn against us, and tell lies about us, the way people like them always have."

"Does it matter so much if they do? Even if it's just you and me, we'll still have each other," India said. "And if you don't come now, it could be too late. I'm getting older, Izzie. I'm finally growing up. I can feel it."

ICK took a step closer to the portal. Her nose was now inches from her sister's. She studied India's face, her eyes passing over every inch of skin. Whatever ICK saw, it horrified her. "It's true," she said, her voice cracking. "I see it. We'll be different soon. We won't be identical anymore."

"It doesn't have to be that way," India pleaded with her sister.

"No," said ICK. "It doesn't. I'm going to come get you, whether you like it or not. I'm not what I used to be, Indy. Since you left, I've discovered the power of fear. And I'm going to make everyone on that side feel what *I've* felt all these years."

"Izzie, no!" INK cried, but her sister was already stomping away.

India took a step forward, but Charlie reached out and stopped her from going through the portal. "We tried and it didn't work," he told her. "If you go back to the Netherworld, you may have to stay. Is that what you really want?"

"But my sister!" India sobbed. "You don't understand what she's been through."

"What difference does it make now? You heard what she said," Charlie told her. "She's going to spread fear throughout the Waking World. I have to stop her. It's my job to protect the portal, India. We'll have to burn the tower down."

India's eyes were wide with fear.

"Just one night," she begged. "Please, Charlie, just give me one night to find another solution. Imagine it was your brother. What would you do?"

CHAPTER TWENTY-SIX

SILAS SPEAKS

Charlie didn't know if he'd be able to sleep. The tower was still standing, and India Kessog was spending the night on one of the sofas downstairs. But he drifted off only minutes after laying his head on the pillow. And when he opened his eyes, he found himself sitting in a purple room with purple furniture and a purple carpet laid out on the floor. The walls and the furnishings looked newer than he was used to, but he recognized his surroundings right away. He was inside a copy of the purple mansion, and the golden sun streaming through the windows told him he'd been transported to the Dream Realm.

"Hello, Charlie," said a man sitting across the room from him. Pale and thin, with sharp cheekbones and a thick head of jet-black hair, the man was instantly familiar.

Charlie gasped. "I know who you are."

"I should hope so," Silas DeChant replied with a chortle. His voice was deep, and he spoke like a character out of an old movie. "You live in my house and walk by my portrait a dozen times every day. If you didn't recognize me, I would worry that my mansion was being guarded by a dimwit—or a *nincompoop*, as you modern children say. Fortunately, that is not the case. Thank you for taking such good care of the portal."

"You're welcome, sir," said Charlie. "It's been an honor."

"Yes," said Silas. "And a terrible responsibility—one the inhabitants of this house should no longer be burdened with. For one hundred and fifty years, the DeChants have acted as guardians of the portal. We knew that the day might come when the only way to protect it would be to destroy it. I'm afraid that day is here."

It felt like his words had taken a weight off Charlie's shoulders. "Wow, I'm really glad you said that," he told Silas. "I've been thinking the very same thing."

"Yes, you should destroy the portal. Just as soon as you rescue the human girl who's trapped on the other side."

Charlie groaned miserably. He should have known there

would be a catch. "We tried to do it tonight, Mr. DeChant," he said. "I thought India Kessog might be able to talk her sister into coming to our side, but my plan didn't work."

"Perhaps Isabel's sister wasn't the right person to convince her," Silas said.

"Then who . . . ," Charlie started to ask. Then he realized what Silas DeChant was hinting at. "You mean *me*? Why do you think I'm the one who can convince her?"

"I don't know *why* you're the one," Silas said. "I only know that you are."

"How?" Charlie demanded.

"I know because you're the only one who's been inside Isabel Kessog's nightmare. Even her twin sister hasn't seen it. But you have, haven't you, Charlie?"

"Yes, but her dream's completely crazy!" Charlie almost shouted. "It's all about these big smelly sheep in the most disgusting field on earth. It's freezing and stormy, and some invisible person in the distance is humming a lullaby."

Silas seemed to consider what Charlie had told him. "I'll admit it's unusual, but nightmares often don't make sense," he said. "That doesn't mean you can't understand them. And if anyone is able to understand Isabel Kessog's nightmares, it's you. Let me ask you a question—how did you *feel* while you were inside her worst dream?"

Charlie thought a moment. Cold. Bitterly cold and miserable. But there was more to it than that. He'd felt alone in ICK's nightmare—like the world had turned against him. And he'd felt angry, as if the rage and frustration that were building inside him were the only things keeping him from freezing to death.

Silas was right; Charlie knew just how the girl felt. He'd experienced the same feelings long before he'd ever met Isabel Kessog and her sister. After his mother had died, Charlie had suffered from bad dreams too. In his nightmares, he was trapped in a cage at the top of a witch's belfry. While he'd swung there, he'd felt alone and abandoned—like the world would be better off without him.

A chill ran down Charlie's spine when he remembered the part of his dreams that had scared him far more than the witch or her cage. In his nightmares, there had been something lurking far below the witch's tower—something that was searching the forest for him. . . .

Suddenly Charlie had the clue he needed. He knew ICK's worst fear had nothing to do with sheep or lullabies. Her worst fear was coming face to face with the woman who hummed.

"I think I've figured out what frightens Isabel Kessog the most," Charlie told Silas. "It's—"

Silas held up a hand to stop him. "It's not for me to know," he said. "You and the girl share something powerful. If you've found it, Charlie, you may be able to save her."

CHAPTER TWENTY-SEVEN

THE PROPHECY

"Charlie! Wake up!" Jack was shaking him.

Charlie opened his eyes. It was still dark outside his bedroom window. "Is it morning already? What time is it?" he grumbled.

"Just after midnight," Jack said. "You've got to wake up! We need to get to the tower."

Charlie sat up in the bed, his heart pounding fast. "What's going on?" he asked.

"Tonight I was supposed to be having a nightmare about the Red Skull," Jack said, talking a mile a minute. "I fell asleep as usual, but Jed never showed up. I was getting really bored, so I went out to find him."

"Wait—who's *Jed*?" Charlie asked.

"My favorite Nightmare!" Jack said. "He plays all of Captain America's enemies in my bad dreams. Tonight he was supposed to be the Red Skull."

"I should have known," Charlie muttered. Only Jack would go out *looking* for his own Nightmare. "Did you find him?"

"Yeah," said Jack. "Jed was with most of the other Nightmares, in the middle of town. Charlie, ICK is taking over the Netherworld! She's captured President Medusa and Dabney and she's holding them hostage. I'm pretty sure she'll be coming to the Waking World soon. The Nightmares are saying that the prophecy has begun."

Charlie was suddenly completely awake. He slid off the side of his bed and grabbed a sweater from his bureau. His dream about Silas DeChant couldn't have come at a better time. If the prophecy had begun, then it was time for Charlie Laird to play his part.

Less than twelve hours had passed since Charlie's last trip through the portal. The barricades on the tower door had been removed then—and Charlotte hadn't seen the point in replacing them. They all knew that the next time a Cyclops wanted to get through, a few nails and some wood weren't going to stop it. So Charlie and Jack had no boards to remove or chains to unlock. They simply climbed the stairs to the tower room and stood in front of the portal. Then Jack did the honors and opened it. Beyond the doorway, they saw a massive crowd gathered around the Netherworld courthouse. A group of fierce-looking Nightmares stood atop the courthouse stairs, guarding the doors. Charlie recognized the Cyclops that had tried to break down the tower door. There were also several werewolves, a giant gorilla, and a family of yeti.

As they watched, a sluglike creature scaled the steps to confront the rebels. The Cyclops picked him up and hurled him past the crowd of Nightmares. The slug hit the ground and splattered a bunch of dreamers who were nervously watching the scene.

"Look! Over there!" Jack cried. He was pointing to another group of humans standing at the edge of the crowd. It was Paige, Alfie, Ollie, and Rocco, all of them in their pajamas.

Charlie and Jack hurried over to their friends, and Paige greeted Charlie with a frightened hug.

"Did you guys just get here?" Rocco asked. "Things are about to get ugly. You were right about ICK, Charlie. She's really bad news."

"I know. But *you* were right about India," Charlie said.

"She's innocent. And I'm sorry I got so angry at you and Alfie and Jack for figuring it out before I did."

"Apology accepted," Alfie said. "You've always had a terrible temper. We like you anyway."

"I have a bad temper?" asked Charlie. He'd always thought of himself as rather laid-back.

"Are you kidding?" Jack asked.

"Don't worry—your good qualities outweigh the bad," Paige added, threading her arm through his.

"True," Alfie agreed. "And right now we've got bigger problems than Charlie Laird's hot head. We were all dreaming when our Nightmares left us to go fight ICK's army. None of them ever came back."

"Wait a second!" cried Ollie. "There's my Nightmare. He's right at the front of the crowd. Dingleberry! Hey, Dingleberry!"

A small brown monkey with a white face was hopping across the heads and shoulders of larger creatures, screeching angrily at the rebel Nightmares on the courthouse steps.

"Yeah, but where are the others?" Rocco asked. "We have no idea where they went. I hope they're okay."

"I'm sure they're fine," Charlie consoled him. "Remember, Nightmares don't die."

"No, but I bet ICK can think of something much worse than death," Paige said.

"Maybe she's making them eat the nuggets from our school cafeteria," said Ollie, but Charlie didn't laugh. He'd just watched Dingleberry the monkey climb to the top of an ogre's head. The monkey appeared to have a large brown ball in his hand, and he was preparing to throw it.

"What's he doing?" Charlie asked.

"Uh-oh," said Ollie.

Dingleberry hurled the ball at the Cyclops guarding the courthouse doors, and it exploded as it hit the monster's one-eyed face.

"Was that what I think it was?" Alfie asked.

"I don't really have any way of knowing what you *think* it was," said Ollie. "But I can tell you—that was poo."

The Cyclops issued a deafening roar and charged into the crowd after the little monkey. But the Nightmares who'd gathered at the courthouse weren't going to let him take one of their own. Soon a brawl had broken out among the creatures of the Netherworld. Vampires latched on to the necks of yeti. Ogres did their best to stomp spiders. Pterodactyls dropped guano bombs on skeletons wearing pirate suits. Two different versions of Godzilla nearly crushed Alfie as they wrestled each other to the ground. Charlie and his friends were quickly backing away from the battle when three words brought the madness to a sudden halt.

"STOP THIS INSTANT!"

The Netherworld monsters lowered their fists, retracted their claws, dropped their battle-axes—and immediately turned their attention to the stage. The voice was so clear and so powerful that they didn't appear to have any choice but to obey.

Then a small creature appeared on the courthouse steps. Dressed like the little toy soldier that Ms. Abbot had discovered in her garden shed, its face was hidden by a terrifying gas mask that made it resemble an alien insect. When the creature pulled off the mask to address the crowd, the face underneath belonged to Isabel Kessog.

"I wonder if she got that from Medusa's costume collection," Jack whispered to his brother. "It's a good one."

"Yeah," Charlie said. "Where was *that* when I needed a disguise? It's a million times better than a yurei costume."

"What's a *yurei*?" Jack asked.

"Never mind," Charlie told him.

"A yurei is a girl ghost from Japan," Alfie replied.

Jack snickered. "Charlie had to dress like a girl ghost?"

"He looked gorgeous," Alfie whispered.

"Shhh!" Paige ordered the boys. "This is no time for jokes."

"Greetings, Nightmares!" Isabel Kessog shouted at the crowd. "My name is ICK. President Medusa has been overthrown. I am your new leader."

A Nightmare near the bottom of the steps began booing, and was quickly plucked from the crowd and dragged away by ICK's thugs.

ICK continued as if she hadn't noticed a thing. "As I've promised before, Nightmares who choose to join my army will accompany me to the Waking World. There, we will ensure that the human race spends its days in fear. When the Netherworld is no longer necessary, a giant hole will open up once more. Those of you who stay here will share the fate of the Netherworld. This time the hole will swallow you and your entire world."

"Why should we believe any of this?" a one-armed zombie called out. "You're too puny to be an evil mastermind."

ICK's army made a move toward the zombie, but ICK raised a hand to stop them. She seemed calm on the surface, but Charlie knew that inside, ICK had to be seething.

"I'm small because I am a human child, you imbecile. And I have come to the Netherworld in the flesh! You've all heard of the prophecy. Well, I *am* the prophecy!" ICK shouted. "And that means the end of the Netherworld is nigh!"

Charlie cupped his hands around his mouth. "Oh yeah?" he shouted as loud as he could. "Well, if you're the prophecy, then I'm the prophecy too!"

He hadn't planned the outburst. The words had sprung from his mouth unexpectedly. But now, to Charlie's great surprise, he realized that what he'd said was *true*. A week earlier, if someone had asked Charlie which Laird brother was more likely to save the Netherworld, he would have insisted it was Jack. But it turned out that Charlie was the one who was going to make all the difference. Not because he was fearless or charming, but simply because he understood why ICK was the way she was. And he understood ICK because if it hadn't been for his friends and family, Charlie Laird might have become a villain too.

"What are you doing?" Jack squealed. The crowd had gone completely silent, and every last Nightmare was staring directly at Charlie.

"Charlie!" Paige cried.

"Trust me," Charlie told her. "Let me through!" he shouted at the crowd, and the Nightmares in front of them parted, clearing a path between Charlie and the girl standing atop the courthouse stairs.

"Charlie Laird," ICK said, her lip curled into a sneer.

"Isabel Kessog," Charlie replied. "I'm here in the flesh, just like you."

The Nightmare nearest Charlie reached out and pinched his arm. "It's true! He's here in the flesh! And he reeks of human!"

"Is that Jack's brother?" someone else asked.

An ogre leaned down to sniff the air in Charlie's wake, and his nose wrinkled with disgust. "Smells like him," the monster replied.

"Bring the boy to me!" ICK shouted.

Two enormous yeti approached Charlie. "Hands off, gentlemen," he told them calmly. "I can escort myself, thank you very much."

As he walked confidently toward ICK, the Nightmares began to chatter away, and Charlie could hear the hope and excitement in their voices. So, it seemed, could ICK. And she was furious.

"This ridiculous boy cannot be the prophecy!" she insisted. "Where is *his* army? What is *his* plan? Tell us, Charlie Laird. How do you intend to destroy the Netherworld?"

Charlie climbed the stairs until he was face to face with the girl. "I'm not going to destroy anything," he announced.

"Then how can you claim to be the prophecy?"

"The way I've heard it, there are *two* parts to the prophecy," Charlie replied calmly, but loudly enough for everyone in the crowd to hear. "It says that there will be a child with the strength to destroy the Netherworld. But it also says there will be a child with the power to save it. I'm *that* kid."

ICK looked as if she could kill him right there with her own two hands. "What powers do you have?" she shrieked. "You're just a horrid little boy."

"My power is here," Charlie said, tapping his temple with a finger. "I know something."

"What do you know?" ICK asked. She was trying her best to hide it, but Charlie could see she was worried.

Charlie leaned over and whispered in her ear. "I know who's humming the lullaby in your nightmare."

There was a clap of thunder and the lights went out. Suddenly Charlie and ICK were no longer atop the steps of the Netherworld courthouse. They were up to their ankles in mud and sheep poop. A cold wind was blowing across the field, carrying the sound of a woman humming.

"No, no, no," ICK whimpered, holding her hands over her ears. Her bravado was gone. She was no longer the prophecy come to life. She was just a terrified girl. "Why did you bring me back to this place?"

She seemed on the verge of bolting until Charlie took ICK's cold hand in his. "Listen to the song, Isabel. What does it remind you of?" he asked gently.

ICK answered the question with a sob. "My mother used to sing that lullaby to me and Indy every night when we were little. But then she died."

"I thought so." Charlie put an arm around the girl. "And do you know how I figured it out?" he asked. "Because my mother died four years ago. Everything you feel in this nightmare, I've felt too. And I know what you need to do to make it stop. You need to say goodbye to her, Isabel."

One of the black sheep wandered up to them. It paused and looked up at ICK as if wondering what she would do.

"How can I say goodbye? I never even got a chance to see her," ICK sobbed, pulling away from Charlie. "Indy and I knew she was sick. We did everything we could to get back home to her. But she died and left us here in this horrible place all alone."

"Why were you and India away from your parents?" Charlie asked. "Were you sent to live in America because of the war?"

ICK nodded. "We never wanted to leave England. Then, in 1939, a plane dropped a bomb on our school, and our parents sent us to stay in Orville Falls with Uncle Alfred. I suppose they thought we would be happier here, but they didn't know our uncle."

"I've heard about him," Charlie said. "He sounds like a very strange man."

"He never left the castle," ICK said. "And he hated children. We spoke to him less than a dozen times—and the only reason he spoke to us then was to punish us."

"For the pranks you pulled around town?" Charlie asked.

"We just wanted to go home, and he wouldn't let us! After we heard that our father died in the war, we knew Mother would be in London by herself. Then she sent us a letter telling us she'd come down with pneumonia. We thought if we did enough terrible things, they wouldn't care if we were safe or not and would send us back to England."

"So that's why you blew up the town square in Orville Falls?"

"No!" ICK cried. "We glued locks shut and put baking soda in ketchup bottles, but we had nothing to do with *that*! We didn't even have the right supplies to create an explosion as big as the one that destroyed the fountain. But the people in Orville Falls needed someone to blame, so they chose me and Indy. It wasn't the first time either. A few months earlier, people claimed we'd spiked the punch at the fair with syrup of ipecac, which made everyone vomit. But it wasn't us. It was the bad mayonnaise at the hamburger stand."

Charlie could understand now why ICK had been so angry with the people of Orville Falls. "Sounds like you and your sister ended up being the town's scapegoats."

"That's precisely what we were. After the explosion, they tried to drag us out of the castle—even though there were people in the crowd who must have known we were innocent. Uncle Alfred made us sleep with the sheep that night in case the townspeople came back to get us before dawn. And before he put us in this pen, he told us there was no point in pulling any more pranks because our mother was already gone." Isabel sniffed in a big sob. "She'd been dead for weeks, and we didn't even know."

Charlie could feel the tears welling up in his eyes. At least he'd been able to see his mom in the hours before she passed away. He couldn't imagine what it must have been like for the girls to be stranded on the other side of the ocean while their mother was dying.

"Indy cried all night. But I was so angry, I did the only thing I could think of. I set all of those stupid, smelly sheep free. And in the morning, Uncle Alfred told us that the sheep were the final straw."

"And he sent you to live in that lighthouse in Maine."

"Yes," ICK said. "A governess was with us at first, but she fled after a few weeks. I can hardly blame her. The place was revolting. Everything was damp all the time, and the walls were covered with mold and mildew. But Indy and I stayed, and we didn't tell anyone that the governess had gone. Groceries were dropped off every Monday, and if we needed something, we left a note downstairs and the supplies would be delivered the next week."

"So it was just the two of you?" Charlie asked.

ICK nodded. "Indy and I didn't have anyone else. Our parents were dead, and Uncle Alfred was our only relative. Indy wanted to leave the lighthouse. She wanted us to make our own way in the world. But I refused to go. I just kept getting angrier and angrier until, one day, a portal to the Netherworld opened up in the lighthouse and I passed over to the other side."

"I accidentally opened a portal too," Charlie confessed.

ICK's eyes went wide with surprise. "You did?" she asked.

"I did," Charlie said. "I was furious at the world after my mother died. Then my dad got married again and made us move to the purple mansion. I hated my stepmother, and I said some pretty terrible things to my brother. I was so scared and so angry that I opened the portal in the mansion's tower without knowing I'd done it. I could have ended up being stuck in the Netherworld too."

"How did you escape?" ICK asked.

"I had friends who helped me figure out what was really scaring me. Everything changed after I faced my fear. I wasn't as angry anymore, and I stopped having bad dreams like this one."

Charlie looked around at the fat black sheep milling about the field. "So this is where you were hiding the night you were accused of a crime you didn't commit—the same night you found out your mother had died," Charlie said. "That's why you dream about the sheep?"

"Yes," ICK said.

"I think I can help you leave this place for good," Charlie said.

"How?" ICK asked.

"For starters, we're going to clear your name. It's time the people of Orville Falls knew what really caused the town square to explode. And we need to find your parents in the Dream Realm so that you can visit them whenever you need to."

"I can visit them?" ICK asked, her eyes wide with wonder.

"Yes," Charlie told her. "And I'll show you how. But first, you'll have to do something very difficult, Isabel. In fact, it may be the hardest thing you'll ever do. You need to find your worst nightmare and say goodbye."

"I don't understand," ICK said, looking around. "This *is* my worst nightmare."

"I don't think so," Charlie said. "I think your worst nightmare is the same as mine. I think it's saying goodbye to your mother. She's here somewhere, Isabel. And if she's anything like mine, she's been hoping you'll find her. You need to stop running away."

"I can't do that," ICK said, clinging to him. "Please don't make me."

"You have to," Charlie told her. "Say goodbye, Isabel. You won't be alone. You'll have your sister and you'll have friends."

"Friends?" ICK asked skeptically.

"I promise," Charlie said. Then, once again, they heard

the sound of humming on the wind. "That's her. It's time, Isabel. You need to go find her."

"Will you come with me?" ICK begged. "Please?"

"I can't," Charlie said. "You have to do it by yourself. You won't want me with you when you see her. But I promise I'll wait right here for you. I won't move a muscle until you get back."

"Thank you," said ICK. And before she set out in search of her mother, she wrapped Charlie in a giant hug.

CHAPTER TWENTY-EIGHT

THE REUNION

Charlie never asked Isabel what happened—and she never told him. But when she returned to the spot among the sheep where she'd left him, she was different. The fires that had been burning inside her were out. She looked sad and exhausted but completely at peace.

They found their way out of the sheep pen quite easily. On other nights, Charlie had spent hours searching for the gate without ever managing to find it. Now it appeared in front of them as if it had been there all along.

Once they were out, Isabel leaned over the fence to pet one of the giant black sheep that had come to see them off.

The girl and the sheep had spent eighty years together, and now it was finally time to say goodbye.

"Don't take this personally," she told the sheep. "But I don't think I'll ever be able to wear wool again."

The sheep bleated loudly. At first Charlie wondered if it had understood Isabel's joke. Then he realized it was calling attention to the gang of Nightmares that had been sneaking up behind them.

"Isabel Kessog," said Dabney the clown once he'd stifled a high-pitched giggle. "Your army has been defeated, and you're under arrest for crimes against the Netherworld."

Without saying a word, Isabel held out her hands and allowed one of Dabney's men to put cuffs on her. She must have known the risks that came with visiting the land of Nightmares in the flesh. You could get stomped, squished, or eaten. You could also get arrested.

"Well, that was a lot easier than I expected," Dabney said, a little confused. He looked down at Charlie. "Are you all right?" he asked.

Charlie smiled. "Never better," he told the clown. He felt stronger and happier than he had in ages. By saving Isabel, he'd faced the fear that he hadn't yet faced—the fear of the darkness inside him.

Jack found Charlie and Isabel in the hallway of the Nether-world courthouse, nervously waiting for the girl's trial to begin.

"Isabel, meet my brother, Jack," Charlie said, introduc-ing the two. "Jack is good friends with India."

Charlie saw Isabel frown at the mention of her sister's name, but she still reached out to shake Jack's hand.

"I apologize for what I did to you a few months ago," ICK said to Jack. As her Tranquility Tonic had taken its toll on the Netherworld, she'd tried to pin the blame on Jack. Many of the Nightmare creatures he'd befriended during his secret trips to the other side of the portal had turned against him.

"That's okay," said Jack. "It taught me a pretty impor-tant lesson."

"What was that?" Charlie asked.

Jack looked up at his brother. "That I'd rather have one person who really loves me than a million who pretend to like me," he told Charlie.

The door to the courtroom opened, and the three of them were ushered inside. Sitting at the far end in the red velvet judge's chair was Medusa. Her snakes rose for a look at the girl who'd just entered. Charlie and Jack stood back while Isabel was escorted to the front of the room. She glanced anxiously over her shoulder, and Charlie gave her a thumbs-up. If someone had told him three days earlier that he'd be standing where he was, Charlie would never have believed it. But this was where he was supposed to be.

Medusa lifted a hand to her glasses, and the spectators gasped. For a moment it looked as if the girl once known as ICK would be turned to stone as punishment. But then Medusa's fingers dropped to the desk in front of her.

"Isabel Kessog. Once again, you have attempted to destroy our world," Medusa said, her imperious voice echoing through the courtroom. "What do you have to say for yourself?"

Standing before the giant gorgon with a halo of angry snakes writhing about her head, Isabel looked terribly small.

"I am very sorry, ma'am," she said.

"YOU'RE *SORRY*?" Medusa bellowed. "YOUR ARMY AMBUSHED MY LIMOUSINE, KIDNAPPED ME, AND THEN LOCKED ME IN A CLOSET!"

Isabel cowered at the woman's words. And Charlie's heart went out to her. He couldn't just stand there when he knew what Isabel had gone through. He now understood what had driven her to such desperate actions.

He stepped forward to address the president, the way he'd seen people speak to judges in movies. He was going to plead Isabel's case. He'd been preparing his speech since

the moment they'd arrived. "Madam President, may I say a few words on the defendant's behalf?"

Medusa sat back in her chair and crossed her arms. "If you must," she said.

"Isabel Kessog is an orphan," Charlie began. "Her parents died tragically. She was abandoned by her uncle, accused of horrible crimes she didn't commit, and hunted like an animal by the people of Orville Falls. After a while, she became so terrified of the Waking World that she opened a portal to the Netherworld, and she's been stuck here for eighty years. Madam President, you once told me that no human being should stay frightened for that long. Isabel Kessog has suffered more than anyone I know."

It was a truth that couldn't be denied. Medusa nodded, and her expression softened. "I visited your lighthouse many times over the years," she said gently. "So did my son, Basil. We tried to rescue you, but you wouldn't let us in. Why didn't you let us help?"

Isabel looked up at the fierce monster staring down at her from the judge's chair. "You have snakes for hair, Madam President. And your eyes turn people to stone. How was I supposed to know you were there to *help*?"

"I see," said Medusa thoughtfully.

Charlie took advantage of the silence that followed. "Isabel faced her fears tonight," he told the president. "It's time for her to go home to the Waking World."

Medusa drummed her fingers on the desk in front of her. She seemed to be considering the idea. "If I allow her to go free, how can we ensure that she will never return in the flesh to the land of Nightmares?"

"Isabel will come with me through the portal in the mansion," Charlie said. "Once we reach the other side, we will destroy the tower and the portal inside it."

Several loud gasps came from the crowd, and the Nightmares began to whisper among themselves. Dabney the clown giggled sadly.

"But that means you and Jack will never be able to return in the flesh," Medusa said. "Are you certain this is the best course of action? Have you discussed this with your brother?"

"He has." Jack stepped forward. "Charlie's right. It's got to be done."

"My family is willing to make the sacrifice. I spoke to Silas DeChant, the man who built the purple mansion, and even he agrees. As much as Jack and I will miss you, Madam President, we both think we will all be safer if the portal is closed for good," Charlie told her.

"Since you've brought up the subject of safety," Medusa said, "how can we be sure that this child will not do more terrible things once she's set free in the Waking World?"

Charlie straightened his spine and stood as tall as he could. "I am the second part of the prophecy, and I will vouch for Isabel, ma'am. My friends and I will help her stay out of trouble."

Medusa nodded. "Very well, then. Isabel Kessog, otherwise known as ICK, your sentence is banishment from the Netherworld. You shall live out the rest of your days as an ordinary human."

Medusa struck her gavel against the desk, and the trial of Isabel Kessog was over.

The presidential limo drove Charlie, Jack, and Isabel to the Netherworld mansion. Along the way, they passed what was left of the old Laird family house with the cavern beneath it. Charlie was happy to see that the building was already collapsing bit by bit.

When they reached the Netherworld mansion, Medusa and Dabney saw them all to the front door. There were hugs all around, and Dabney cried, but Charlie knew it wasn't goodbye forever. The gorgon and the clown would always be there for him in his nightmares.

When their friends had finally gone and the door of the mansion had closed behind them, Charlie solemnly led the way up the stairs. Inside the tower at the top of the building, he and Jack stood at one of the windows and gazed out one last time on the nightmare land below. Across the room, Isabel Kessog stood at the tower's other window, and Charlie wondered if she too was saying goodbye.

"Are you going to miss it?" Charlie asked his little brother.

"Nope," said Jack. He sounded surprised to hear himself saying it.

"Me neither," Charlie agreed. As exciting and rewarding as his journeys in the strange world had been, it felt good to be leaving it all behind.

"That's because you did what you were supposed to do," Jack said. "You fulfilled the prophecy. You saved the Netherworld, the Dream Realm, and the Waking World. I think you deserve to go home."

Charlie looked over at his brother. "*We* fulfilled the prophecy, Jack. I couldn't have done any of this without you."

They were interrupted by the sound of feet thundering up the stairs. For a moment, Charlie wondered if ICK's Nightmare army had come to get them. Instead, the ugliest baby in the Netherworld walked through the door. It was wearing a snug, beet-stained onesie that showcased its hairy arms and legs—and smoking the stub of a cigar. A giant bird with a woman's head flapped in behind it.

"Oh dear. What are *you*?" Isabel asked the smaller creature.

"Just call me Prince Charming," said the baby in a gruff

voice. Then it winked at Isabel and laughed at its own joke. "I'm a changeling, toots. What are *you*?"

"She's the girl who burned down the lighthouse," said the bird woman.

"Hi, Ava. Hi, Bruce," said Charlie. "Actually, this girl is that girl's *sister*. Her name's Isabel Kessog. We're taking her home to the Waking World."

"And you two thought you could leave without saying goodbye to us?" Bruce demanded. "Come here, ya little monster," he said, grabbing Jack by the shirt collar and pulling him down for a hug.

Jack embraced the changeling with one arm and pinched his nose with his free hand. "No offense, Bruce, but after we're done here, I think your diaper is ready for a change."

Dawn had already broken by the time Charlie, Jack, and Isabel stepped through the portal and into the Waking World's purple mansion. They found the room on the other side filled with people who'd been waiting for them to arrive. Charlotte, Rocco, Alfie, Ollie, and Paige were all there in their pajamas. And standing in front of them all was India Kessog.

Isabel walked up to India. The two sisters stood face to face, each the mirror image of the other. This was the moment of truth. The girls had been on opposite sides of an epic battle, and there was no telling whether it had left lasting wounds.

"You're older than me now," Isabel said.

India grinned and Charlie began to relax. "By one whole month."

"How does it feel to be ordinary again?" Isabel asked.

"You tell me," India said. "You're ordinary now too."

Isabel thought about it for a moment. "It's terrifying," she said. "But exciting."

"It's scary for everyone," Charlotte told her. "Even old ladies like me."

"Pshh," said India with a dismissive flick of her wrist. "You think *you're* old? We're so old that when we were growing up, water was *free*."

"Water's not free anymore?" asked Isabel.

"Oh no," said her sister, taking Isabel by the arm and leading her down from the tower. "They charge a dollar a bottle! Can you *imagine*? And they have computers the size of a ration booklet!"

"You're joking!"

"Not at all. And they've improved the design of Soxhlet extractors. And added twenty-eight new elements to the periodic table."

"How did you learn all this so quickly?" Isabel asked.

"Well, you see, there's this teacher. . . ."

CHAPTER TWENTY-NINE

THE SCOOP

The road to Orville Falls had a million twists and turns. Every time the bus from Cypress Creek went around a curve, Charlie and Paige had no choice but to lean against each other. Charlotte would have driven the two of them, but Charlie had convinced his stepmom that she had better things to do. Someone needed to stay home and plan the demolition of the purple mansion's tower, he'd said. Charlie didn't tell her that after the excitement of the previous week, he and Paige needed some quiet time alone.

And it was quiet. They didn't talk very much during the ride. The sun was shining and the leaves were just beginning to turn red and yellow. It was a beautiful day, the Waking World was safe, and Paige's hair smelled just like strawberries. The forty-five minutes they spent on the bus were the happiest Charlie had spent in quite a while.

When they reached Orville Falls, the pair hopped off the bus and made their way through the town toward Paige's aunt Josephine's house. It took longer to reach their destination than Charlie had expected. Every block or so, someone would stop to thank them for saving Orville Falls from the Tranquility Tonic. They were all so nice that Charlie found it hard to imagine that these pleasant people could be the children and grandchildren of the townsfolk who had accused two little girls of crimes they hadn't committed.

It was midafternoon when they reached Josephine's house. They walked the stone path through her neat little lawn, past the pretty red mums that were growing in the flower beds, and up to the front door. They knocked three times before Josephine opened the door in her robe.

"Hey, guys," she said with a yawn so wide Charlie could count her fillings. "Sorry I'm not dressed yet. I was up all night working and I ended up sleeping late. Come on in."

She led them into her homey living room, where a large framed advertisement was now hanging over the sofa. The product being hawked was a tonic that came in a sapphire-blue bottle. Written above the product was one line:

Dreamless Oblivion Can Be Yours When You Try Tranquility Tonic!

Over the summer, Josephine had been the first person in Orville Falls to be turned into a Walker by Tranquility Tonic. And while under its influence, Josephine had painted the ads that convinced many of her neighbors to try it.

She blushed when she caught Charlie studying the advertisement on her wall. "Some of my friends think I'm a bit weird for having that sign in my living room, but believe it or not, it keeps me hopeful," she said. "Every time I look at it, I think about the people who love me—and how far they went to save me from the tonic. Plus, it's darn good work for a Walker, wouldn't you say?"

"It certainly was effective," Paige said.

Charlie nodded. He was sure he'd never shake the memory of seeing the entire town of Orville Falls waiting in line for a chance to purchase one of the blue bottles.

"Yeah, *too* effective," Josephine said. "That's why I'm through with advertising. I'm focusing more on my writing now."

Paige dropped down on the sofa, put her feet up on the coffee table, and made herself at home. "Is that why you were up all night? Are you writing a big story?"

"Yep," said Josephine. "Did Charlie ever tell you about the two little girls who used to live in Kessog Castle?"

Charlie shot Paige a look as he sat down in a chair across from her.

"He did," Paige said. "India and Isabel Kessog."

"That's right," said Josephine. She popped into the kitchen to pour herself a cup of coffee. When she returned to the living room, she was carrying a plate of banana bread, which she offered to the kids. "I've been searching for the twins since we found a chemistry set that once belonged to them. I figured if either of the Kessogs was still alive, I'd have a wonderful story for the paper."

"Did you find them?" Charlie asked, though he knew the answer. Then he shoved a chunk of banana bread into his mouth.

"No," said Josephine. "I've traced them as far as a lighthouse in Maine, but the building was destroyed a couple of months ago, and the trail goes cold from there. But I did discover something quite interesting."

"What?" Paige asked.

"The girls were from England, and both of their parents died during World War Two. Their father, George Kessog, was a famous chemist who developed a formula that could treat people who'd been poisoned in certain ways. He also developed something he called Liquid Sunshine. It was a vitamin cream for people who didn't get enough sun in the winter. He didn't live long enough to see what happened to his invention, but it was a huge hit in Finland. The cream made the family a fortune."

"Wait—so the girls are rich?" Charlie felt a jolt of excitement.

"Well, see, that's the funny thing," Josephine said. "The Kessog girls never claimed the money. It's been sitting in a bank for the last eighty years. If they're still alive, they probably don't even know about it."

"They're both alive, and I know where they are," Charlie said. "They're in Cypress Creek. That's why Paige and I are here. We came to tell you."

Josephine sprayed the coffee she'd been sipping across the room. "You're kidding!" She set the cup down and wiped her mouth on the sleeve of her robe. "Charlie, that's amazing! How did you find the Kessogs? When can I meet them?"

"You can't meet them," Charlie told her. When Josephine's face fell, he rushed to explain. "They're very private ladies, and they're both extremely shy. But if you write down some questions, I'm sure they'd be happy to answer them for you."

Josephine looked relieved. "Do they have any idea that they're heiresses?" she asked.

"I doubt it," Paige said. "I don't think money has crossed their minds much in the last eighty years."

"Wow!" Josephine's eyes sparkled. "This is going to be quite a story!"

"There's more," said Charlie. "The Kessogs told me they're ready to give you a full account of all the pranks they pulled in Orville Falls, but they're very clear on one thing. They say they had absolutely nothing to do with the explosion in the center of town—the one that destroyed the fountain in front of the courthouse. The girls claim they were falsely accused."

"You know, I wondered about that," Josephine said. She jumped up and grabbed a bunch of papers off the dining table. They looked like official reports, and Charlie could see a blueprint or two sticking out of the pile. "The more I read about the explosion downtown, the more it sounded like something must have happened to one of the natural-gas lines beneath the square. They'd been repaired a week earlier, and the mayor hired his dim-witted brother-in-law to do the job. There's a chance that one of the pipes ruptured because of faulty repair work and the people responsible let two little girls take the blame. If that's what happened, the Kessogs must have been furious. They probably still are."

"I'm sure they are," Paige said. "But if you can manage to clear their names, I bet they'd both be incredibly grateful."

Josephine did seem very determined. "I'm definitely

going to do my best," she said. "If I write a list of questions for the Kessogs, do you think you could deliver it to them?"

"Absolutely," Charlie told her. "We were planning to visit them this afternoon. In fact, that's the other reason we're here. You have something that belongs to the Kessogs, and we were hoping to return it to them today."

"I do?" Josephine's brow wrinkled with confusion. "Ah!" she exclaimed when inspiration struck. "I do! Let me get it." She knew exactly what Charlie was talking about.

Charlotte met Charlie and Paige at the bus station and drove them through the woods to the old Livingston place. Charlie lugged the chemistry set up to the front door and knocked. Ms. Abbot answered, wearing a pair of safety goggles and long black rubber gloves. In her left hand was a bubbling test tube.

"Charlie! Paige!" she said. "Welcome!"

The living room was a laboratory once more. Charlie recognized a few pieces of equipment from the lab that had once been in Alfie's room. The Kessog twins were inspecting a complicated apparatus while Alfie watched in admiration.

Charlotte had come in behind the rest of them. "I can't believe it. I just dropped the girls off here this morning, and you guys are already hard at work?" she said. "Doesn't anyone but me need a rest?"

"Rocco and Jack ate an entire pizza and passed out in the back room," Alfie offered.

"But the girls and I have no time to waste," Ms. Abbot said. "India and Isabel's father was working on a few new formulas when he went off to war. The one we're trying to re-create right now was a treatment for the flu. If it works, who knows how many lives we'll be able to save."

"Maybe this will help." Charlie held up the chemistry set. "Recognize it?" he called out to the twins.

Indy and Izzie looked up from their work.

"Hey, is that what I think it is?" Alfie asked in astonishment.

"Our chemistry set!" cried the girls in unison. They rushed over and opened the box.

"Oh, this is a good one," Alfie said, rubbing his hands together as if he were standing in front of a spectacular feast. "They don't let kids play with cool, dangerous stuff like this anymore."

"They don't?" Isabel asked. "Well, that's silly. Don't they know *life* is dangerous?"

"People are very safety conscious these days," India said. "They don't let kids make their own fireworks anymore either."

Isabel looked scandalized. "Why not?"

"Something about losing fingers."

"Oh heavens," said Isabel with a roll of her eyes. "They've all gone a bit soft, haven't they?"

"Well, aside from the fact that kids aren't allowed to play with cyanide anymore, how are you liking the twenty-first century?" Paige asked Isabel.

"It's wonderful," Isabel said. "And you've all been so kind to us. Alfie gave us laboratory equipment. And Rocco and Jack brought us pizza. Ms. Abbot has allowed us glimpses of the television. So many singing competitions! And Ollie is decorating our new bedroom."

"Your new bedroom?" Charlie asked. It hadn't even

occurred to him yet that Isabel and India would need a place in the Waking World to live.

"I've invited the twins to stay here with me," Ms. Abbot said. "We'll see how far we can make my salary stretch!"

"Oh, I don't think you'll need to worry about that," said Paige. "You've just adopted two very rich little girls."

But her announcement was overshadowed by the appearance of Ollie Tobias. He had a pastry brush dripping green paint tucked behind one ear and several eye shadow brushes clenched in his fist like a bouquet. "Done!" he announced. "I think this may be my masterpiece."

CHAPTER THIRTY

THE DREAM

That night, Charlie paid one last visit to the tower. He sat on the floor where Charlotte's desk had once been and thought about everything that had happened to him in that room. The first time he'd entered the tower, he'd been an angry, frightened boy. Now he'd faced his fears and he felt like a different kid. The portal had saved him. And he, in turn, had saved the Netherworld. Which was weird, now that he thought about it. Crossing over to the land of Nightmares could have been the worst experience ever. But it had ended up being exactly what Charlie needed.

It just went to show that you never really knew, Charlie

thought. Most things could be good *or* bad, depending on how you looked at them. He would try to remember that in the morning when the construction workers arrived to pull down the tower.

Charlie yawned and dragged himself up off the floor. It was time for bed. The portal was swirling, beckoning him to the other side, but he ignored it. He was through with the Netherworld. The Dream Realm was waiting. And as soon as Charlie was in bed with his eyes closed, he was there, standing in golden light on the porch of the purple mansion. His mother was there too. She'd been waiting on the steps for him.

"Charlie!" She jumped up to greet him. "You did it! I knew you would."

He hadn't seen his mother since the black sheep dreams had begun, and he hugged her like they'd been apart for years. "How did you hear?" he asked.

"Jack stopped by earlier," Veronica Laird said. "He's so proud of you, Charlie. He told me how you helped ICK— sorry, I mean *Isabel*—face her fears, and how you convinced Medusa to let her return to the Waking World. He said you were incredibly brave."

Charlie could feel himself blushing at the praise. "I really thought Jack would be the one who'd figure everything out."

Charlie's mom put an arm around him. "Oh, I'm sure

Jack will save the world someday too," she said. "But I always knew the ICK and INK dilemma was yours to solve. It needed someone who'd felt enough fear to open a portal, and Jack doesn't know that kind of darkness the way you do. It's amazing, isn't it? Your dark side helped you save three worlds."

"But in order to bring Isabel back to the Waking World, I had to promise Medusa we'd destroy the portal so the twins can never return to the Netherworld," Charlie said. "The purple mansion's tower is being demolished in the morning."

He hadn't known how his mother would take the news, but she seemed thrilled to hear it. "It will be worth it," she said. "I can't imagine how happy those two girls must be."

"Yeah, and it's a good thing it all ended when it did. It was getting pretty hard to keep hiding everything from Dad," Charlie said. "I can't believe he didn't figure out what was going on."

His mother raised an eyebrow. "Do you really think he didn't suspect anything?" she asked.

"Did he?" Charlie asked, surprised.

His mom shrugged mischievously. "Don't worry. I think I smoothed everything over."

"What do you mean?" Charlie asked, but there was no time to probe for an answer. Isabel and India Kessog had just appeared together at the bottom of the drive. They spun around on the sidewalk, taking it all in. "Indy! Izzie! Up here!" Charlie shouted down to them.

The two girls ran up the hill to the porch. "Is this it?" Isabel asked.

"Are we here?" India added. "Is this really the Dream Realm?"

"You've made it," Charlie told them. "I'd like you guys to meet my mother."

"Hello," said Veronica Laird, holding out a hand to each of them. "It's a pleasure to finally meet you both. My sons have told me all about you."

"It's our pleasure, ma'am," Isabel said. The words were polite, but she was staring at Charlie's mom with a strange expression. "We owe your sons everything."

"It's true. We're very grateful," India said. She had the same unusual look in her eye. "May I ask you a question, ma'am?"

"Of course," said Charlie's mother.

"Are you . . ." She couldn't seem to finish.

"Dead?" asked Veronica Laird. "Yes, in the Waking World, I'm dead. But in Charlie's dreams, I'll always be alive."

"Does that mean . . ." It was Isabel's turn to be flummoxed, but Charlie knew exactly what she wanted to say.

"Yes," he told her. "Your parents are here too. If you want to see them, you just have to imagine them."

The girls gave each other a nervous look. "Do you remember what they looked like?" India asked Isabel.

"Down to the buttons on Mum's favorite dress," Isabel said.

"Try it," Charlie's mother urged them.

The girls closed their eyes. In an instant, a man in a uniform and a pretty auburn-haired woman in an old-fashioned dress appeared in front of them. When the girls opened their eyes, they all stared at each other as if they couldn't possibly be real. Then the twins' parents each grabbed a girl, and the four of them threw themselves into a hug powerful enough to make up for the last eighty years.

"Come on," said Charlie's mom, nudging her son with her elbow. "Let's give the Kessog family some time alone."

The next morning, the guests began arriving around seven-thirty. They gathered in the kitchen, where Andrew Laird was making the world's biggest batch of waffles. He was in a good mood, Charlie noticed. It was almost as if he knew what it meant that the mansion's tower was being torn down.

At eight o'clock, the small crowd moved out to the front yard of the purple mansion. There was no laughing and little talking. They had gathered for a very solemn event.

"Are you ready?" shouted a man holding a sledge-hammer.

Charlotte didn't answer at first.

"You okay?" Andrew Laird whispered to his wife, and she nodded. "Are you sure the tower's too damaged to save?"

"'Fraid so," Charlotte said sadly. "You have no idea how much it's been through in the last one hundred and fifty years." She cupped her hands around her mouth. "We're ready!" she called up to the man.

He lifted the sledgehammer and brought it down with a crash on the side of the purple mansion's tower. Three of his colleagues did the same, and soon there was a gaping hole where one of the tower's eight walls had once been.

Charlie felt a hand slip into his. He didn't need to look to see whose it was.

They watched as the tower came down, bit by bit and board by board. When it was gone, Charlie saw his dad turn to Charlotte.

"Is it over?" Andrew Laird asked his wife. "Are we going to be a regular family now?"

"I'm sorry?" Charlotte asked, as if she didn't understand. "What are you talking about?"

"The secrets and the ghosts and all the monsters that go bump in the night?"

Charlotte's jaw dropped. "You knew?" she asked.

"Charlie tried to tell me, but I didn't believe him. It sounded so crazy. Evil twins and Nightmares and portals to other worlds. I thought he'd made it all up. Then I found out that it was all true," Andrew Laird said. "I just wish you guys had let me help."

"I'm so sorry. I didn't want to burden—"

"I know," he said softly. "It's going to sound strange, but I had a dream and someone explained it all to me."

Charlie knew who had told his father the truth.

"So is it over now?" Andrew Laird asked again.

"Yes, honey," Charlotte told him. "It's over. I promise."

CHAPTER THIRTY-ONE

BACK TO (SOMEWHAT) NORMAL

On a Tuesday just before Christmas break, the Orville Falls newspaper published three big scoops. Charlie and his friends read the news on Paige's phone as they trudged through the snow after school.

TWO CHILDREN WRONGFULLY ACCUSED OF EXPLOSION THAT DESTROYED TOWN CENTER

In 1939, the fountain in the center of Orville Falls was destroyed in a massive explosion. For almost eighty years, two little girls have taken the blame. Their names are India and Isabel Kessog, and today those names have finally been cleared. After an extensive investigation by this reporter and the *Orville Falls Gazette*, it can now be said with absolute certainty that the explosion was the result of a ruptured gas main, and that the mayor's office was directly responsible. . . .

SEVENTH GRADER'S ARTWORK BRINGS BIG BUCKS

A mural created by Oliver Tobias, a seventh-grade student at Cypress Creek Elementary, was recently purchased by a Russian business-woman for a price that is rumored to be in the high six figures. The mural came to the attention of the art community earlier this year after a photo of it went viral. Painted on four walls of a small house that was once located at the end of Freeman Road in Cypress Creek, the mural shows twin girls on an epic journey through a human body, battling viruses and "kicking some serious bacteria butt," in the words of the twelve-year-old artist. The artwork's new owner purchased the entire house and is having it shipped to the outskirts of Moscow, where she lives.

LOCAL TEACHER FINDS THE CURE

A teacher in nearby Cypress Creek is being credited with one of the most important scientific discoveries of the decade. Ms. Samantha Abbot, who gives equal credit to her two adopted daughters, has developed a formula that treats some strains of the flu. . . .

. . . Ms. Abbot's daughters have been offered scholarships to Columbia University, and Ms. Abbot has been granted her own laboratory. The three will be departing for New York City in a matter of weeks.

Jack passed Paige's smartphone back to her. "I can't believe Izzie and Indy are leaving Cypress Creek," he complained. "They only just got here!"

"I can't believe they get to skip high school and go straight to college," Alfie groaned even louder.

"Oh, don't be jealous," Paige chided him. "The Kessogs are eighty years old. I bet in five or six decades, you'll be almost as smart as they are."

"Gee, thanks," Alfie said, sticking his tongue out at her. "But *seriously*! Ollie's going to be a famous artist. The Kessogs are in college. Ms. Abbot cured the flu. Charlie saved the Netherworld. You're practically MacGyver. Rocco will probably get drafted to play professional football any day now, and what am I? Totally, hopelessly *normal*."

"Nobody would ever call you *normal,* Alfie," Charlie assured him. "I saw what you're wearing under that coat. How many other kids would go around wearing a shirt that says SUPER FUNGI?"

"Charlie's joking," Rocco said. "But you're definitely not normal. Everyone in Cypress Creek knows it's your special water that's gotten the football team on this winning streak. Even Jancy Dare says so. I bet there are a million people who'd kill to know what's in it."

"You think?" Alfie said.

"Yeah, I heard Jancy's dad saying he'd love to sell that stuff at his sporting goods store—as long as the competition couldn't buy it," Rocco told him.

"Hmmmm," said Alfie. "I always thought I'd be an astrophysicist, but maybe I should go into business instead."

"Just what the world needs," Paige joked, giving Alfie a wink. "Another scientist turned entrepreneur."

When they reached Main Street, Charlie and Jack said goodbye to their friends and headed for Hazel's Herbarium. They reached the store just as the mailman was preparing to shove a load of mail through the slot. A sign in the window said TREATMENT IN PROGRESS. OPEN AGAIN AT 3!

"I'll take that, if you don't mind," Charlie told the mailman. "I work here."

"You guys Charlotte's kids?" the man asked.

"We are," Charlie said without a second thought.

"I sure was sorry to see the tower on your house get torn down," said the mailman. "You know, when I was growing up, I was convinced it was magical. Sometimes I'd see a light coming from the windows, and I figured there might be a door to another world in there."

"Can I tell you a secret?" Jack asked. "You were right."

The mailman laughed. "I don't know about that," he said. "But it sure would make life more interesting. Have a nice afternoon, boys, and give Charlotte my best."

"We will," Charlie told him. He opened the door and put the mail down on the counter. As he did so, something caught his eye. He picked up the letter on the top of the pile. It was a nice, thick envelope, and even Charlie could tell that the paper was fancy.

He read the name on the return address. It belonged to one of the biggest publishers in New York. He couldn't help but peek. He tore the top of the envelope a little—just enough to see that the first word of the letter was *Congratulations*.

The keys to Hazel's Herbarium dropped out of his hand.

"Charlotte!" he shouted.

She stuck her head out of the examination room. "What's going on?" she asked. "I'm just treating Mr. Hainey."

"Forget the fungus—you've got to get out here!" Charlie told her. "Your book is going to be published!"

PUT YOUR NIGHTMARES TO BED
ONCE AND FOR ALL!

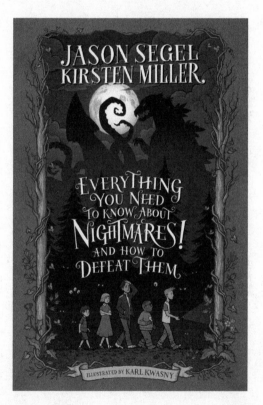

Turn the page for a sneak peek at the handy

guide every sleeper needs. . . .

THE TRUTH ABOUT NIGHTMARES

Each evening when we fall asleep, our minds embark on a journey. If we're lucky, we make our way to the Dream Realm, a wonderful world where we're able to live out our fondest fantasies—like riding a unicorn, scoring the winning goal at the World Cup, or sneaking into a cheese shop after dark. But more often than we'd like, we close our eyes and find ourselves trapped in a sinister world filled with Werewolves and Giant Scaly Things and everything else that goes bump in the night.

This is the Netherworld, the land of Nightmares. We all visit the Netherworld countless times in our lives—and by now you've probably learned that it isn't always easy to leave. Night after night, you may find yourself being chased or gobbled or stalked by creatures that seem determined to scare you. The bad news is these Nightmares are every bit as real as you and me. Fortunately, there's some good news too. No matter how gruesome they are, Nightmares can't hurt us—and they don't want to either. When they make you shiver, scream, or wet your bed, they're only doing their jobs.

You see, Nightmares force us to face our fears. Everyone is scared of *something*. (We could personally list a *hundred* things.) The Netherworld is where our fears come to life. When you see them, your first instinct is to flee. But that would be a *big* mistake. You can't run away from a Nightmare. You might manage to escape one night, but your fears will be back to taunt you the next time you fall asleep.

As terrible as this sounds, there's no need to despair. Even the worst Nightmares can be beaten—you just need a little grit, some cleverness, and the courage to stand your ground. If you face your Nightmares—if you don't run away—you can find a way to make them vanish for good.

This handbook will give you the advice you need to beat the most common species of Nightmares. You'll learn all about their strengths, weaknesses, and quirks. With this book by your bedside, you can rest assured that you're totally prepared for your next trip to the Netherworld.

Good night, and good luck!

LURKERS AND STALKERS

Lurkers and Stalkers are some of the Netherworld's creepiest residents. Unlike other species of Nightmares, they're rarely seen. The trouble is, they can always see *you*.

Lurkers and Stalkers like to hide in dense forests, at the bottom of large bodies of water (lakes, oceans, Olympic-size swimming pools), or in dimly lit metropolitan areas. Masters of disguise, they can blend into any background. Lurkers will usually watch you from a distance, while Stalkers prefer to follow you. The good news is, neither group is dangerous. They (almost) never attack. They prefer a slow, steady scare. Nightmares starring Lurkers and Stalkers have been known to drag on for days.

PRO TIP!

You don't need to *see* Lurkers or Stalkers to know they're nearby! Look for these warning signs.

- ◆ Cold, clammy hands
- ◆ Hair standing up on the back of your neck
- ◆ Extra-large goose bumps (spider bite–size)

If you're suffering from one or more of these symptoms, there's probably a Lurker or Stalker around!

THE THING IN THE WOODS

You don't know what it is, but you know it's out there. Maybe you see yellow eyes glowing in the dark, or hear something prowling among the trees. Or perhaps you catch the unmistakable scent of mushrooms, rotting leaves, and terrible BO. If so, you're dreaming about the Thing in the Woods (TITW).

The star of countless camping-themed nightmares, the Thing has tortured every city kid who's ever gone to summer camp in the country. Call it a monster. Call it a beast. Just don't call it Bigfoot. Its feelings get hurt when it's confused with its famous neighbor.

Nightmares about the Thing in the Woods are common when people are expecting big life changes. If you're about to start a new grade at school, move to another town, go to prison, or set off on an expedition along the Amazon River, you may soon find yourself dreaming about the Thing.

Nothing's more frightening than the unknown (whether it's the future or whatever's under your bed right now). But hiding from things you can't see doesn't work. In the case of Lurkers like the Thing in the Woods, you should take immediate action. Don't cower, and don't run away. Find a flashlight and go out and greet it. (Consider bringing a s'more or two in case your Thing is hungry.) As soon as you can see it, you'll probably realize that it's really not scary at all!

STRENGTHS

- It knows the woods far better than you do.
- Unlike you, it can see perfectly well in the dark.
- You won't hear it unless it wants you to hear it.
- It can unzip a tent.

WEAKNESSES

- The TITW may act tough, but it's really quite shy. It may run away the first time you introduce yourself.
- It can easily be bribed with s'mores, chocolate-covered granola bars, or burnt campfire marshmallows.

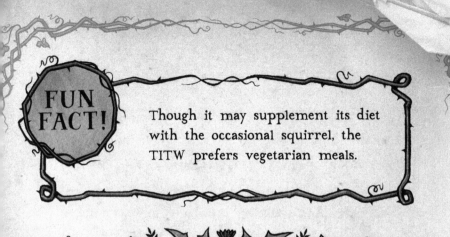

Alfie Bluenthal and the Thing in the Woods

Alfie Bluenthal first spotted the Thing in the Woods at the end of May, about two weeks before he was due to head off to cooking camp for the summer. In his nightmare, Alfie was picking vegetables in his garden when he heard a beast panting in the woods at the edge of his backyard. He couldn't see the Thing, but it sounded big. And when he detected a horrible stench on the breeze, he knew anything that smelled *that* awful had to be *huge*.

Alfie ran into his house and slammed the door. But the panting didn't stop. It only grew louder. Soon he could hear the Thing on the other side of the door.

Alfie shouted for help, but his mom and dad didn't answer. (As parents in nightmares so often do, they'd abandoned their child to a terrible fate.) He rushed to his bedroom and pushed his bureau against the door, but he could still hear the panting—along with heavy footsteps in the hallway. Seconds after he'd crawled under the bed, he heard the bureau slowly sliding across the floor.

Alfie woke up from his nightmare before the Thing got him. And the very next morning, he paid a visit to the purple mansion. Charlie had an idea that he thought might help. "Your Thing sounds really hungry," he said. Alfie preferred the word *ravenous*. "Maybe you should stop running," Charlie advised, "and invite it over for dinner."

The following night, Alfie couldn't work up the courage to prepare a meal. After all, he was only just learning to cook. But the evening after that, he decided the nightmare needed to stop. Before he fell asleep, he found a recipe online that seemed easy to make, and when he got to the Netherworld, he felt completely prepared. In his nightmare, he whipped up a big batch of cacio e pepe. Then he set up a table in the backyard and waited for the Thing to arrive.

The delicious aroma of pasta and cheese lured his dinner guest out of the woods. As the beast slunk across Alfie's backyard toward the table, Alfie was amused to see that it was about the size of a toddler (though much furrier, and with an impressive set of teeth). Turned out the Nightmare's name was Bernard, and he and Alfie had a lot in common. They ate the pasta (which was absolutely delicious), talked about the latest advances in astrophysics, and discussed their summer plans.

The next night, Alfie cooked cacio e pepe for dinner in the Waking World, which blew his parents' minds. Then he went to sleep and dreamed of cooking camp. When he woke up, he couldn't wait for summer break to begin.

HANDY RECIPE!

CACIO E PEPE

INGREDIENTS

1½ cups grated Romano cheese
1 cup grated Parmesan cheese
1 tablespoon black pepper
salt
¾ pound dry spaghetti noodles
olive oil

INSTRUCTIONS

Dump the cheeses and pepper into a bowl and mix them together. Add some water a little at a time and stir until the mixture is as thick as glue.

Boil a big pot of salted water. Add the spaghetti.

Right before the pasta is completely cooked, use tongs to transfer it from the cooking pot to the bowl with cheese and pepper. Save a cup of the cooking water.

Stir the pasta, cheese, and pepper together. Add a little olive oil—and a little cooking water to make it creamy.

Eat and enjoy!!!

OTHER "THINGS" YOU MIGHT MEET IN THE NETHERWORLD
(AND WHAT TO HAVE ON HAND WHEN YOU DO!)

The Thing in the Attic

Even if it's not frightening, it's probably pretty annoying. Things in the Attic tend to thump around quite a bit. Occasionally they'll thump so hard that they crash right through the ceiling. If you'd like to get rid of yours, try scattering a pocketful of acorns across the attic floor. The acorns will attract squirrels, and Things in the Attic *hate* squirrels. (They never developed a taste for them like the Thing in the Woods.) As soon as the furry little beasts move in, your Thing will move out. The only downside? You'll be left with a bunch of Netherworld squirrels, who aren't known to be particularly friendly.

The Thing Right Behind You

It's so terrifying that you can't bring yourself to turn around. But you have to face it! That's where a small mirror comes in handy. Use your mirror to look the Thing Right Behind You in the eye and tell it to hit the road. Odds are, you won't have to say much more. The Thing will be so horrified by the sight of its own appearance that it will already have bolted.

The Thing You Fear Most

Whatever it is—a giant millipede, the existential void, or Hickory Smoke Spam—you're sure to come across it in the Netherworld. To prepare for this meeting, you must be brave! Try imagining yourself standing face to face with your Nightmare. Now imagine reaching out and giving it a hug. (If your Nightmare is Spam, this could get pretty gross, but try it anyway.)

SHADOWS

Shadows are by far the most common species of Stalker in the Netherworld. They're just about everywhere you look! Most of the time they play a supporting role in other bad dreams, helping to make those nightmares spookier and more atmospheric. Occasionally, however, a Shadow will become the star of the show. And when that happens, you better look out. ('Cause it's right behind you!)

Most Shadow Nightmares begin with the sensation that you're being followed—and you *are*. There's something creeping up on you, but when you spin around, nothing's there. All you can see is a strange patch of darkness on the ground. The truth is, you could be staring straight at a Shadow Nightmare and you'd never suspect a thing. Then, as soon as you're not looking, it'll reach out and stroke the nape of your neck, sending shivers down your spine. When you run, it will stay right on your heels. No matter how fast you book it, you'll never get away.

Here's what you need to know about Shadows: They don't want to hurt you. They *like* you! That's why they're always following you around. So think of your Shadow as your biggest fan—and try to get used to its company. Once a Shadow has found you, it's highly unlikely that you'll ever get rid of it for good. (But whenever you need a little alone time, all you have to do is turn on some lights.)

STRENGTHS

- Can go anywhere
- Can assume any shape (even yours)
- Can make any setting seem creepy

WEAKNESSES

- Light (of course)
- Always a split second slower than you
- Low self-esteem

FUN FACT!

Shadows are the children of the Netherworld's oldest Nightmare—the Dark. Try to imagine how hard that must be! Shadows know they'll never be as famous or as frightening as their world-renowned parent. Most are desperate to be something other than Shadows—they'd like nothing more than to be solid and real. That's why they're always taking the shapes of other objects!

PRO TIP!

If a Shadow is behind you, for heaven's sake, don't run! The Nightmare will chase you wherever you go. It's best to continue at a slow pace and try to enjoy the Shadow's company. In fact, why not have a little chat with it? Your Shadow won't be able to talk back, but it will appreciate the effort. It's probably a good idea to get to know each other—you're going to be hanging out together for a while!

THE BEASTS FROM BELOW

Commonly known as sea monsters (a name they truly despise), the Beasts from Below can be found in any large body of water. Classic Stalkers, they enjoy following ships, swimmers, and recreational water craft. Despite their terrifying appearance, they're playful and enjoy physical contact. They are known to bump rowboats, flip kayaks, and brush up against legs.

If you find yourself being stalked by a Beast from Below (BFB), there are several things you can do:

- **Sing it a song.** BFBs are suckers for sea shanties and classic Motown.

- **Avoid peeing in the water.** They hate that! And your Waking World mattress may suffer as well.

- **Hitch a ride.** (Note: It's important that you tell your BFB how long you can hold your breath.)

STRENGTHS

- The element of surprise. BFBs are masters of timing and can pop out of the water when you least expect it.

- Many BFBs have long necks or tentacles, which are perfect for snatching people from boats with no warning.

WEAKNESSES

- You have size on your side. You're not really big enough to be much of a snack.

- BFBs are not the largest creatures in the ocean. There are things down there that scare them to death too.

FUN FACT!

Every Netherworld lake has its own Beast from Below. They're less common in the Waking World, but you can find them here too. (Just not in Scotland. The Loch Ness Monster is nothing but a silly legend.)

PRO TIP!

If you expect to encounter a BFB, wear your swimsuit to bed. You might feel silly, but you'll be far more comfortable and your Nightmare will recognize (and respect) your preparedness!

THE CHASERS

You know the feeling. There's something after you. You're running as fast as you can, but you can't seem to lose it. It's right on your heels—so close you can hear it panting or groaning or slurping the spit off its lips. You could be racing through a burnt-out city, a Romanian forest, or a Bed Bath & Beyond. It doesn't matter where you are or which kind of Chaser Nightmare is after you. If you stop, trip, or slow your pace, you're in serious trouble.

Chasers are among the Netherworld's most popular Nightmares. Some (such as saber-toothed tigers) have been around since human beings first began having bad dreams. Others regularly change their appearance to suit the latest trends.

If a Chaser is hounding you, there's a simple question you'll have to answer before you can shake it off: what the heck am I running from? As with all Nightmares, knowing what you're really scared of is half the battle!

FUN FACT!

Many people think Chasers and Gobblers belong to the same family of Nightmares. They do have many similarities, but there's one important difference. Chasers chase, but they don't always *catch*, and when they do, they rarely eat. Gobblers, on the other hand, may pursue you, but most would rather wait for you to fall into their traps. And once a Gobbler's got you, it will *always* chow down.

PRO TIP!

Not sure what's after you? Here's a foolproof way to find out: simply lure your Nightmare into a booby trap! (A basic net trap usually works well.) Your aim is not to injure the beast, just to find out what it wants (some only want a little attention). Once you do, the chasing should stop immediately.

ZOMBIES

It's important to remember that Zombies are people too. Sure, they may be falling apart, but underneath all that rotten flesh, they're just like you and me.

Don't take it too personally if the Netherworld's Walking Dead are after you and your brains. Zombies suffer from acute *hanger,* and the human brain just happens to be an excellent source of the vitamins and nutrients the Walking Dead crave. Fortunately, so is chopped liver.

The best way to avoid an attack is to prepare a big batch of chopped liver and slip it under your pillow before you drift off to sleep. (Vegetarians, take note: Cooking liver may be unpleasant, but when it comes to Zombies, a nice kale casserole will *not* do the trick. The authors of this chapter learned that the hard way.)

As soon as you're in the Netherworld, whip out your dish. Chopped liver should look and feel like brown Play-Doh, and if you have enough time before the Zombies attack, go ahead and get creative. Mold it into the shape of brains! They always appreciate the extra touch.

After your Zombies have eaten, you might be surprised by what pleasant company they are. Though it's probably a good idea to leave pretty soon after dinner. Those with bellies digest their food quickly, and you don't want to be around when it's time for their next meal.

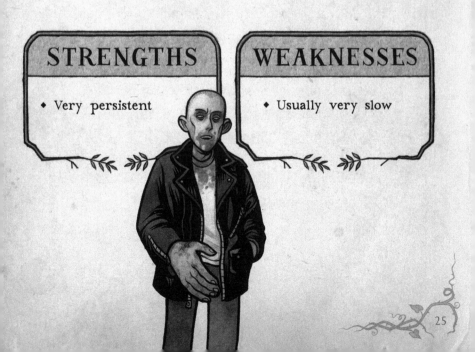

STRENGTHS

• Very persistent

WEAKNESSES

• Usually very slow